Praise for Heidi Cullinan's
Carry the Ocean

"Heidi Cullinan continues to amaze with vivid characters who leap from the page into my heart."

~ *K. A. Mitchell, author of* Bad Behavior

"A memorable and moving love story that reminds us there's someone for everyone!"

~ *Laura Kaye,* New York Times *bestselling author of* Hard to Come By

Look for these titles by *Heidi Cullinan*

Now Available:

A Private Gentleman
Family Man *(written with Marie Sexton)*

Love Lessons
Love Lessons
Fever Pitch

Minnesota Christmas
Let It Snow
Sleigh Ride

Special Delivery
Special Delivery
Double Blind
Tough Love

Carry the Ocean

Heidi Cullinan

SAMHAIN
PUBLISHING

FIC
Cullinan

Samhain Publishing, Ltd.
11821 Mason Montgomery Road, 4B
Cincinnati, OH 45249
www.samhainpublishing.com

Carry the Ocean
Copyright © 2015 by Heidi Cullinan
Print ISBN: 978-1-61922-711-8
Digital ISBN: 978-1-61922-520-6

Editing by Sasha Knight
Cover by Kanaxa

First Samhain Publishing, Ltd. electronic publication: April 2015
First Samhain Publishing, Ltd. print publication: April 2015

Dedication

for all who navigate the waters of life's superpowers
may you ever stay afloat

Acknowledgments

Thank you to Dan Cullinan, Saritza Hernandez and Maura Peglar for beta reading. Your nudges, comments and suggestions made the book better and more authentic. Thank you also to the Mad Spaz Club, particularly Graham, for honesty, humor, and more information than I could have ever hoped to ask for.

Thank you, Damien, wherever you are now. I hope you're happy and full of love and that you still sing to the mirror in the car. May you still be stepping out with Joe Jackson and always be surprised you never knew you could feel love like this before.

We certainly hope that you all enjoy the show, and remember, people, that no matter who you are, and what you do to live, thrive and survive, there are still some things that make us all the same.

—Elwood Blues, *The Blues Brothers*

Chapter One
Emmet

It took me ten months to meet Jeremey Samson.

I saw Jeremey the day we moved into our house in Ames, Iowa. We moved there before I started my freshman year at Iowa State University. Jeremey's house was across from ours in the back, on the other side of the train tracks that ran through where an alley should have been. When I walked with my aunt Althea to the organic grocery store down the street, I made her go the long way so I could memorize his house number and the license plate of the car in his driveway. It took a lot of online digging, but I learned his family's name, and eventually I discovered his too. Jeremey Samson.

I didn't approach him, though. I watched him from a distance. I studied him across the yard. I found his Instagram. He was quiet online, which is smart but makes it hard to learn about someone you're too shy to say hello to in person. I would have introduced myself in social media, sent a message and gotten to know him first in text, but he only posted maybe one picture a month, and he never left comments.

He was a high school senior then. He had a friend named Bart, which is probably short for Bartholomew. Bart liked to post selfies on Instagram with his tongue sticking out. I followed Bart's account because sometimes he took pictures of Jeremey.

Jeremey never stuck out his tongue, and his smile was always small, with his lips closed.

Sometimes I tried to find a logical reason why I liked Jeremey so much, but romantic feelings have nothing to do with logic. Sometimes what I liked best about Jeremey was the way he spelled his name. *Jeremey*, with an extra e. I made a computer program to spell his name out in a pretty font, and I always smiled at the third E. It made him special—ordinary Jeremys weren't good enough to have all the Es.

Sometimes I liked him for his smile. Sometimes I liked him because he didn't smile. Sometimes I got an erection because of the way he brushed his hair away from his face. It didn't matter to my brain that these were odd reasons to care for someone. My brain, my body, my everything wanted to be Jeremey's boyfriend.

I wanted to introduce myself, but I was nervous. My first year of college was challenging, and I didn't have energy enough to deal with so many new things and making a new friend too. I kept hoping I would run into Jeremey on the street or at the library, but it never happened. As the school year wore on, Jeremey came outside less and less, and he posted fewer pictures, sometimes not posting anything for over a month. One day in May he had a graduation party, but not many people came to sit on his back deck with him. When I did see Jeremey, he looked sad.

I wanted to meet him and find out why he was sad, maybe make him happy. But I couldn't. The truth was, I had a crush on Jeremey Samson. I didn't just want to be his friend. I wanted to be his *boy*friend.

Most people would say, *Good job. You go get your boyfriend.* If I went online to a message board, I could get anyone in the world to root for me. People hardly mind anymore if I'm gay, and nobody cares in Ames.

There's one little issue though, something that would change most people's minds about me. It's the reason I had to wait so long to introduce myself to Jeremey, the reason I didn't want to tell my family I had a crush. This tiny problem is the reason moving made me nervous, made college a struggle for me. Though I have tons of online friends, one fact about me changes what everyone thinks when they meet me in person. Because even though the me who writes like this is the same me who walks and talks and rides the bus to college, nobody believes it when they see me face-to-face.

My name is Emmet David Washington. I'm nineteen years old, and I'm a sophomore at Iowa State University studying computer science and applied physics. I got a perfect score on my ACT. I'm five feet nine inches tall with dark hair and blue-gray eyes. I enjoy puzzles and *The Blues Brothers*. I'm good at computers and anything to do with math. I remember almost everything I read and see. I'm gay. I love trains, pizza and the sound of rain.

I also have autism spectrum disorder. It's not even close to the most important thing about me, but as soon as people see me, watch me move, hear me speak, it's the only thing that seems to matter. People treat me differently. They act as if I'm stupid or dangerous. They call me the R word or tell me I should be put in a home, and they mean institution, not the house where I live.

When people find out I have autism, they don't think I should be allowed to be in love, not with Jeremey, not with anyone.

Which is crap. It's like Elwood Blues says: everybody needs somebody to love. I'm an everybody. I get a somebody.

The problem is, getting a somebody is trickier if you have autism. If I wanted to introduce myself to Jeremey to see if he would be my friend, maybe something more, I couldn't ignore him or let my autism make me uneasy about possible rejection. I tried to tell myself someone with such a quiet face and nice smile wouldn't say mean things to me or call me the R word. I told myself to be brave.

It took me ten months to introduce myself to Jeremey Samson. To learn and memorize the etiquette, to find the right words that would show *me* to Jeremey, not my autism. It took a long time and a lot of work, but I did it.

I shouldn't have worried so much about it. Frankly, I'm awesome, and anybody who doesn't agree should get out of my way.

Before I talk about how I met Jeremey and became his boyfriend, I have to explain how my autism works. The first thing you have to learn about autism is that everyone's is different, and doctors don't know everything about the disorder. Some people argue about whether or not it's actually a disorder at all, or if disorder is the right word. My mom says *disorder* makes it sound as if there's something wrong with me, and there isn't. I'm wired differently, but she says so is everyone if you come right down to it.

Honestly I think the word is correct. The word *disorder* means disruption of normal physical and mental functions. I understand no one is truly normal, but as I've told my mom, I deviate liberally from the mean. I'm not wired a little differently. I'm wired *a lot* differently.

It's hard to describe how autism is different than the brain functions of people on the mean since I don't know how a brain on the mean feels. The best summary I can give is to say I'm more sensitive than most people, and I don't mean feelings getting hurt. My kind of sensitivity is if my socks have a seam on the inside of the toe it feels as if someone is scraping a trowel across my brain. A fan blowing on me can feel like ten million ants are crawling all over my skin. Noises don't bother me, but flashing light makes me feel sick. Strong smells do the same thing, and certain food textures make me throw up. When I look at things, I see them extra bright, and every detail distracts me. All the sounds are louder, even someone's breathing. Being with people too long often overwhelms me, because people can be highly over-stimulating. This is my problem at school. I don't understand why I'm the only one who gets upset when people shove in the hallway or talk too loudly with sharp voices. Why would anyone enjoy that? Who wouldn't be upset?

My aunt Althea has what when she was little they called mild Asperger's, but they call Asperger's autism now. When you talk about autism, you say someone is "on the spectrum", like we're all in this line and we all have different kinds of autism. Mostly I agree this is a good metaphor, for as much as I understand the concept of metaphor. Althea can function quite well. Most people don't know she has autism at all. She can drive a car, which I'm jealous of. They say I can't ever, no matter how many times I write out the *Iowa Driver's Manual* from memory.

Althea lives with us, though, since she is as bad at math and organization as I am good at it. She can't keep her room clean at all. Mom and I help her every Saturday, but I can't go in for the first hour until Mom makes it less gross. Althea can have conversations more easily than I can, but she tests very poorly and has a difficult time focusing at most jobs, which is why she changes so often. Meanwhile, I focus too much. So you see, you can't say *autism* and know what someone is. Any more than you can say *boy* or *man* and think you know a guy.

Althea says ASD—that's shorthand for Autism Spectrum Disorder—makes our filters thinner than most people's. She says loud voices and smells bother everyone, but thicker filters mean people on the mean can ignore them. She and I can ignore bad stimuli too, but it takes effort.

She showed me a website about a woman with lupus who talks about spoons, how we all get so many spoons for each day of our lives, but people with intense physical or mental disability have to use more spoons to get through each day. I don't understand what spoons have to do with anything, but I do know stimuli wears me out faster than it does most people. I've read the website *But You Don't Look Sick* seven times, but I still don't understand why the friend is crying over silverware. Althea says it's because my brain doesn't get metaphors, which are representative stories to explain something instead of giving a literal answer. My brain is about as literal as brains get.

There are some fun things about my autism though. For example, I remember everything I see. My brain is like a camera, and if I see something, especially a number, I remember it forever. My mom always asks me to find things for her, and I can do it not because I'm magic but because my brain is amazing. If I see her put something down, I know where it is unless someone else moves it without me seeing. I can remember recipes, phone numbers, license plates, math formulas. I can memorize fifty lines of computer code in one read-through. I understand math well, and what I don't know I can learn quickly.

My eyes see differently too. In addition to seeing everything at once, my mom says I'm more aware of detail, like texture and color. This means sometimes I find objects and art beautiful where other people find them ugly, and sometimes what is beautiful to people on the mean is ugly to me.

People, though, are trickier than numbers or remembering where Mom's keys are. I can't understand people at all. Not what they're feeling, why they behave the way they do, what they'll probably do next. It makes me sad sometimes, because in my head I can talk to anyone, and they always understand me. It's fine to have autism superpowers, but most times it means I'm lonely.

I try to interact with people, and I'm okay when it's online or in text, but when I have to use my mouth, everything gets messed up. It's not only words, either. I touch at the wrong time but don't touch when someone wants me to. I say and do things that make people angry. *Very* angry. Worst of all, though, is while nobody else can do what I can with math and computers, *everyone* can do people—except me. It doesn't matter how big a math problem I do or how many lines of code I fix. If I say the wrong thing to a person, usually they hate me forever. People are more important than numbers or seeing colors sharper or remembering every ingredient of our Thanksgiving dinners for the past ten years. And people are the hardest things in the world for me.

I didn't want Jeremey Samson to hate me, but the statistics were not in my favor. First of all, to be my boyfriend, he would have to be gay too. Data is unclear, but it's estimated two to five percent of American men are homosexual. In standard circumstances, reciprocated attraction isn't measurable as a potential percentage, but I didn't need a case study to know autism wouldn't help even if I beat the rest of the odds.

I wanted to approach Jeremey, but first I needed to improve my chances of a positive interaction. It wasn't as if I could stop being autistic—but I *could* choose to introduce myself in an advantageous environment. I did a great deal of research on dating advice, which was hard because I'm not always the best judge of this kind of reporting. I got lucky and found a few message boards where other autistic people had successfully dated, and they offered advice. I measured their input against the advice of the Internet as a whole. I applied myself to the study of asking Jeremey Samson out as diligently as I did my physics homework or my coding projects.

The trouble was, whenever I looked at him, I forgot all my research. I could only think about how much I liked him and wanted him to like me back.

The nice part about having autism is I could look at Jeremey without him knowing I was doing it. One of the things that bugs people on the mean the most about autistic people is we often don't meet people's gazes when we talk to them. I can't speak for every autistic person, but the thing is, I don't have to look right at someone to see them. Direct eye contact is way too loud and intense, and it feels wrong even though my mom and dad and aunt say it's rude not to look someone in the eye.

When I watched Jeremey, my autism was a superpower. I could sit on my deck for hours, tracking him as he moved around his yard. Nobody ever knew what I was doing.

My family didn't know I watched Jeremey, because they thought I was waiting for a train. I loved how we had a train track in our backyard, and my favorite way to relax was to count the train cars as they passed. When it rained and a train came, I was pretty much in heaven. I didn't just count the trains, either. I noted the numbers of the cars and the engines, tried to find patterns in the way they were arranged, checked how many of the cars came through and when, and in which direction.

I did watch the trains. But I also watched Jeremey.

I didn't see him outside often, but I always paid attention when he appeared. He moved gently and carefully in a way that made me think he was sensitive too. He didn't smile much, but his face was quiet and calm, like my dad's. Sometimes he seemed sad, but I couldn't tell since I was too far away. He did chores for his dad—taking care of the garden, mowing the lawn, mulching plants. Sometimes he sat outside with his mother, and once with his sister when she visited. Bart came over sometimes, but not often. Mostly he sat outside by himself.

I never saw Jeremey anywhere but in his yard, though, and he still was never online anywhere I could strike up a conversation. To meet him, I would have to make the first overture, and I'd have to do it in person. I would have to be brave and watch for my chance.

It came in early June, at our neighborhood block party.

I didn't want to go to the party. There would be lots of people and many shouting children, but Mom said it would be good to be with our neighbors. Normally I would have had an argument with her and told her where she could stick her block party, but then I read the flyer and realized the name was a misnomer. More than one block was included at this party. A blocks party.

Jeremey's block too.

Of course for me to meet him there, he would have to attend, but it was a risk worth taking. The night before I practiced all my facial recognition charts and went through my flash cards of appropriate getting-to-know-a-boyfriend conversation. When I got dressed the next morning, I took extra care to make sure my shirt was nice and my hair was combed. I'm not always good at that, but when I came down, Althea smiled and told me I looked handsome.

I sat on the front porch and rocked for an hour, waiting for the party. When my family gathered lawn chairs and potluck bowls, I carried the bag of potato chips and walked along, humming all the way.

Mom watched me. "Are you nervous about something, Emmet?"

I *was* nervous, but I didn't want to tell her about Jeremey. "I don't want to talk to you."

She kept staring at me, making her face that meant she was going to ask questions, so I covered the ear nearest her with my hand.

She sighed, but she turned away and didn't ask me anything. Which was good. We were almost to the picnic area, and I wanted to see if Jeremey had come.

When I saw his parents, my heart beat funny. Laughing at something someone said, Mrs. Samson stepped toward a table and reached for a bowl. My pulse kicked again, and I felt dizzy. This was adrenaline, my body's hormones kicking up in a fight-or-flight response, which was annoying. What I needed right now was focus, not chemical confusion.

Except I knew why my body acted illogically, why it disregarded all my plans and turned my super-brain into super-soup. In the place where his mother had disappeared, standing under the tree, his blond head bowed as he stared at the ground, was Jeremey.

Chapter Two
Jeremey

When you have an invisible disease, your sickness isn't your biggest problem. What you end up battling more than anything else, every single day, is other people.

It took me a long time to understand this, because the truth is, for years I didn't know I was sick. When I look back, I've had depression since middle school, and the anxiety started in high school. Or maybe they were swirled together all along, and I only noticed those feelings more specifically at those times. That's the thing with both depression and anxiety. They're entirely *in your head*. People who don't have depression or anxiety think this means you can erase negative feelings as soon as you realize they're present. To those of us living with mental health challenges, we know it simply means your demons never take a day off.

In the first months after I graduated, I wasn't able to think so articulately about what was going on with my brain and what might or might not be making me worse. For a long time I wasn't able to name my conditions, and when I finally did, I felt ashamed and wrong. At that point I was largely surviving, and not well. People had always alarmed me, even when they didn't notice me. There had been some teasing in seventh grade, and it culminated in an incident in the locker room, when a bunch of boys laughed at me and threatened to shove me naked into the hallway so the girls could laugh at me too. I started getting stomachaches every time I had PE. The nurse thought I was making it up, so I made myself vomit too when I complained. Eventually I had to go back, but I got good at hiding in the bathroom until everyone else was out. I think the teacher figured out what was going on, since he never called me out for being late.

This became the way I dealt with school. People were dangerous and usually mean, so I avoided them. I had one friend, sort of, but I think I was more a prop for Bart than an actual buddy. He certainly dropped me fast enough when my depression started getting the better of me, which was the whole of my senior year. I kept it from everyone but him until May, when I broke down during a presentation in my government class.

This earned me a trip to our family doctor, who diagnosed me with major depressive disorder. He kind of tossed off the diagnosis like I had a cold, and I got the feeling he was slapping a label on me and offering some pills more than anything else. It didn't address the anxious feelings, but it wasn't like I wanted *another* label around my neck. I was embarrassed and ashamed, and when my mom got angry and told him he didn't know what he was talking about, I didn't object. Mostly I was grateful they let me finish the rest of my school from home due to stress. I didn't have to go to graduation, either.

It all sounded great at the time, like I was getting out of jail free, but the truth was now the person I battled all the time was my mother.

She hated how I kept retreating from the world, and she made it her personal mission to shove me face-first back into it. Though she'd let me skip church since confirmation, she began dragging me there by the hair again every Sunday. Talk about battling other people—after every service it was a constant barrage of my mother's friends, whom I didn't really know, smiling overeagerly at me, asking where I was going to school in the fall and if I was dating anyone. If I reacted badly to this onslaught and had a panic attack, Mom scolded me, and Dad glowered. Had I known losing my shit in government class would have this kind of reaction, I'd have worked harder to contain my meltdowns to the bathroom stall between classes like usual.

The neighborhood block party was another opportunity for my mom to force me to be normal—and for me to fail.

She showed me the flyer three days before and said, "We should go. It would be good to meet more of the neighbors. So many young couples have moved in." I didn't say no, which should have counted as me being good. I let her drag me shopping for food, even though the store always gives me a panic attack. I didn't plead sick the day of the party, but I cried through my shower when my dad's angry right-wing radio and TV playing at the same time overwhelmed me.

But simply being present wasn't enough for my mom. "Help me make the salad, Jeremey." "Run to the store for me, Jeremey." "Go help the hostesses set up, Jeremey." Of course I fucked all that up—I hadn't been able to get out of the car at the store, and Dad had to go instead.

She came with me to the picnic area to help set up, nudging me with her elbow and murmuring at me to stop being so nervous. When too many commands and the loud woman from three houses down made me jumpy, the hostesses saw I wasn't feeling well and told me to rest. "We can finish without you, don't worry."

Mom didn't worry, but she was mad. According to her, my behavior embarrassed her in public.

Mom wanted a bright, smiling, charming son. She wanted me to have a different answer to the question everyone kept asking—*Where are you going to school this fall?* She wanted me to lie, or evade, or better yet magically not be so depressed and exhausted I usually wanted to get back in my bed instead of making it. Saying *I don't have a school picked yet* was a compromise, I thought, since we all knew I wouldn't make it anywhere, but that wasn't the son my mom wanted.

I wasn't the son my mom wanted.

I didn't smile and flirt and anticipate what the hostesses needed. I cowered and averted my gaze and dropped casserole dishes. Every time someone laughed too loudly, I startled. All the conversations in so many directions made me panic, so I did my best to shut everything out—which meant when someone asked me a question, I didn't hear it.

The hostesses and other party guests patted me on the shoulder and teased me about stress from wild teenage schedules, but my dad frowned and my mom set her lips into the thin line that promised trouble for me later. I didn't have a wild teenage schedule. I hadn't stayed out too late the night before. I never did. I wasn't shy because there were girls my age at the party. That was a whole other issue, one my parents didn't know about yet.

It wasn't as if I didn't try. I went to the horrible block party and was as normal as I could be. It wasn't enough, of course. My parents weren't ever going to listen to me. I could see the future ahead, and it was terrifying and dark and paralyzing, me in a strange dorm room in a strange city with everyone laughing at me or making uncomfortable faces and asking what my problem was. I thought, not for the first time, about how it would be best for everyone if I simply wasn't around.

I was trying to calm myself with a plan of how I would make everything stop when the boy came up to me.

I'd seen him arrive with his parents, but basically I'd paid attention to him long enough to decide he wouldn't bully me or make me uncomfortable, and then I'd dismissed him. Vaguely I'd noted he was different, that something about him seemed off, but otherwise I hadn't given him a great deal of thought, only pushed him into the fog of my focus with everyone and everything else. Except suddenly he was coming up to me, clearly intending to initiate conversation.

The weird thing was, he didn't look at me. He looked *near* me, but he didn't look me in the eye and smile. He stopped in front of me, planting his feet heavily on the ground. Leaning to the side, his hands clutched and bent at an odd angle in front of him, he stared at the air beside me and spoke.

"Hello. Allow me to introduce myself. My name is Emmet Washington. How do you do?"

I blinked at him, not exactly understanding. I mean—I understood what he said, but the *way* he said it was so strange. He sounded slightly robotic, all his words stuffed together in a string, all the vocal inflections put in the wrong places. Even the question was off—he made his voice go up at the end, like he was aware it had to do that to be a question, but it wasn't the *right* kind of up.

There's something wrong with him, the panicked voice in my brain whispered. I drew back, rounding my shoulders and shrinking into myself.

Emmet kept speaking, and I started to wonder if he had a teleprompter in the space beside me he stared at, as rehearsed as his words were. "It is a lovely day for a picnic, isn't it? Not too hot and not windy."

I had to say something. It was clearly my turn to talk, but I was so confused. Why was he talking to me? What was I supposed to say?

He's just being polite. Maybe his mom made him come to the picnic too, and told him to go be social. The thought relaxed me a little. Obviously Emmet was special needs. Would it kill me to be nice to him?

"H-hi." I blushed, embarrassed at my own ineptitude. *Who's special needs now, idiot?*

If Emmet thought I was a tool, he didn't show it. He waited patiently, rocking gently on his heels, staring at the place beside my head. His posture was so odd. His shoulders were too high, and his hands were all twisted in front of him. Sometimes he moved them, but only for a moment, and then they'd go rigid again.

He was cute. His hair was light brown and a little long, fanning around his face like he was in a boy band. His eyes were pale blue, with a lot of lines in them, like refracted crystal.

"You're supposed to introduce yourself now," Emmet said at last.

"S-sorry." I started to hold out my hand, then retracted it, not feeling brave. I tucked my fingers under my arms. "I...I'm Jeremey."

"It's a pleasure to meet you, Jeremey." He waited a beat, and I half-wondered if he wasn't counting, like he knew he should pause and was waiting it out. "I'm a sophomore this fall at Iowa State University. I study applied physics and computer science. I enjoy puzzles and games and taking walks." Another pause, as measured as the last. "What about you?"

I felt jumbled, torn between discomfort at his disinclination to go away and astonishment at what he had told me. "You...you go to college?" And studied applied physics?

Suddenly I felt unsure about my special-needs assumption. Which made me feel guilty, and shamed, and made the panic around the edges of my consciousness close in tighter.

Emmet continued on as if I weren't quietly freaking out. "I do go to college. We moved here last fall so I could attend school. It's not a good idea for me to live in a dorm or on my own, and Mom said it was time for a change anyway. My dad works at ConAgra as a research specialist. My mom is a general practitioner part-time at Ames Medical Clinic. My aunt Althea works at West Street Deli and is an activist. I want to be either a programmer or a physicist. I haven't decided yet." Pause. "What do you do, Jeremey? Do you go to school?"

Physicist. I swallowed hard, feeling confused and lost and inadequate. "N-no. I...graduated in May. H-high school."

"Do you plan to go to college?"

It was nice he didn't *assume* I was going to school, but the shame of saying no, I was running as far from college as I could, was still too much. "I...don't want to. But my parents—" I glanced around to make sure Mom and Dad weren't listening. "They're making me go to the University of Iowa."

Emmet frowned, and his rocking became more pronounced. "That's too bad. They should let you go to Iowa State. It's a good school, and it's right here in Ames."

It was funny—I'd been spiraling into guilt at speaking badly of my parents, but Emmet simply breezed over it. It inspired me to confess more. "I don't want to go to school at all."

His gaze never wavered from the space beside my ear. "What do you want to do?"

"I don't know." It was too much to keep looking at him—made me feel overwhelmed—so I stared at the ground in front of me. "I want to rest. This last year has been difficult, particularly the last month. But I guess real life doesn't work that way."

"What's been difficult?"

For a little while talking with Emmet had been okay, almost pleasant, but now I wanted to stop. I tried to think of how I could get out of the conversation.

Emmet stopped rocking. "I'm sorry. I think I've made you uncomfortable. Was that a bad question?"

I glanced up at him, surprised. He rocked overtly now. *He* was upset. I needed to make him not feel bad. "It wasn't a bad question. I'm...kind of a mess."

"You've seemed sad lately, when I see you in your yard."

Whoa. "You—see me in my yard?"

"Yes. You live across the train tracks from me. I see you sitting on your deck or working in the garden. Sometimes you seem sad."

I probably did appear sad in the backyard a lot—it was where I went when I needed to get away from my parents. The idea the neighbors had been watching me freaked me out and made me embarrassed again. "I'm...sorry."

"Why are you sorry for being sad?"

I *needed* this conversation to stop. "I...don't know."

"You're uncomfortable again."

I was. I was starting to breathe too fast too, and I could feel my heart banging like it wanted out of my rib cage. I shut my eyes. Oh God, I was going to have a panic attack here, at the picnic. My mother would never forgive me. "I—I have to...go." I glanced around, realizing how many people had arrived, how close they were to me. My breath got shallower and shallower, and I wanted to cry. "I can't get out of here. I'm trapped. They're going to be so angry."

"Will you let me help you?"

I blinked at Emmet, not understanding what he was saying at first. He still didn't look at me, but he had his hand out, and he'd stopped rocking, waiting.

I put my hand in his. I don't know why, but I let him lead me away from the tree, away from the picnic. He navigated me around some garbage cans at the corner of the house, parked me on a bench and sat beside me. He let go of my hand, and he left plenty of space between us. He said nothing, only sat with me as I took deep breaths and calmed myself down.

"Th-thanks," I said, when I could speak again.

He sat straight in his seat, staring at my knees. "I'm sorry if I said the wrong thing. I tried to practice, but it's hard, meeting someone."

"You—practiced?"

"Yes. I've wanted to meet you for a long time."

"You...wanted to meet me?" *For a long time?*

"Yes." He rocked on the seat, moving his gaze to a tree. "I wanted to make a good first impression, but I gave you a panic attack. I'm sorry."

Shame filled me, thick and unpleasant. "You didn't do that. I'm...a mess. I was embarrassed to admit I didn't want to go to school."

"It's a big transition. You should tell your parents you need to move more slowly."

My bitter laugh caught at the edge of my throat. "My parents tell me I need to get over it."

"I'm sorry. That's a mean thing to say."

I don't know why I did it. Even as the words formed on my lips, part of my brain tried to shut me down, but Emmet scrambled all my expectations and assumptions, and apparently when that happens, my sensors get tripped. Instead of making an excuse for them, instead of murmuring *yeah, tell me about it* or something else like that, I said, "I have depression."

"Oh. Do you mean MDD? Major depressive disorder? Clinical depression?"

I nodded, ashamed to my toes. "I...had a breakdown at school. I didn't go to class for the last two weeks. I graduated, but since I didn't go to the ceremony, sometimes I'm not sure it actually happened. I'm still stuck in the front of the class, blacking out because I'm not getting enough air." The memory of that horrible day hung on me like fog. "My doctor wants me to take drugs, but my parents won't let me."

"Modern antidepressant medication increases monoamines in the synaptic cleft, and they're clinically proven to elevate mood and alleviate depressive symptoms in many cases. Sometimes it takes time to find the right drug, and for some people they never work, especially without the addition of talk therapy, but they're effective for a number of patients."

This was the same thing the doctor said to me, I was pretty sure, but I didn't understand it any more now than I had in May. It kept weirding me out how smart Emmet was—he *seemed* like someone I should have to compose small sentences for, but obviously that wasn't the case. I wished I could ask him about that, but all I could think of was *what is wrong with you*, which was awful.

"How do you know so much about depression?" I asked instead.

"I read about it. I had a depressive episode when I was thirteen, so I researched my condition. Drugs aren't advisable for teens except in severe circumstances, so I practiced mindful meditation and exercised. I also started homeschooling, which helped. Sometimes I have anxiety now, but most of the time I can make modifications to my daily life and avoid stressful situations."

How was he rattling all this off like it was no big deal? Both the technical mechanism of depression and how it took him out of school? "Modifications?"

"Yes. I have a lot of modifications. I have a regular schedule and signs I use with my family to let them know I'm getting upset. At school it's harder, but mostly I keep to myself and don't talk to other people, and they leave me alone. Since I'm a genius, my professors like me and help if other students are mean. My peers call me names sometimes, but I put my earbuds in so I can't hear them, and it's fine."

"Why...do they call you names?"

"Because I have autism."

I don't know what I'd expected him to say, but it wasn't that. I'm pretty sure I stared, possibly with my mouth open. "You—you're autistic?" I bit my tongue before I could add, *you can't be.* Something was off about him, yes, but...autism? Weren't autistics unable to speak, unable to touch people?

Emmet kept staring at the tree. "Yes. I have autism spectrum disorder. My brain is wired differently than most people's. But it's not like depression where they think it's about monoamines. It manifests as social disorder and in how my body behaves, my mannerisms. I'm intelligent, more so than most people, but I have a hard time interacting with others. So most people act like there's something wrong with me, that I'm stupid."

Which is basically what I'd done. I felt awful. "I'm sorry."

"It's okay. They're the ones missing out." He paused again, but this time I was pretty sure he was working out what to say, not waiting because he felt he was supposed to. "I was hoping you'd want to be friends with me."

I remembered he'd said he'd been wanting to meet me for a long time. I realized he'd worked up the courage to introduce himself to me, as if I were someone people clamored to get to know. The thought made me feel wonderful and self-conscious at once. "I'm not interesting. I...don't have many friends."

"Me either." He turned his face so he almost looked at me, and he held out his hand. "What do you think? Should we give friendship with each other a whirl?"

I stared at his hand, unsure of what to do with it. Confused, flattered, terrified, and above all hypnotized, I put my hand in his. When he squeezed my fingers, a thrill raced through me.

For the first time since my meltdown, I wasn't thinking about how to make the world stop, how to escape the failure that was my life. I thought about Emmet Washington, and physicists, and autism, and monoamines.

I thought about what it would be like, being Emmet's friend.

Chapter Three
Emmet

I was thrilled with how well meeting Jeremey had gone. I'd worried his panic attack was a bad sign, but even that had worked out. Jeremey was everything I'd hoped and *more*.

I felt bad, though, that he had depression and his parents weren't helping him with therapy. I worried about him leaving for college in the fall, with no friends to help him.

It wasn't fall yet, though. We'd exchanged cell numbers, and I already had an appointment in my calendar to text him in the morning and arrange a date. Except Jeremey made an appointment to text me first.

I was working some math problems at 9:18 p.m. when my phone buzzed. It was the single buzz that meant someone new had texted me, which meant it might also be spam. Usually I ignore those and let my dad sort them out because once the spam was bad and it upset me. But then I remembered I hadn't assigned Jeremey a vibration pattern or set up his contact at all beyond his name and number. That was unusual for me, and I don't do anything unusual.

Jeremey was not usual to me.

I hummed for a minute and rocked in my chair while I tried to decide what to do.

Here's the thing about my brain—it acts like an octopus, my mom says. This is another metaphor, but unlike the spoons, I understand this one. I don't actually have a mollusk inside my skull, but part of my brain acts like one. It sits quiet until something pokes it, and then it puts tentacles all over and makes me feel nervous. I don't like this metaphor. An octopus on your brain is bad, even a pretend one, but Mom says we can't take it out without hurting me, so I live with an octopus. It's gross, but I can't change it. So I hum to it and rock and flap my hands.

I had to do everything—hum, rock and flap—until 9:23 p.m. I wanted to talk to Jeremey, but I couldn't know if it was Jeremey until I looked to see if it said Jeremey Samson or unknown or nasty bad spam. I could ask my mom, but she would want to talk, and I didn't want to talk to her right now. I wanted this to be *my* thing, with Jeremey. No Mom, Dad or Althea.

If it is bad spam, I will ask for the foam hammer to bang on my bed with, I promised the octopus, and that worked. I flipped over my phone and touched the home button.

I saw Jeremey's name and number appear in the preview notification with the word *hi*.

Now I hummed because I was happy. I unlocked the phone with my fingerprint, and when I opened the text app, I laughed. There was my text to myself, my joke I'd sent when I'd entered my number into his phone and sent a text so I'd have his number in mine.

Hello Emmet, this is yourself from Jeremey's phone. It was still funny. I tell good jokes.

I wanted to text back, but first I filled out his contact information and gave him a vibration pattern so I would know it was him when he texted next time. I gave him the heartbeat pattern because he made my heartbeat go funny, and because I wanted him to be my boyfriend. You use hearts for boyfriends. Or girlfriends, if you're not gay or if you're lesbian.

I hoped Jeremey was gay. I wished I could ask him, but Dr. North and my parents all told me with serious faces I could not ask people that right away. It is something I don't understand. If it's natural and okay to be homosexual, why is it such a big deal to ask if someone is or not? Except they tell me it's because of the people on the TV and in the bad churches. Their hearts are sick, which they can fix but they usually don't want to. It's dangerous to be around them. They project hate onto people they don't understand, and it can hurt me and other gay people. Some countries kill gay people.

I'm glad I live in Iowa, not those countries, and I'm glad our church is not a bad one. Iowa is a good state with lots of equality. It has same-sex marriage and had the first female lawyer and said people of different skin colors could get married to each other before the Civil War happened. Iowa is a good place. Some people here still have sick hearts, but most people are okay.

I worried if Jeremey was okay. I would need to use the foam hammer for a long time if he had a sick heart.

I was done entering Jeremey's contacts, so I texted him.

Hello Jeremey. This is Emmet. You don't need to say it's you in a text, but I prefer to. I like the way it looks, as if I'm there in the words. *I'm glad you texted me.*

He didn't text back right away, but I was patient because he might have had to go to the bathroom, or his bedtime might be earlier than mine. But I didn't wait long before I felt the heartbeat vibration in my hand.

Thank you for introducing yourself today. I enjoyed meeting you.

The text made me smile. Not as big as when he wanted to be my friend, but it was still a nice stretch on my face. I hummed as I replied. *I would like to meet you tomorrow. What activities do you enjoy? What time are you free?*

I wanted to see Jeremey tomorrow. I had several open spaces in my schedule. It could work.

He replied again. *I don't have anything going on. Wide open.*

I hesitated as I tried to understand what was wide open. Before I could figure it out, he texted again.

What do you enjoy doing?

I relaxed. I understood this question. *Many things. Math is wonderful, but so are computer games. Sometimes I make computer games. Minecraft is good, but not on the server. I don't care to shoot things in games. I like reading. I enjoy poker, but people don't want to play poker with me.*

Why not? he texted back.

They don't like it when I count the cards, but it makes me nervous to play without counting.

Huh. Well, I don't know how to play poker anyway. I play some computer games. But I like old ones, like Pharaoh.

I put down the phone and Googled *Pharaoh computer game.* You have to add computer game, or it will tell you about Ancient Egypt. I looked at the game pictures and read some reviews, then texted Jeremey. *I found it online. It looks fun.*

Do you want to come over tomorrow and see it?

Also a hard answer. Yes, I did, but I got nervous thinking about going into Jeremey's house. I would rather he came to mine. But Pharaoh was a PC game, and I only have Apple products, because they're better. I hummed and rocked while I tried to think of what to do.

Jeremey texted back before I could answer. *Or we can go to your house.*

That made me feel better. But I remembered Jeremey had panic attacks. *Will you be nervous to come here?*

Yes, but I'm nervous all the time.

It made me sad to think Jeremey was always nervous. His brain octopus must be bad. I wanted to say I could go to his house so he wouldn't be nervous, but I didn't think I could. We were stuck. I didn't want to go back to only watching him in his yard when he mowed the lawn. If it didn't rain, he only mowed once a week, and never in a scheduled pattern, so sometimes I missed it.

Then I had an idea.

We could meet at the train tracks. Whoever is less nervous will go to the other person's house.

Jeremey wrote back in thirty seconds. *That could work. What time do you want to meet?*

I opened my calendar to my schedule. It's always full, but the events are colored. Red events can't be changed. Like bedtime. Yellow events mean I have to talk to my mom before I alter them. But green events are okay, and I can change them on my own. I had green events at nine, ten, eleven, one, two, three and four. I wanted to maybe use several events to be with Jeremey. So I would pick an early one. But I didn't know if it should be morning or afternoon.

Do you wake up early, or do you sleep late? I asked him.

Usually I sleep late, but I can set an alarm.

It made me feel good to think he would change his sleep schedule for me. Though he shouldn't. Sleep was important. *Let's meet at 1 p.m. Does that work with your schedule? I am free until 5 p.m.* I wanted to explain I go shopping for dinner with Althea at five, but this is extra information, and people don't always want to know. Plus I'd have to explain Althea, and that's not always easy.

One o'clock sounds good. I'll meet you at the train tracks.

I smiled. I had a date. My first date. But then I remembered the train.

Sometimes there is a train at 1 p.m. They have an irregular schedule, but sometimes there's one at the time we agreed to meet. If a train comes, wait in your yard and we can meet when it's over. You shouldn't go too close to trains. Accidents can happen.

Okay. I'll watch for the train. And for you.

My mom knocked on my door—four knocks, so I'd know it was her. "Bedtime, sweetheart."

She was right. My 9:50 p.m. alarm was about to go off to tell me to brush my teeth, get into pajamas, lay out tomorrow's clothes and go to bed. I texted Jeremey. *I need to get ready to sleep now. I will see you tomorrow.*

Okay. Good night. Thanks for talking with me.

Jeremey could make me smile so much. My smile made my face stretch as I replied to him. *You can text me in the morning if you want, if you don't sleep too late. I can't talk at noon because it's lunchtime, but I have a vibration alert for you, and I will always know when you text me. I'll answer unless I'm in a place inappropriate to answer a text.*

I wanted to tell him about the heartbeat vibration pattern, but it was extra information. It also would mean I would have to explain I wanted him to be my boyfriend. Which it's too early to say out loud, even I knew that. Sometimes feelings have to wait.

Jeremey texted back. *Thank you. Maybe I will text you.*

Good night, Jeremey.

Good night, Emmet.

Chapter Four
Jeremey

Nobody ever asked me what it's like to have depression. Not Bart, not the school guidance counselor, not our doctor, not my parents. Everyone treated me like a freak and wrote me off.

Everyone until Emmet.

A train did come at one when we were supposed to meet, but I could see him waiting in his yard, rocking on his heels and tapping his finger on his leg as the cars rolled by. He didn't look at me, which still felt strange, but the truth was, sometimes when people stared at me, I felt overwhelmed and had to look away.

I wondered if he was overwhelmed, or if with autism it was different.

I wondered if I could ask him about it.

When the train passed, I started down the ditch to the train tracks, and so did he. He still didn't meet my gaze, though he glanced at me a few times. A tiny smile played around his lips.

"Seventy-seven cars, three engines. One at the back." Emmet wrapped his arms around himself and stood rigid, fixing his gaze over my shoulder and rocking slightly on his heels. "I'm sorry. That's a rude way to greet someone. Hello, Jeremey. It's good to see you again."

I smiled and wrapped my own arms around my body, mirroring his pose. "It's good to see you too."

He seemed agitated, but when he spoke, his voice was clear and even. "It's a nice day. Seventy-seven degrees, only seventy percent humidity. No chance of rain. I enjoy rain, but today I'm okay without it. It's sunny, but we have an umbrella on the deck and large trees. It's shady and comfortable. Would you like to sit outside on our deck?"

The no eye contact wasn't half as difficult as the wall of words he threw at me. I did my best to sift through for the question. Did I want to sit on the deck with him? I did, but it took me a minute to answer. "Yes, thank you."

"If you're too nervous, we could sit on your deck. Except my mom made banana bread. Gluten free, no sugar. We use stevia. The effects of gluten on ASD are unsubstantiated, but it doesn't hurt to cut it out in case there are hidden benefits. Sugar is inflammatory and bad for your brain and your body. Health is important and food is health. Except sometimes my dad takes me for ice cream anyway because he says fun is important for health too." He paused and started to rock again. "I think I am giving you too much information. I'm sorry. I'm nervous. It's hard to remember what not to say to you."

This, his bluntness, was what had drawn me to him yesterday, and it pulled me in just as much today. To say Emmet was honest was as understated as saying the surface of the sun was warm.

Plus, he was cute, and I could stare at him because he wasn't looking at me. His lips were not too thin, not too plump and a soft pink. But more than anything I liked his neck. The cords, the divots of his clavicle, his smooth skin. I worried if it was okay to think he was cute. I worried, a lot, that it made me a perv to crush on him. Then I worried it was rude *not* to perv on him, since he'd demonstrated clearly that autism wasn't mental retardation.

Though this is pretty much me in a nutshell. I worry about all the rules, and then panic because there's no definitive answer to anything.

I hadn't said anything back to him. Except he wasn't angry or agitated. Only waiting.

I took a deep breath and replied. "I'm nervous, but I always am. It's okay. Let's go sit on your deck. The banana bread sounds good."

He relaxed. "Okay. Let's go." He started toward his house, but he kept talking, turning his head so I could hear. "She makes two kinds. One with walnuts and one without. I don't care for walnuts in food. The texture is too strange. You can have whichever kind of bread you want. But she'll probably make us have water to drink."

I nodded, realized he couldn't see, since he wasn't actually looking at me, so I said, "Okay."

He kept talking, explaining all the ingredients in banana bread and how different flours behaved in baking and the binding properties of egg versus gluten, and I listened, but mostly I was thinking. I'd never met anyone like Emmet. He reminded me of a guy in our class, Kyle, who had cerebral palsy. With CP sometimes there's brain damage and sometimes there isn't, but the physical defects made him seem different. In middle school Kyle and I were friends, but he moved away in ninth grade. Kyle wasn't dumb any more than I was. But it was easy to forget that his barking laugh and strange noises and flailing hand gestures outside didn't accurately reflect his insides.

It's the same with me. I'm quiet, and it's hard for me to explain what I'm feeling, but I feel a lot of things, and I do want friends. It was tricky with Emmet, though. I usually watch people for cues to know how to behave around them, and Emmet didn't give any. I wished I could ask him about autism, but I worried it would be rude. I didn't want to hurt his feelings.

As we came onto the deck, Emmet pointed at a chair. "You sit here. I'll put up the umbrella and tell my mom we're ready for a snack."

He turned the crank on the umbrella until the canvas spread above us. He watched the crank as it turned, and I thought I heard him hum, but only once. When he was finished, however, he didn't go inside the house. He pulled out his phone. He texted something, then put the phone on the table and sat down.

"I'm leaving the phone out, but I'll only answer if it's my mom. She might have questions. Oh. Which kind of bread did you want? With the walnuts or without?"

I had a moment of panic, trying to decide which was the right or wrong choice, but it was difficult to stay nervous when Emmet was so nonthreatening. Besides, I didn't like walnuts either. "Without, please."

"Okay. I'll tell her." He typed another text, then pushed the phone aside. He sat on the edge of the chair, and I got the idea he was deliberately not rocking. "What should we talk about?"

It was a simple question, but it felt like a land mine, or rather a big rushing chute, sending me down a river into waters I didn't know how to navigate. I didn't know what to talk about. I never did. This was going to be a disaster. I felt sweaty and uncomfortable, and I wanted to go home. Then I felt horrible for feeling that way. The dark waters pulled me harder.

"You have hunched shoulders. You're nervous. Did I say the wrong thing?"

His question drew me out of the mire enough to blink in surprise. "What? No. I'm...sorry. I'm not good at this."

Emmet stared at the umbrella crank. "That is not specific. The word *this* is a pronoun, but you gave me no antecedent. What are you not good at?"

He was so *intense*. I wasn't sure what to do, or say. "I'm not good at much. I have a hard time talking to people."

Emmet nodded. "Me too. I want to talk to people, but they don't understand me. They get mad a lot. Or they get mean, which is worse. This is because of the autism, why I can't understand. I can't read faces, and people say confusing things. You said, *I'm not good at this,* but you didn't tell me what *this* is, so I can't understand you. I try to be clear and exact when I talk, but sometimes that's bad. Talking with people is tricky for me. Why is it difficult for you?"

It took me a second to digest the fact that he'd spoken of his disability as casually as he might a paper cut. Plus he'd given me so much information about himself, helpful information. Intense and direct. It was, honestly, refreshing.

I wondered if I could dare to be the same.

"If I say the wrong thing, I'm sorry," Emmet said. "If you tell me what was bad, I won't say it anymore to you."

I made myself look at his face while I answered. "It's okay. I'm trying to find my answer is all. That's one of the reasons it's hard for me to talk to people. I worry about saying the wrong thing, and sometimes it means I can't say anything. It takes me a long time to give an answer to a question."

Emmet brightened. "This is why we can be good friends. If you say the wrong thing to me, I'll tell you. Then you can stop, and it will all be fine." He rocked in his chair, clearly a subconscious gesture. "Thank you for telling me how sometimes it takes time for you to answer. I will try to wait. You'll have to tell me if I'm not being patient enough."

He made it sound so easy. "I wouldn't want to upset you, though, even by accident."

"Accidents happen. Even if we all stick to a schedule, the world is unpredictable. Sometimes I'm late to an appointment because of traffic. Sometimes the power goes out because of a storm or the weather closes the roads. It upsets me, but I can't let it ruin my life. If you said the wrong thing and upset me, I would tell you, and then you would stop, and it wouldn't matter that you had said something wrong. We're friends. Friends forgive each other." He started rocking, then stopped. "Does it bother you when I rock? It bothers people sometimes, but it calms me down."

"I don't mind." I watched him begin to rock slightly in his seat. "Are you nervous, though?"

"Yes, and I don't know why, which makes me more nervous. But I don't want to end our date. So I'm calming myself down."

The more I sat with Emmet, the more fascinated I was. Basically he kept saying out loud what I was feeling, except where I scolded myself and felt awkward, he...rocked. Or reached for some kind of pragmatism I could barely dream of.

I didn't want this date to end either. Though that gave me pause, that he called it a date.

Obviously he didn't mean *date*.

Except, maybe he did. The thought made me feel jumbled and heavy, and I had to push it away.

His mother appeared then with a tray bearing two plates and two glasses of water. Emmet took his own plate and glass from the tray, but I let his mother serve me, and I told her thank you after.

"You're welcome." She smiled at me and held out a hand. "Hi. I'm Marietta Washington. It's good to meet you."

I accepted her hand. "J-Jeremey. Good to meet you too."

Her face was as animated and bright as Emmet's was cool. "If you need anything, let me know."

"Mom, go away. I want to be with Jeremey by myself."

I startled at his rudeness, but Marietta took it in stride. She turned to Emmet and without a word extended two closed fingers in front of him.

He grimaced and touched three fingers to her two.

"I'll be inside if either of you need me," she said, and went into the house.

Emmet rocked in his seat, staring at the umbrella crank. "Do you want to eat, or do you want to keep talking?"

I was confused. "We can't do both?"

Emmet shook his head. "No. Separate is better. I want to keep talking, but it's rude to keep a guest from their food. I can wait if you're hungry."

"Talking is okay," I told him. I wasn't actually hungry at all.

Emmet remained agitated. "I wish she would have texted. The interruption was unexpected. I wanted to ask you more about being nervous, and about depression."

I blinked. "You did? I mean, you do?"

"Yes. I want to know about you. So I don't make mistakes."

Well. That was...pragmatic. I leaned back in my chair, thinking. "Can I ask about your autism?"

He smiled. Not big, not long, but it was there. The gesture arrested me.

"Yes. You may always ask me about my autism. Then you'll know. Knowledge is important." His rocking was gentle now. It made me think he was happy-rocking. "But I've told you some things about autism already. It's your turn to tell me about depression. I refreshed my research about it this morning. It's fascinating, but there seem to be few determinable causes, which makes treatment difficult. Which medicine do you take?"

"I don't take any medication. They've talked about it, but...I'm not taking anything now."

"There are many kinds, but some of the side effects are bad. It's inefficient that they have to use trial and error to find the right one, and then there is relapse. You should consider exercise and Omega 3 fatty acids. My mom is a doctor. You can always ask her questions about depression if you want. And health food. It's all she wants to eat. Except my aunt Althea is worse. She's vegan. Mom and Althea have fights about paleo and vegan diets. Sometimes my dad and I let them fight and we go to Subway and get meatball subs and watch *The Blues Brothers* together."

I smiled, then ducked my head to hide it.

He continued to rock gently, but sometimes now he flapped his hands too. "How does depression feel? The article talked about low mood and self-esteem, but they weren't specific. Does it mean you're sad all the time? Also, it said clinical anxiety and depression are often present together. Do you have anxiety too?"

"I—don't know." *Clinical* anxiety? What the hell was *that*? I wanted to say no, I didn't have it, whatever the hell it was. It wasn't as if I needed anything else wrong with me, but it was hard to argue I wasn't anxious when I hid in the school bathroom and got nervous about going to the store.

Except *clinical anxiety* was probably the flip side of *major depressive disorder*. Why hadn't the doctor asked about that? Was it because I didn't tell them about the panic attacks? If I told them, would they say I had clinical anxiety too? Would that mean I was too messed up and they'd put me in an institution?

Tiny claws of terror sank into my brain, and I thought, *Yeah, you totally have clinical anxiety. You have both. That has to be bad.*

I picked at the bread, mostly for something to do with my hands. "I didn't always have depression. But I was always quiet. It got bad in high school."

I tried to think of how to answer Emmet's question, about how it felt. I put the anxiety question away in a box inside my head and sealed it shut with mental duct tape. "Depression feels like there's a bowl over you. A glass bowl you can see out of, but it makes the world further away. It feels lonely and heavy. But sometimes the bowl gets cloudy."

I could see the bowl in my head, myself in the glass. "Even though I'm inside the bowl, everything from the outside still gets in, too loud. So I'm under glass, full of clouds, with a loudspeaker piping in all the sounds, and the smells and lights get in too. Sometimes they make me panic, but sometimes there's all the sound and it makes me feel flat and dull. Or nothing at all. It makes it difficult for me to be with people, but if I'm not with people, I feel more lonely."

Emmet leaned toward me, earnest. "You need people, Jeremey. Humans are social animals. We get sick without contact."

Didn't I know it. I loved this contact right now. It was weird—I kept forgetting he had autism, though it was obvious every time I looked at him or he spoke. Mostly, though, he felt like someone who wasn't annoyed with me or awkward around me. Someone who made me feel like a real person.

A friend.

"I'm glad we became friends." His gaze flicked to my chest.

I smiled at him. "I'm glad we're friends too."

Emmet rocked gently. "I want to eat my banana bread now. Would it be okay if we stopped talking long enough to eat?"

"Sure." I kept smiling. It was so easy—he was easy. This felt good.

"We can keep talking after we finish. I enjoy talking with you."

The nerves which had troubled me all day began, by inches, to fade away. "I enjoy talking with you too."

Emmet and I didn't meet every day, but we always texted. At first it was random, but by the third day he asked if we could schedule time to chat with each other at 9 p.m., and he got me to do it on Google Talk instead of phones.

I wish you had an iMac or an iPhone, he texted me one night. *The iMessage interface is much better, and if you were on Apple products too, we could switch between phone and computer more easily.*

I don't even have a smartphone, I replied.

We have an old iPhone you could use, if it worked with your plan.

I lied and told him I'd look into it. I didn't want to tell him my mom and dad would never go for it.

Things had been tense with my parents since the picnic for a lot of reasons, but it didn't take long for Emmet to be the focus of our recurrent arguments. They'd seen me talking to him at the block party and asked about him when we got home, but I mostly blew them off. I could tell Emmet would rather be at his place, so we hung out there, and honestly I felt better at the Washington house too. When I got home from visiting him a third day in a row, I was glad I hadn't had him over to my place and vowed it would be a cold day in hell before I did.

"Where were you?" my mom asked me as I came in the door. "I searched the whole backyard, but you weren't anywhere. Were you walking on the tracks again?"

I thought about lying, but it felt wrong to lie about Emmet. "I was visiting a friend."

"Bart?" My mom's whole demeanor changed. She smiled, and her shoulders went back, like the world was coming into the right orbit. "I hadn't realized you two were hanging out again. How's he doing?"

Now I wished I'd gone with my original impulse to deceive her. "It's not Bart. A new friend." I could see the question forming on her face, the judgment and censure about Emmet, and I decided to trap her. "He's a sophomore at ISU. Double major in computers and advanced physics." Or maybe it was applied physics. I didn't care—*advanced* sounded better.

She paused, thrown off her game. "A university student, here? This far from campus? Is there a rental house in the neighborhood?"

"No. He lives with his parents. Might as well, to save money. And we're actually close to ISU, if you cut through the park." I decided to lay it on thick. "He's wicked smart. Programs on his computer for fun."

"Oh." Mom relaxed, comforted by the idea I might be making a decent friend who could straighten me out. "What's his name? I can't believe I didn't know about a boy your age in the neighborhood."

Boy? What was I, twelve? "Emmet Washington," I said, and watched her tense up.

"*Jeremey Andrew Samson.*" She closed the distance between us and loomed over me. "That's horrible of you, lying about a retarded boy. What are you *doing* with him? Babysitting?"

I blinked at her, blown away by her cruelty and insensitivity—except she wasn't being mean. She was *that* clueless. "Mom, he got a perfect score on his ACT. He really is a double major in physics and computers. I'm not babysitting. I'm hanging out with him. He's not retarded, and you're not supposed to use that word anymore anyway."

She rolled her eyes. "Don't give me that PC nonsense. Retarded means *delayed*. You can't tell me that boy is normal."

No, I couldn't—but sometimes I thought he was a lot more normal than me.

Emmet had his tics, yes, but he had a pragmatism I didn't just admire—I found it *soothing*. If nothing else, I always knew where I stood with Emmet. If he didn't want to do an activity, he said so. If something was important to him, he let you know. He was kind though too—he noticed things about me I wouldn't have expected anyone to notice, and he regarded what I considered my most awkward oddities as simply part of who I was.

The greatest example of this was the day we walked to Wheatsfield, the organic grocery store at the end of my street. Emmet's mother needed some things for dinner, and Emmet asked if we could run the errands for her.

"How kind of you to offer, Emmet. Thank you." She kissed him on the cheek. "I'll get the list and the wheeled shopping bag."

I don't know why, but I was ridiculously excited to run the errand with him. We'd taken walks around the block before, usually in the evening when it was cooler, but shopping together was kind of domestic and grown-up. This wasn't hanging-out shopping, either. We were helping make dinner, which I'd already been invited to stay for. The whole episode made me feel like part of the family. A real family. A good one.

No sooner did we start down the street, though, when Emmet stopped us. "No. You like the inside." He pushed me to the far side of the sidewalk, the one closest to the houses. "You get nervous when you're by the street."

"I do?"

"Yes. You jump when a car goes by. You still do when you walk on the inside, but you relax more."

I had no idea I did that. How many other people had noticed this? "I didn't know. I'm sorry."

"Don't be sorry. But you need to be on the inside, so don't take the outside."

We didn't talk the rest of the way, but we didn't usually talk a lot when we walked. I used the time to think, to enjoy being with him. Also, it was fun to find out what he was counting. I'd learned he was always counting *something* when he was so quiet. I had asked him so often on our walks that now he simply told me when we arrived at our destination.

"Nine hundred thirty-one cracks in the sidewalk," he announced when we made it to the store. He pushed a multicolored striped wheeled trolley ahead of him, which Marietta had explained would hold the grocery bag. "One hundred twenty-four irregular. Eight hundred and seven straight lines."

"Sidewalk cracks? Surely you've counted those between here and your house before."

"Yes. But there were four new ones today."

I wondered what it would be like to have a brain that counted so many things. I would think it would be exhausting, but Emmet enjoyed it.

I was going to ask him more about the cracks, but then we went into the store—and hit a wall of noise.

I'd been in this store before, and I enjoyed it because it was so small, but I'd never come when a live band played in the corner. The store was full of people talking and laughing as they shopped. I wasn't laughing. All I wanted to do was run. It felt like someone was slamming cymbals against my head over and over. It was hard to breathe.

I was so embarrassed—I was having a panic attack in front of Emmet.

And then, abruptly, I wasn't. Or rather, the cymbals were gone and I was breathing rough, but we were outside and Emmet was sitting me down on a bench.

He touched my face awkwardly. "It's too loud in the store."

"I'm sorry," I tried to say, but mostly I wheezed.

He pushed my head between my knees, his warm hand on my back. "Take deep breaths. Go to a happy place in your head."

He was so calm and logical it frankly surprised me partially out of my attack. It took me a minute to regain full control, but I recovered more quickly than I had in a long time.

I was sad when he took his hand away.

"You're better. You need something to drink. Will you be okay?" I nodded. "Good. I'm going to find Carol."

I thought he would go inside, but he loitered by the door, rocking back and forth until someone came outside—a middle-aged woman with red hair and a bright smile and an apron marking her as a store employee.

"Hello, Emmet. Where's your mother?"

Emmet didn't look her in the eye, and he kept rocking. "She's at home. I'm here with my friend Jeremey. But your music is too loud, and there are too many people. He had a panic attack and needs something to drink. It's too loud for me too. I have good adaptations because I've practiced, but I don't like the store either right now. It makes both of us uncomfortable."

Carol turned to me, all empathy. "Oh, honey. I'm so sorry."

She spoke to me as if I were a four-year-old. I shut my eyes and tried to wish her away.

Emmet gave her no quarter. "Your music is too loud, Carol. You upset people. It's bad for your business. Althea would lecture you about ableism. I want to lecture you too. But I can't right now. We need to take care of Jeremey. He's upset. He needs something to drink."

I tried to say I was fine, but I wasn't. Carol and Emmet spoke for a minute—he asked for two mineral waters with raspberry, and he gave her the list of groceries and his mother's debit card. Then he sat beside me. "I'm sorry for her music. I'm angry with her for upsetting you."

He was the calmest angry person I'd ever met. I still felt embarrassed, though I was touched Emmet took my side. "It's okay. I'm sure the normal people enjoy the party."

"No one is normal. Normal is a lie. The store should be for all people, not only people who like loud music. It's rude. I'm telling my mother. She's a board member of the co-op. All people should be included. They make the aisles big enough for wheelchairs. They should make the stimuli low for people who need things calmer. If our sensitivity had a chair, they'd make room for it."

He spoke in the same flat tones he always did, but he rocked a lot, and his hands opened and closed in a rhythm on his lap. This was angry Emmet. Angry, protective Emmet.

Angry for me. He'd stood up for me.

"Thank you," I told him.

He glanced at me. Well, near me. "What did I do?"

"You took care of me. Thank you."

He looked surprised. He stared at the pavement with one of his almost-smiles. "You're welcome."

Soon Carol appeared with more apologies, a full shopping bag, and chocolate gluten free vegan cupcakes for Emmet and me. We ate them before we started walking, washing them down with the last of our mineral waters. By the time we got to his house with the supplies for dinner, I'd forgotten all about my panic attack.

In fact, I felt great until I went to my house, where my mother pursed her lips at me and my dad failed to emerge from the den, too engrossed in his TV. I thought about the Washingtons, who as I left had been doing the dishes together and arguing good-naturedly about politics, all but Emmet who made it clear he planned to spend the rest of the evening programming in his room.

I'd always known my family wasn't the most amazing in the world. It had been better when Jan still lived at home, but not much. I didn't realize until that day, though, how lonely my house was. How it was technically my home...but I felt safer and happier and more accepted for who I was and who I wasn't in the living room of the family I'd known for less than a month.

I tried to tell myself this would be the bright side of moving to Iowa City, getting away from my parents. Except I'd never find another Emmet there. With every day I hung out with him, anything less than that kind of happiness didn't feel like a life worth pursuing.

Chapter Five
Emmet

By the Fourth of July, Jeremey was my best friend.

I'd felt he could be my best friend for a long time, but the holiday was when it all came together. We went to the downtown parade—just us, not with either of our parents. We wandered around the carnival in Bandshell Park. We thought about swimming at the aquatic center, but there were too many people, so we biked out to Ada Hayden instead. It's a park with a water reservoir you can boat on, with lots of paved trails. It was a hot, hot day, but I didn't mind. I was with Jeremey.

He went with our family to watch fireworks on the Sixth Street hill—the tree line means we miss a few, but it's not crowded, not loud, and all our neighbors are there. While we were sitting on the blanket, covered in vanilla bug spray, watching kids run with sparklers down the hill to the soccer field at the bottom, my feelings became intense. I was happy, so happy. I still wanted Jeremey to be my boyfriend, and sometimes maybe I thought he might be gay too, but even if we were only friends, it would be okay. He was my best friend, the kind of close friend it's a challenge for a person with autism to have. We can be tricky to get to know. But already Jeremey knew more about me than anyone, even my parents and Althea.

As the fireworks exploded above us in the sky, the urge to tell him how I felt was huge inside me. I was scared to end my happy feelings if he didn't feel like we were best friends too, and I worried my autism would wreck the moment. So though he sat right next to me, I texted him.

Jeremey, you're my best friend. My chest got tight with nervousness. *I hope that's okay,* I added, then hit send.

His phone made a soft chime. I held my breath, for once hating my superpower of seeing out of the corner of my eye. I couldn't help watching him pull out his phone, read the text and answer back. When my phone made the heartbeat pulse against my hand, I almost didn't read it. I was sorry I'd sent anything. If he said it wasn't okay, all my happiness would crash.

But when I got brave enough to read the text, it said *me too.*

I smiled as I rocked on the blanket. I had a best friend.

I wished he were my boyfriend. If he had been, I would have asked to hold his hand. But I didn't. I only enjoyed the rest of the fireworks with my best friend.

We hung out together every day, usually in the afternoons. Usually we played games or took walks. Sometimes we sat on my deck and didn't say anything. Jeremey enjoyed reading, and when my mom found out, she gave Jeremey her old Kindle full of all kinds of books. Jeremey wouldn't take it to his house, but every afternoon if I suggested we sit on the deck, he brought the Kindle out and read the whole time unless I talked to him. I loved those afternoons.

I also showed Jeremey *The Blues Brothers* movie, which he said he hadn't ever seen. I liked showing him the movie, but at first when we started watching together, I didn't have much fun. I was working so hard to not be autistic.

The Blues Brothers isn't just my favorite movie. It was one of the first things I memorized. My dad loves the movie too, and he played it around me when I was little. My mom got mad at him for that, because I would walk around quoting the whole movie, or using the movie to speak. If I wanted something from my mom, I asked her, "Did you get my Cheez Whiz?" I didn't want Cheez Whiz, but to my brain, it was the only way I could ask for something, using the line from the movie. When I played with my blocks, I would line them up in a row and count them by quoting the part where the guard (who is Frank Oz, the guy who gave the voice to Miss Piggy and other Muppets) lists the inventory of Jake Blues' personal effects. "One Timex digital watch, broken. One unused prophylactic. One soiled. One black suit jacket." And when I didn't want to do something, I didn't simply say no. I crossed my arms over my chest and said, "No. Fucking. Way."

I don't remember doing this, but Mom says I used the whole movie as speech from the time I was four until the first half of kindergarten. I don't do that anymore, but sometimes my brain whispers the lines from the movie in places it thinks would be a good time to say them. Sometimes people on the mean quote movies, and other people on the mean laugh at the joke. But they laugh differently at me when I quote *The Blues Brothers*, so I don't do it in public.

My dad likes it when I quote, though, because he says I do an amazing Elwood Blues. Sometimes when we're in the car, he says, "What's this?" and I know I'm supposed to do the part about trading the Cadillac for a microphone. I keep telling him that for it to be right he needs to let me drive, since Elwood always drives. He says no, I'd try to jump a bridge. Which isn't true. Ames doesn't have any moveable bridges.

It's fun to quote the movie with my dad, but there's one problem about watching the movie, especially with someone not a member of my family. Every time I watch the movie, I say the lines along with the actors. I've gotten better about not saying every line out loud, but I say every single one in my head. I read a script of it online when I was in high school, and now when I watch it, I say the stage directions too. My dad says the lines with me when they're his favorites, and he never cares how much of the movie I recite.

When autistic people quote TV and movies the way I did when I was little, they call it echolalia. I don't have echolalia now. When I speak, one hundred percent of what I say is my words. Some autistic people, though, can't ever stop parroting either TV or movies or what the person in front of them just said. It's because of their brain octopuses.

People shouldn't laugh or make rude faces at autistic people when they parrot. Some can't help it, and most who can have to work not to. It's difficult for me not to quote *The Blues Brothers* all the time even now. When I watch the movie, it's almost impossible to resist.

I was nervous to find out how Jeremey would feel about my autistic quoting. I didn't want him to think I was weird and decide we shouldn't be best friends. So all the way until Elwood and Jake left the nun they call The Penguin, I sat on the edge of the couch, trying not to rock, trying not to hum, and more than anything else, trying not to parrot. It was the first time I ever didn't like watching *The Blues Brothers*.

Then my dad walked into the TV room, and said, "Boys, you gotta learn not to talk to nuns that way."

I rocked back and forth. "Dad, they already did that line."

"I know. But it's one of my favorites." Dad sat down all slouched in his favorite chair, the big fat one with an ottoman to the right of the TV. He grinned as he watched Curtis tell the boys they had to get to church.

This was another tricky part for me. Usually I sing along with James Brown. This time I didn't sing, didn't quote anything. Not when my dad did. Not even when he said, "Jesus H. goddamned bastard Christ, I have seen the light!" And I didn't dance along with Elwood, which was the hardest part of all.

When they were talking about putting the band back together, Dad frowned at me. "Emmet, you feeling okay?"

I nodded and stared at the floor. I was watching the movie, but usually I watched the movie by looking at it. I couldn't today, because I would start parroting for sure.

Dad didn't say anything else at first. Eventually he smiled at Jeremey. "How are you liking the movie? I hear it's your first time."

"It's good." Jeremey smiled back. "It's funny."

"You've got to get Emmet to do his Elwood for you. He knows every line. Every incline of Dan Aykroyd's head. Once on vacation he did the whole movie for me when we were stuck waiting for a tow truck. Best two hours of my life."

I stopped rocking and glanced by my dad's head. I remembered sitting by the car on the dark road, doing the movie for my dad. I hadn't realized it was the best moment of his life. It certainly wasn't mine. The rocks had been hard to sit on.

"Usually," Dad went on, "when Emmet and I watch together, we do all the best quotes back and forth. Which, since the movie is so great, means we quote the whole movie. You'll have to forgive me if I do some anyway. Emmet's being kind and letting you watch it without our commentary, but he has more self-control than me."

Jeremey's smile got brighter. "Oh, please do the quotes! I wish I were good at memorizing so I could play along too."

"Emmet memorizes enough for the whole world." Dad winked at me. Then he raised an eyebrow and spoke along with John Belushi. "'First you trade the Cadillac for a microphone, then you lie to me about the band, now you're gonna put me right back in the joint.'"

I was still nervous to parrot in front of Jeremey, but my brain octopus was so angry at me for not being able to quote, my dad was looking right at me, and it was my second favorite line from the movie. "'They're not gonna catch us. We're on a mission from God.'"

Jeremey laughed—and my chest went *flutter flutter flutter*. It was the kind of laugh people on the mean got when they quoted and made good jokes. "Oh my *God*—Emmet, you sounded just like him."

"You wait," my dad said. "If we can talk him into dancing during the Palace Ballroom scene, it'll be your best day all year long."

I started quoting a little more. I didn't want to quote all the time, but Dad did, and pretty soon Jeremey watched me more than the movie, looking at me as if he hoped I'd say something, so I gave in and parroted.

"'You want out of this parking lot? Okay.'"

I loved watching Elwood drive, and the scene in the mall makes me laugh. It looks so fun to drive a car. I've driven go-carts at amusement parks. It's fun. I crash into the walls a lot, and sometimes other drivers, but nobody gets hurt. It's the best.

We kept quoting, and Jeremey kept laughing, and pretty soon *this* became my favorite two hours of *my* life. When we got to the Palace Hotel Ballroom scene and the Blues Brothers theme started to play, Dad and I got up and did the dance. He pretended to unlock a handcuff from my wrist, and I handed the silver thing (I've watched it over one hundred times, but I don't know what that thing is) to the pretend drummer behind me.

Dad passed me the broom handle with a cardboard microphone we keep beside the TV, and I did Elwood's speech before the big number.

I love the song "Everybody Needs Somebody to Love", but I love the speech Elwood does before it best of all the lines of the whole movie. He says everyone is somebody, and we're all the same.

I think Elwood Blues is on the spectrum. He's higher functioning, but he has the signs. Only eating white bread—that's something an autistic person would do. Then there's the bad driving, and some of his tics. Also, I can parrot a lot of characters in movies, but I don't do anybody better than Elwood.

I don't know if he's gay too or not, but he never gets excited about girls, so maybe.

I sang along with Elwood into the pretend microphone, and my dad got up and sang into his. Dad likes to play Jake. He says John Belushi was a genius taken down before his time. We do a good Blues Brothers, and only Belushi and Aykroyd do the dance better, Dad says.

I don't know if Jeremey agreed, but he laughed and clapped and whistled, and when the movie was over, he had a funny look on his face. I didn't know what it meant, but Dad is good at faces.

He leaned forward in his chair and grinned at Jeremey. "You want to see the Palace Ballroom dance again, don't you."

Jeremey blushed, but he nodded.

We did the dance three more times. And now when we watch the movie together, I quote the whole thing. He's not as bad at memorizing as he says, either, because he quotes it now too.

He does a great Curtis.

I saw Jeremey every day, but some afternoons I couldn't sit very long on the deck with him, because I had to go to school.

I didn't have to take summer courses, but Mom and Dad said it would be a good idea for consistency. The class I took was Calculus III, so it wasn't hard for me and made a smart choice for a summer program. It was in Carver Hall, in a nice room with a lot of light. Most of the time I rode my bike and locked it up at the student union, but if it was raining or too hot, I rode the CyRide bus service. I can't drive, but I'm an excellent bus rider. I enjoy being independent enough to bus to school, but I don't spend extra time on campus.

I did take walks on campus with Jeremey, though. It was only a half mile from my house to the edge of campus, and cutting through it was the best way to West Street Deli, where we'd grab lunch if Althea was working. We didn't talk much while we walked, since Jeremey knew I didn't like to walk and talk at the same time. When he wanted to say something, he asked if I minded if we took a break, and we sat on a bench or curb and talked for a few minutes. This meant he wanted to talk, not rest, but he never said, "I want to talk to you, let's stop."

That's pretty much how Jeremey is, though, so I don't mind.

A few days after the Fourth of July, we were walking through campus, and Jeremey asked if we could take a break. We were outside of Beardshear Hall, which is administration offices, and we sat on the steps, looking across the grassy commons. I waited for Jeremey to talk, but this time it took a long time for him to start.

"My parents keep trying to make me apply to college. They finally stopped pushing Iowa City and said I could apply here. That would be okay, I guess, since you'd be here too."

He fiddled with his fingers in the way non-autistic people do when they're nervous. I always notice it because I can't see how it's different than flapping, and I liked when people did the fiddling thing. It meant they felt strong emotions. I was pretty sure Jeremey was having nervous emotions. "Yes, I'll still be here. Will you take science or math or computer classes?"

"I don't know what I'll take. I don't want to go to college at all."

"What do you want to do?"

"I don't know. Rest. I wish everything would calm down."

Jeremey often said that he wanted to rest. Except he went to bed at the same time as me and often slept until noon. Some days he didn't get out of bed at all and had to cancel our time together. But he didn't have much on his schedule ever. I didn't understand what needed to calm down, but before I could decide if it was an okay question to ask, he started talking again. This time his voice shook, he was so nervous.

"This is—probably... I mean..." He shut his eyes and took a breath before continuing. "I don't know if you'd be interested, but I thought maybe we could be roommates in a dorm."

I had many thoughts and feelings at once. I'd asked if I could live in a dorm when I first applied to college, but Mom had taken me on a residential tour, and I knew right away it would never work for me. Too loud, too many people, too much sharing of public space. I think that's why she did that, because I wanted to be the same as everyone else, but not once I saw what college dorm life was. But when I thought about living with Jeremey, all I could think about was being in the same room with him, all the time.

If I lived with him, I was pretty sure I could get up the courage to kiss him and ask if he wanted to be my boyfriend.

"I'm sorry." Jeremey hunched his shoulders and stared at the ground. "That was a stupid thing to ask."

I hated how often Jeremey said he was stupid. "It's a good question. I was trying to think if it would work. I would like to be roommates with you, very much." I remembered the shouting young men and public, dirty showers and began to rock. "A dorm isn't good for my autism, though. But ISU has apartments similar to dorms."

"Probably expensive, though."

I didn't know. I pulled out my phone and made a note on my to-do list to look up the apartments. "I'd have to talk to my parents. The problem is I'm not good at remembering all the things I should do in a house, Mom says, and cooking all the time would be difficult. But I think Frederiksen Court has on-site dining." I hummed a little, trying to imagine it. A nice quiet apartment with Jeremey.

I could kiss him on the couch. If it turned out he was gay too. And wanted to date me, not just be best friends.

"I wonder if there are a lot of parties in those apartments. That might not be good for your autism. Or me either."

No. Parties would be terrible. I hummed and rocked harder. This was a tricky problem. I would have to think about it and do some investigating—but I wanted it to work.

As I sat rocking and humming, a group of guys walked by, and I heard one murmur, "Fucking freaks."

I shut my eyes so I could focus on controlling my anger.

I understand I can't lash out when someone calls me a name. Every now and again it would happen to me when I was with Jeremey, though, and it upset me. I hated not defending myself in front of my best friend who I wanted to be my boyfriend. It made me frustrated and angry and embarrassed.

"What assholes," Jeremey said.

I felt better knowing he hated them too. "I shouldn't have rocked and hummed. That's why they said something."

"Why *can't* you rock and hum? You were thinking. That helps you. People have funny little tics all the time. What's so bad about yours?"

All my feelings swelled up. They were good feelings, but sometimes those make it more difficult for me to talk. If I'd been with my family, I'd have made one of my signs, but I hadn't taught them to Jeremey. So I got out my phone. He never seemed to mind when I texted him instead of talking out loud.

Jeremey, this is Emmet. You are a wonderful friend. Thank you.

Jeremey smiled when he read that, and he leaned toward me as if he were going to put his head on my shoulder. I went still, not sure if I wanted him to do that or not. Before I could decide, though, he sat up straight, very quickly. He texted back.

This is Jeremey. You're a wonderful friend too. I'll talk to my parents about the apartments. That would be so awesome, if it

59

worked. But don't do it if you think it would be bad for your autism.

Normally I was okay with my autism, but right then I hated it. All I could think about was how if I weren't autistic, I could live in the dorms with Jeremey. That was bad logic, because if I didn't have autism, my family wouldn't have moved to a new city so they could be with me as I went to school, and I likely wouldn't have met Jeremey at all. I wouldn't be me, either.

But it wasn't fair that autism made it so hard to be roommates with Jeremey.

When I asked Mom about getting an apartment, I wore my Stitch T-shirt, which was code for my question being important to me.

I have signs and codes I use with my family and they use with me. I can't always understand subtleties of vocal inflections, and of course faces are impossible, and Mom says this is where communication usually breaks down. She says it's why the Internet is full of misunderstandings. I actually do well on the Internet, but maybe that's because I don't rely on verbal and visual cues for comprehension.

When I talk to people in real life, though, they expect me to act like non-autistic people, and Mom says even she forgets not to assume. So we worked out the code. I have shirts that mean different things, and when I wear them, everyone knows I'm feeling something in a big way. We have hand signs so Mom can tell me in public if I'm rude, and she stops me from making everyone mad by accident. When I'm overwhelmed, sometimes talking is hard, so we all learned American Sign Language long ago, which is so handy. Everyone should learn it as a second language, really.

My Stitch shirt says *ohana means family, and family means no one gets left behind.* I wear that one when I want to talk about something important to me. So when I sat her in our talking chairs in the living room and she saw me in that shirt, she didn't tell me she didn't think it was a good idea to get an apartment or remind me of what the dorms were like. She said, "Tell me more about why this is important to you, Emmet."

I had practiced my reasons with notecards in my room, and I wrote an essay about it I could have read aloud or handed to her, but I wanted to show her how hard I was trying and did it the talking way instead. "Jeremey is my best friend. He's nervous about going to college, but his parents are making him. I think his depression is as nervous about being in the dorm as my autism is. Also I think he has an anxiety brain octopus he doesn't know about. Plus I want to live in an apartment with him like a regular college student. Frederiksen Court has on-site dining and groceries. It is the perfect place for us to start our independent living experience."

"Sweetheart, do they have openings this late in the year?"

I didn't know, and I worried about that. We would want the two-person two-bedroom, which the site said was very limited. They capitalized and bolded the word *very*, so they were serious. "Mom, I need to do this."

"I understand. Unfortunately the world doesn't always work itself out simply because we need it to be a certain way." She rubbed her leg as she leaned back in her chair. "This is a sticky one, sweetie. I'm not sure you're ready for a regular apartment, even on campus. You work hard and you try, but when you get frustrated by something, you need help in a hurry. We would do our best to prop you up, but it's not as easy when you don't live upstairs. Maybe we could talk to your dad about finally turning the basement into an apartment."

"I don't like the basement. It smells funny."

"Your choices might be the basement or nowhere, honey."

"Then I want to live in the dorm. We can find a quiet one."

Mom sighed. "I appreciate how much you want this. Please remember I want this for you too. I can promise I'll start looking into options as soon as we're done talking. But I need you to understand it might take a long time, and my solution might not be the exact answer you want."

I understood the logic of what she said, but it made me angry and sad. I thought of the guys calling me freak, of how something like that always happened if I was myself in public. I thought about how nervous Jeremey had been when he asked about living together, because he wanted this as much as me, and he needed help.

I don't like to hate myself, and hating my autism is hating myself, but right then I was so angry, I wanted to be a different person. I worried Jeremey's parents would send him away to Iowa City and we'd stop being friends. I worried he would meet someone not autistic and like them better. I hadn't seen his friend Bart tag him on Instagram or come to his house, and Jeremey never talked about him, but I always worried Bart would take Jeremey away. I thought of all the not-autistic Barts at college who would be brave enough to tell Jeremey they were gay and maybe try to kiss him.

"Emmet." Mom's voice was gentle, and she put her hand by my leg, her way of touching me without adding sensation. "I know how you feel about Jeremey. I know how important he is to you, and that's why this hurts so much, not being able to give him what he asks." She held her hand out flat, her sign for *I need you to listen to this part.* "I am your advocate. I watch for you and fight for you even when you don't notice. I know you're upset, and I think you need some quality time with the foam hammer once we're done talking. But don't you let those bad voices tell you I'm not helping you."

I know she's my advocate, and I'm glad. But I was *so angry.* Maybe my face didn't show it, but inside I felt like fire and sadness. "I'm too different, Mom. I don't want to be so different."

"Everyone's different. Some people are more able to shove their differences into the dark, to blend in and be sheep, but that isn't always a good thing."

"I'd rather be a sheep than be alone."

"But that's the big secret. The sheep are more alone than everyone."

She was right. But I was still pissed off and wanted the world to stop getting in my way. "You're right. I need to go use my hammer."

"And I need to go make some phone calls. Can I have a hug, jujube?"

I am not a fruit from China, which is what a jujube is, and I was too angry for hugs. But *can I have a hug, jujube* is my mom's code for when *she* needs a hug. She's a mom with lots of superpowers, but she says they're powered by hugs.

I really needed her superpowers at full blast right now. So I hugged her and let her kiss my hair, which she also cried on.

I did not cry. I went upstairs, got my foam hammer from the closet and pounded on the bed and yelled for fifteen minutes. I said a lot of bad words.

When I was done, I did some algebra. It's always soothing. I can't live in the dorms and I can't stop people from calling me a freak, but I can always solve for X.

Chapter Six
Jeremey

By the end of July, I was registered for classes at Iowa State, and my parents and I fought all the time.

I felt as if everything they asked me to do was impossible, but even when I did it anyway, my efforts were never enough. I let them register me for classes, but I got in trouble for not taking initiative in getting school supplies or furnishing my impending dorm room. My dorm room where I'd live without Emmet. He'd told me, gaze fixed on the floor, that he was sorry, but his autism wouldn't let him handle a dorm or a campus apartment.

"My mom is looking into other options," he assured me. "She says to sit tight. She has a lead."

I wanted her to have a lead, more than I could express with mere words, but until it became a reality, I had to assume I'd be living in a dorm with a stranger, and I had to prepare. According to my mother, I wasn't prepared remotely enough, and when she got tired of waiting for me to take care of things, she took charge. She dragged me to Target after yelling at me for an hour about responsibility, but I think I would have had a panic attack in the middle of the college prep aisle even if she'd smiled and told me it would all be okay.

Don't think she held my hand afterward, though. She shouted at me the whole way home.

"How could you embarrass me like that? Everyone looking at us. Everyone looked at *me*, as if it were somehow *my* fault."

I felt guilty, though she *was* the reason I got upset. She made me go. I couldn't do the large discount grocery store or any store bigger than Wheatsfield, and some days *it* was too much. But I hate disappointing anyone, and I hated the way everyone looked at me too. I *despised* that I couldn't walk farther than the greeting cards in Target without hyperventilating, but it didn't matter how I tried, I always broke down.

I broke down all the time now, even at home. Not often with Emmet, but we had to stop walking on campus, because it only made me think of how awful living there would be without him, and I would get a panic attack.

"I think you should not go to college yet," Emmet said. "I think you should talk to my mom about medicine. She could prescribe it for you."

He was right. But I always told him I didn't want to talk about medicine. Honestly, part of me *wanted* to go be a mess at school, to show my parents how wrong they were.

Then I would realize how many strangers would see me break down, and I'd have another panic attack. So mostly I tried not to think about school at all.

Marietta worried about me, I could tell. She didn't tell me I should take medication, but she gave me lots of attention every time I was over, assuring me she was looking into alternate housing for Emmet and me, that she was making me an extra-special going-to-school care package. Books began to appear on the Kindle I always borrowed from her too. *The Noonday Demon. Shoot the Damn Dog. From Panic to Power.* They were books about depression and anxiety.

I didn't read them.

It wasn't that I didn't want help. I *did*, but mostly I wanted my parents to stop pushing me, and I didn't see how *me* taking drugs or reading was going to change *them*. I needed *them* to take drugs or read books or at least listen to me.

They didn't listen, no matter what I said or did, no matter how bad my panic attacks became. But one day, my sister called me.

Jan lives in Chicago, and she rarely comes home. My mother complains about this all the time, how whenever she calls Jan, my sister doesn't answer. In Jan's defense, Mom never asks Jan about her life, only complains about her own. I wouldn't answer her calls either, if I were Jan.

Jan doesn't call us, ever, and she *never* calls me. But that day she did, when I was sitting out back waiting for Emmet to be done with class.

"Hey, little brother. How are things?"

"Fine," I said, though they were anything but. Nobody ever wants to know about bad things.

"I hear you're nervous about starting college. And you've been having more panic attacks. You're worrying me, Germ."

My whole body went hot with embarrassment. How did Jan know all this? Her calling me my old nickname didn't make it any better. "I'll be fine." I didn't believe that, but I didn't want yet another person fussing over me. I didn't understand why Jan was. She never did.

But that day, she wouldn't stop. "I know I'm bad about keeping up with the family. I'm sorry for that. I can't handle Mom, so I stay away, but that means I accidentally ignore you. Are you really okay? Do you need me to come home, run interference for you?"

I didn't know what to say. She wanted to come home and help me? I wanted that, yeah, but this whole thing felt weird, and it made me nervous. And embarrassed, that she'd have to bother with me. "I'm okay. Sorry to bother you."

"Hon, you aren't bothering me. I care about you. I want to know what's going on with you. I don't want our parents to drive you out of your mind, and I know from firsthand experience that's a real possibility. Are you seeing someone about all these panic attacks? Are you taking anything, medicine to help?"

Why was everyone acting like I was sick? Like I had a heart condition, not a stupid habit of being upset in public and easily overwhelmed by life? "I'm fine," I told her again. And again.

Eventually she stopped asking, and Emmet started to text me from the bus, so I told her I had to go.

"Okay, but I'm going to keep checking up on you," Jan said.

I was glad she warned me. I told myself I wouldn't be so surprised next time she called, and I'd have better lies prepared.

Two days after Jan's call, Marietta showed up at my house.

She had a cute wicker basket full of banana bread and cookies and a glass bottle of fancy mineral water, and she sat in the kitchen with my mom for an hour, talking about nothing in particular, so I went to my room. But after Marietta went home, Mom was all flushed and happy. The day after, Mom and Marietta went to lunch at the fancy new place in Somerset, and another day they had coffee downtown together at Chocolaterie Stam.

A few days later, Mom suggested I have Emmet over to our house for a change.

She was nervous about it, I could tell, but Marietta had gone on her charm offensive, and she played my mom like a violin. I overheard their discussion on the screened-in porch before the visit. Marietta was telling my mom what to expect with Emmet. "He gets nervous in a new place, and usually I go with him when we try a new environment, but he's insisting on doing this on his own. I've told him the condition for coming over alone is he cannot lose his temper. So if something makes him angry, he'll probably withdraw for a few minutes without telling you anything. If he's doing well, he'll tell you calmly that he's angry. But he's likely far from calm. He's a good boy, though, and he works hard. I'm sure everything will be fine, but if you have any troubles, you have my cell number."

It was huge that Mom was considering having Emmet over. He made her nervous. *Incredibly* nervous.

But she was polite when he came to visit, and so was he. He knocked on the door, only rocked while he waited for me to answer, and he presented my mom with a bouquet of flowers from the co-op, which won her over though he didn't meet her eye while he presented them. He told her, without looking around, that she had a nice home and he was happy to be there. I knew him well enough to know this was all rehearsed.

"I want to see your room, Jeremey," he told me after a little while, and he also tapped two fingers on his thigh in a pattern. He had told me about this—he and his mother had a series of signs and silent exchanges they used to tell each other things without letting anyone else know. The one on the patio that first day I'd gone to his house—her two fingers, his three—was her reprimanding him for rudeness and him acknowledging and apologizing. The two fingers on his thigh meant he was nervous and needed to leave the room, but he didn't want to say it out loud.

I rose from the couch and led him to the stairs. "Sure. It's this way."

He followed me up the stairs without a word. I was looking forward to having him in my room, to show him my things, to be in my space. I'd been to his house many times now, and we'd spent many afternoons in his room. But this would be the first time he'd be in mine.

When I opened the door, though, he took one look inside and jerked, then withdrew into the far corner of the hallway, putting his face to the wall.

I approached him cautiously. "Emmet? What's wrong?"

He held his body rigid, his face hidden from view. "I can't speak right now."

Nerves tangled in my belly. "Why not?"

His neck and arms were tight with tension, and he screwed his eyes shut. "I'm angry. I promised I wouldn't get angry."

I felt hot and cold, as if someone had put poison in my heart and it had spread into my arms and legs. "Why are you angry? At me?"

"Yes. Please leave me alone."

I didn't know what to do. I felt sick—this was pretty much my worst fear, that I would upset someone I cared for but I wouldn't know why, that I would upset *Emmet* and I wouldn't be able to fix it. I could feel a panic attack coming, which would make things worse, but I couldn't stop it. I went to the other corner of the hall, sat down and curled my knees to my chest with my forehead on my arms while I tried to breathe.

His hand fell on my back again.

"Jeremey, you can't have a panic attack right now."

It was such a ridiculous statement I almost laughed, but it was too hard to breathe. It got easier, though, when he rubbed my back. The touch was hesitant, as if he didn't know quite how to do it—but I still liked it. Emmet had a way of cutting through my fog, and I leaned into him.

He let me. He doesn't always want to be touched, but he was touching me now. He kept a heavy hand on my back, and then fingers brushed my hair. He crouched beside me, and he stroked me. Awkwardly, but he did it.

It was wonderful. It made me, as the panic attack ebbed, a little aroused. And when he leaned into me, my leg against his groin—I realized he was aroused too.

I looked up at him—and froze.

He had his eyes shut, his fingers tangled in my hair and his erection pressed into my leg. His expression was still flat, but very focused.

69

He was beautiful.

Eventually he opened his eyes and looked down at me. His gaze was heavy-lidded, and for once he didn't look away.

He touched my lips with three fingers, and I shuddered.

He kept his fingers there, tracing the outline of my lips. His gaze was off to the side, but somehow I could still feel him looking intently at me.

"I need to tell you something important."

I nodded, trying not to dislodge those fingers.

He rubbed the underside of my bottom lip. "I'm gay."

My heart flipped over. I'd figured as much, given the erection against my leg, but it was still a rush to hear it out loud.

His fingers stilled, and I looked up at him. He kept his gaze on my mouth. "I'm not supposed to ask if you are."

I laughed—that was Emmet. Asking a question by saying he couldn't ask it. Well, I could tell him, obviously. But it was still difficult to say the words. I made myself speak anyway. "I am too."

He smiled—again not meeting my gaze, but it made him so beautiful. "Good."

I touched his arm tentatively.

He jerked away. "No light touches. But you can touch me harder."

I put my hand on his arm, a heavy touch.

"Yes." His hand on my back tightened. His erection against my leg grew as he leaned farther into me. "Jeremey, I'm attracted to you."

The words thrilled me though they didn't tell me anything I hadn't been able to figure out for myself. They let the feelings I'd been holding back come forward, made me bold. I gripped his arm. "Let's...go to my room."

But he pulled away. "I can't go into your room. It's too messy."

Too...messy? I blinked at him. "You're angry because my room is messy?"

"Yes. I wanted to come see you, but your room is a disaster. I can't be in there. No wonder you're nervous. Nobody could feel okay in that room."

I didn't know how to respond. It was true, my room was messy. The worst part was I'd picked it up before he came. In fact, I'd worked quite a long time at it. It had taken me all morning, and I'd had to take a nap afterward.

I'd done my best, and it wasn't enough. It might never be enough for Emmet.

We could never live together, be together, because I was too messy. *I* was a mess.

My breathing came sharp and fast, and I wanted to cry. Then I felt stupid for acting this way, which made me more upset. I shut my eyes, feeling the spiral opening in front of me, a dark slide leading into nothingness. Any second my mom would come upstairs, and wouldn't that put the icing on the cake—

Hands, touch—the sharp scent of Emmet filled my senses. When I opened my eyes, he was staring at me, right into my eyes, and I held still, breathless, transfixed.

"Jeremey, we need a code. I can't understand why you're upset, but when you're upset, you can't tell me. Why are you upset right now?"

Why was I upset? God, where did I start? Even thinking it overwhelmed me. How was I supposed to say it out loud?

Emmet opened a notepad app and handed me his phone. "Can you type it?"

Before I met Emmet, I would have said that was silly, typing when someone sat right in front of me. But it was commonplace for us, and I took the phone with shaking hands, tapping out my whirling, churning feelings as best I could. To Emmet, me needing to type because talking was too difficult wasn't an invitation to comment on my freakiness. It was simply an obstacle to overcome.

I'm upset because you're upset about my room. I can't clean it any better than this. I've tried. It was hard for me to do this much. This is my best, and my best isn't good enough for you. I hesitated, shaking, then let out an unsteady breath as I finished. *I want to be with you, be in my room with you.*

In fact, I'd long since kicked guilt over crushing on an autistic boy out the window—clearly he was ten thousand times more put together than me—and had developed some serious fantasies about making out with him. Now that I knew those fantasies could be reality, they were in overdrive.

I kept typing. *I don't know how to fix this, and I'm afraid there's no fix, and—* I stopped, overwhelmed, and passed his phone back, all but dropping it into his hands.

His response at first was no response. He read what I'd written, then stared at it a long time, not saying anything. Not rocking. Eventually he typed something too, and passed it over to me.

E: I will help you fix it. Let me help you clean your room.

What? Clean my—*what*? I frowned and typed back. He'd edited our conversation with a J and an E before our comments, so I put a J: before my reply.

J: Why do you want to clean my room?

He frowned at my comment and typed another quickly.

E: You said that was the problem. I want to fix the problem. It will be tricky because it's messy and that bothers me a lot, but I can get through it. I'm strong.

J: But why would you want to clean my room?

Now he looked exasperated. *E: Your room is messy. I want to kiss you in your room, but I can't until it's clean. So I want to clean your room. Because I want to kiss you.*

I let my breath out in a rush.

I kept staring at the words he'd typed, feeling dizzy looking at them. In my mind's eye I saw Emmet pressing me to my bed, touching my face, my hair, kissing me. It was funny, because in my head he smiled at me in a subtle, rakish manner he never would in real life.

I realized, though, he *did* smile at me like that, in his own way.

I wanted that kiss. I wanted to do whatever I had to do in order to get it. But in the same way Emmet's autism defined him, my depression and anxiety defined me.

J: I'm embarrassed to have you clean my room for me. I should do it myself.

Emmet made a subtle, quirky facial gesture which I'd come to learn was Emmet for raising one eyebrow. *E: But you said you did your best. I thought you meant you couldn't do more, like it was the same as the store, that your room was being too loud. Am I wrong?*

No, he wasn't—I shook my head, too moved to type this time.

He typed more. *I don't mind cleaning. You shouldn't be embarrassed. I enjoy putting things in order. It makes me feel happy. It would make me happy to help you, Jeremey. Let me help you.*

I felt so overwhelmed—but in a good way. I took the phone. *J: Emmet, you're very good to me.*

He smiled, his stretched, lopsided smile, which I loved. He didn't look me in the eye, but he didn't need to. I understood.

I typed one more time. *When you kiss me, it will be my first kiss.*

It felt a little terrifying to say, but only a bit. Emmet read my note, smiled again, though not as wide. *E: My first kiss too.*

Feeling bold, I typed, *J: I want my first kiss.*

Now his grin was as wide as his face, and he hummed as he typed. *E: Then we'd better start cleaning.*

Chapter Seven
Emmet

Here's something only Althea understands, and it's why Jeremey's room upset me so much. People think only humans and animals have feelings, but it's not true. Everything does. And all the things in Jeremey's room, the papers, the baskets, the books, the dirty clothes—they were all sad and angry, like Jeremey.

When I look at an object, I can feel what it's feeling. All things have feelings. I have a hard time knowing what people feel, but objects are a different story. When I was little, I had a favorite pen and a favorite pair of shoes, but I felt bad because the other pens were jealous, and the other shoes were sad when I didn't pick them. I had two pillows on my bed, and I had to rotate between them each night, or they would pout.

Althea and my mom argued a lot when I was little about whether or not this was okay. Althea said she did the same thing and she turned out fine. Mom said it was different for me, that Althea shouldn't encourage me, and they went round and round about it. Usually Dad and I left the house to get ice cream.

Now that I'm older, I don't worry about the chair I'm not sitting in being jealous. That's crazy, trying to make everything happy. They could have explained that instead of arguing whether or not knowing everything has feelings is okay. But picking up my room is a way to take care of my things. My room is never messy. As soon as I get out of my bed, I make it, even to go to the bathroom in the middle of the night. When I'm done at my computer, I line up the keyboard and the trackpad.

Everything is in its place. It makes everything easier, makes the things in my life happier. Makes *me* happier.

A clean room would make things easier for Jeremey, but it made sense that cleaning was a challenge for him, because sometimes everything is difficult for Jeremey. I had to tell my mom to stop offering him choices for refreshments when he came to our house. He always worries he's choosing the wrong thing. Noises are bad too. It doesn't take much to overwhelm him.

Jeremey's room had to overwhelm him simply looking at it. I stood in the middle of his rug, trying to decide where to start. He sat on the edge of his bed, shoulders hunched.

The bed. I decided that would be a good beginning.

He helped me straighten the bedding, though I showed him how to make it perfectly, the sheets iron-straight, the pillows laid out just right. He had a headboard with shelves, which I thought was a bad idea since it made it too easy to be messy, but I didn't want him to feel self-conscious again, so I simply straightened it.

He had a lot of garbage in the room, things he needed to throw away but couldn't. Jeremey *did* understand about things having feelings, but they overwhelmed him. We made piles of things to save, and things to throw away, and things to put away. I told him what nobody ever told me, that you couldn't make all the things happy and could only do your best. That sometimes we have to say goodbye to things and miss them instead of enjoy them. I noticed the longer we worked, the more things he put in the throwaway pile, moving them sometimes from the saved pile. The more he put in that pile, the more he relaxed.

"This is so good," he kept saying. "It's so easy with you helping. How do you do it? Why can't I do this too?"

I couldn't answer that. It was complicated, plus I wanted to keep working, and I don't like to talk while I work. Though I knew we weren't going to finish that day. I suggested we stop, because he looked overwhelmed.

"We can clean tomorrow," I told him. "I'll come over during all my green schedule times."

This only made him agitated, though. "I don't want to stop. I want to fix it. I want—" He looked at my lips, and I knew he thought about kissing. But then he looked away, with a sad face. "I felt normal, while we were cleaning. I want to feel normal. I want to *be* normal."

I felt so many things for Jeremey right then. I wanted to explain to him that he was normal, that we both were, that we were just different. I wanted to tell him I understood about feeling frustrated, about not wanting to wait, but I needed to explain about rushing. I didn't know how to talk to him about the kissing. He needed me to speak, but I couldn't even with the notepad.

That was when I thought of another way I could talk to Jeremey.

On my phone, I pulled up YouTube and went to my video favorites. I played him "Carly's Cafe".

Carly Fleischmann is a real girl, slightly younger than me, who has autism. She has severe autism with motor and speech disability, and she can't talk unless she uses a computer. Until she was eleven, no one knew she could speak at all, until she used a keyboard to share words. Now she uses her computer all the time. She's been on talk shows and has a lot of followers on Facebook and Twitter, and she's written a book with her dad.

She also has a YouTube account, and one of her videos is a kind of ad for the book, where it explains a bit of what it's like to be autistic, for her. It isn't the same for me exactly, but it's still a good video about how disability makes you feel trapped. I thought about how hard it was sometimes for Jeremey to talk, of how much better it was when he typed, so I showed him "Carly's Cafe".

The camera faces out like it's Carly. We listen to her talk inside her head about how much she'd like a coffee, and she makes funny comments about the barista and other people in the cafe, but everyone talks to her as if she's stupid. They don't ask if she wants coffee, they offer orange juice or cocoa, and then they plan an afternoon differently than the one she wants to have. She can't say what she wants, so she gets upset, and suddenly everything is too loud. The coffee grinder, the people talking, the water—everything is too much. Her sister leaves, and Carly reaches for the abandoned coffee, but her dad takes it away. Then he asks how he can help her, and the camera pulls back and you see her face.

Carly's face is wrong. It doesn't match the smart, sassy voice she has in her head. It's this way every day for her, thinking things no one can hear. No one understands how different she feels inside from how she looks on the outside. I understand that. Feeling things I can't express. Like how much I wanted to explain to Jeremey how Carly and he and I are all normal, that it's fine, he doesn't have to be upset. But I couldn't, so I let Carly show him.

Jeremey cried.

When the video ended, he took the phone from my hand without asking and replayed it. I watched his face this time, trying to read it. It was so complicated, and I couldn't. I could tell he felt a lot of emotions, but they were too difficult for me to read. Eventually he put the phone down. He shut his eyes, took a deep breath. When he spoke, his voice was rough and shaky. "That's how I feel. All the time. *All the time.*"

I wanted to tell him I felt that way too, sometimes. I didn't know how, though. So I talked about Carly. "She has a book. I have it. You can borrow it. I have it on Kindle and in paperback. Also audio."

He put his hand on my leg. He started to give a light touch, then remembered and gave a heavy one. It made me feel good he remembered. "Thank you for showing me."

I rocked a little. "Nobody is normal. Life is hard for everybody, sometimes."

"Yes, but not everyone understands like you do, Emmet."

I was the one who had so many feelings then. Loud and hot and cold and spiky and soft. I wanted to tell him, but I couldn't. For the first time in a long time, it wasn't my brain octopus slowing me down. This was *me* unable to talk, unsure of how to tell Jeremey how I felt. It made no sense. He'd told me he liked me too, but those feelings were louder than my octopus. Louder than me.

To be with Jeremey meant managing my autism, my octopus and my feelings. It would be a great deal of work, all the time, more intense than the most complicated math problem in the world. Except this was so much more wonderful than any math problem could be.

For two weeks, every afternoon I wasn't in class, I went to Jeremey's house to help him clean his room.

Gabrielle still didn't like me, but she loved Jeremey's room getting cleaned. She always stuck her head in to ask us if we needed anything, and when I told her we could use some plastic storage bins, she asked me what size and went to the store to get them. She seemed impressed when I knew the exact dimensions without measuring. She tried to feed me, but I get nervous about other people's food, so I always told her no thank you. I usually brought a water bottle and tiny cooler with a snack, so I was fine.

Jeremey was excited to get his room cleaned. By the end of the second day his headboard and space under his bed was all cleaned out, and I noticed he'd made his bed the way I taught him. When we got done cleaning every day, we sat on his bed together.

We didn't kiss, but we were both thinking about it.

I wanted to kiss him, but I was nervous.

I taught him ASL instead. The alphabet, to start, and several common words. He enjoyed it, so one evening I brought him over to my house and gave him my old flash cards so he could practice. I showed him where to find online videos too. We watched several together, so I could help him make sure he had his hands right.

When the woman in the video showed the sign for *I love you*, we both blushed.

This embarrassment was becoming a problem, and I didn't understand it. We were both gay, and he'd said he wanted me to kiss him. Why was it harder now to try doing it than it had been before? I tried to look it up online, but nobody seemed to know. I asked on one of the autism message boards, but they only said I should tell Jeremey my feelings and ask permission to kiss him. I *had* told Jeremey my feelings, but the idea of asking if I could kiss him made me, my feelings and the octopus act like one of those cats in the old cartoons that sticks to the ceiling.

I kept quiet, continuing to help him clean, teaching him ASL and some of my own signs. I showed him all my emotions shirts and told him what they mean when I wear them. I made him a small booklet with all my personal signs and shirts so he could study me. I asked if he had anything about himself he wanted me to learn, but he only shook his head and looked away.

For the first week, going slow was okay, but by the second week I realized we weren't ever going to kiss unless I did something. I told myself I had until we finished sorting out his room to get ready, and then it was kissing time. This made me nervous. That's a lot of pressure, but desperate times call for desperate measures. I masturbated every night, thinking about Jeremey, but it wasn't enough anymore. I needed to kiss him.

I needed to kiss him *now*.

Thursday night of the second week we finished cleaning, and before we sat on his bed as we always did, I shut the door. I would have locked it, but he didn't have a lock, so I closed it until I heard the *click* of the latch. The sound echoed too loudly in the room, and even though it's silly to be nervous because of a door, I was.

I wondered if Jeremey felt the same way.

I sat beside him on the bed, sideways so I could face him. He fixed his gaze away from me. I wasn't looking right at him either, but he doesn't have camera eyes, so he didn't see me at all. I think Jeremey sees feelings so loudly, sometimes looking at people even out of the corner of his eye makes them too intense. Except I understood then how frustrating I was for people without superpowers, because I wished he would look at me so I could try to read his expression and know if it was okay to kiss him.

I hummed, and I rocked.

Jeremey's shoulders relaxed. He still didn't look at me, but he took my hand.

His touch didn't trigger my autism sensitivity. It made me brave, let me lean closer to finally get my kiss.

Starting was tricky. In my head I wanted us to melt together, to move gracefully into each other's spaces, but my body doesn't work that way. It's clumsy. It doesn't listen to me. I'm better than I used to be—I've done all kinds of therapy, but I still move differently. Add that Jeremey's body is hesitant, and it meant our kiss was more of a thump. Jeremey made a noise of surprise. I kept my eyes open until our lips met, and he did too.

He shut his eyes, and so did I, and it was better.

He moved his lips over mine, making them wet. It was a little weird, but mostly it felt good to kiss him. It made my penis erect, made me want to touch him to see if he was erect too, but I didn't. It was too easy to scare Jeremey.

But I promised myself sometime soon I would touch his penis.

When it got to be too much, I pulled back, but not far. When he nuzzled my nose too softly, I didn't let the soft touch bother me.

"I want to be your boyfriend," I told him.

Eyes shut, he rested his forehead against mine. "Emmet...I don't think you get how messed up I am."

"You need to stop saying bad things about yourself."

His laugh was an odd sound. "I don't know how to explain how impossible that is for me to do. I have negative voices all the time. Every day. They never stop."

It made me sad, to think of Jeremey with those negative voices. I put my arms around him, and he put his head on my shoulder. I thought of movies I'd seen, commercials, thinking maybe we looked like one of those couples, sitting there. When I pressed a kiss on the side of his head, I was clumsier than they are in the movies, but that's okay.

It was a great moment, almost perfect. I held Jeremey and counted the patterns in the wallpaper. I was about to tell him how many swirls he had on his north wall when his mom opened the door.

Things weren't so perfect after that.

Chapter Eight
Jeremey

It was all my fault.

I should have put something in front of the door to keep Mom out, should have listened for the creaking board in the hall so I could break apart from Emmet before she came in. I should have done something to stop it. But I was so caught up in being happy, sinking into Emmet's touch—he hates soft touches, but he was touching me so sweetly I thought I would melt—that I forgot to watch out.

I was so lost in the moment of finally getting my first kiss, of having a boyfriend, that I didn't know Mom had come into the room until she screamed.

I guess it wasn't so much of a scream as a yelp and a series of surprised noises. To be fair, I hadn't told her I was gay. In fact I'd worked not to let her know. It was bad enough with me being a depressed loser. I didn't want to know what she'd say to finding out I was a *gay* depressed loser. So not only was she catching me making out with a friend, she was finding out what gender I wanted to make out with.

Also, I was making out with Emmet. I'd underestimated how much she still disliked him, how much she mostly tolerated him.

She stood in the doorway, eyes wide. At first she stared and sputtered. "You—what? Jeremey! Why—? What—? *Oh my God.*" She put her hands over her mouth and backed away. You would have thought she'd caught me stabbing a kitten, not kissing my friend.

Except she hadn't seen that. She'd only seen us cuddling.

My face grew hot, my embarrassment and discomfort spreading down my body like a heat rash. Beside me Emmet had grown stiff, and he rocked back and forth, tapping S.O.S. against his leg in triple staccato. This was one of his signs, and it meant he was upset and didn't know how to react, what he should do.

Me either.

Mom aimed an angry finger at Emmet. "Get out. Get *out* of my house, right now."

Emmet shut his eyes and started to hum loudly, rocking back and forth as he tapped out S.O.S. over and over and over.

I wanted to take his hand, but his left fist was clenched tight against his leg, his right hand absolutely absorbed in his desperate tapping. I ached for him, and it was only the need to protect him that allowed me courage enough to speak. "Mom, stop. You're upsetting him." *Me too.*

Shaking her head, she ignored me and swung her finger from Emmet to the stairs. "Go. *Get out. Get out right now.*" Her face became ugly as it twisted up, her lip curling and her chin trembling in her rage. "How *dare* you come here and take advantage of my son. You *perverted* little creep."

Emmet's rocking made the bed creak, and his hum became a guttural moan as he put his hands over his ears. His whole body posture had changed—everything about the Emmet I knew and cared for had fallen away, leaving a strange, terrifying shell. *This* was what I'd thought autistic people were like before I met Emmet. This wasn't the boy who had kissed and held me.

I hated that he'd been reduced to this. I hated that it was my mother who had done it to him.

I wish I could say I'd stood up and shouted at her. That I'd angrily defended Emmet, protected him. I'm ashamed to admit all I did was cower on the bed. I felt hot and cold, dizzy and nauseous. The panic attack swept me up so quickly I didn't see it coming—one moment I sat there huddled and awkward, and the next I was crumpled to the floor in a fetal ball, sweating and weeping silently as white-hot terror filled my brain and my teeth clacked together.

I don't know how long it took Marietta to arrive, only that suddenly she was there, kneeling in front of Emmet and speaking soothingly to him. He'd retreated into some terrifying internal space, his gaze fixed unseeing at some spot on my carpet, still rocking and making horrifying noises, but she sat in front of him and whispered, her tone so calming it gentled me, though she had yet to so much as glance my way. Her entire being was for Emmet. She didn't so much as lay a finger on him, yet she enveloped him more thoroughly than any physical embrace. Through my panic-pinked gaze, I watched her bring him down, draw my Emmet to the surface.

My mom was in the hall—I heard her talking to Emmet's aunt, heard their sharp whispers rising as they argued. I couldn't make out any words, but I didn't want to hear them anyway. Mostly I watched Marietta and Emmet and wished someone would talk to me that way. I could see how much Marietta wanted to hold Emmet, and part of me wailed and moaned inside the same way Emmet did outside. *Hold me, Marietta. Somebody hold me. Somebody speak patiently and kindly to me. Somebody come running to save me too.*

No one did. No one ever had.

She didn't say anything to me until Emmet left. No one asked if I wanted to say goodbye before Althea and Douglas formed a pair of walls around him and escorted him into their car, which was waiting in front of our house. I watched him go, aching, still dizzy and overwhelmed as I stood at the picture window in the living room and tracked the car until it was gone from sight.

All I'd done was kiss him. Let *him* kiss *me.* I imagine terrible outcomes for everything as simple as opening a box of cereal, but I hadn't seen this coming. It made me want to crawl into my bed and pull the covers over my head.

It made me want to stay there until I died.

They turned on me, Marietta's normally kind face guarded and carefully blank, my mother's quietly furious. My father glared at me as if he'd caught me doing something unspeakable.

"How could you do this?"

I hunched my shoulders and backed against the window, fixing my gaze to the floor as my mother waited for an answer. I had none. I didn't want to talk. I wanted out. If they hadn't blocked the front door, I'd have run out of it.

Marietta took a step closer, and out of fear, I glanced up. Her blank expression gentled. "Jeremey, you don't need to be afraid. We only want to understand what happened." She became guarded again as she went on. "Did Emmet...take advantage of you?"

I blinked, not understanding at first. When I realized what she meant, I hunched further into myself and shut my eyes.

Take advantage. She meant did Emmet force himself on me. I didn't have another panic attack, but shame deeper than anything I've ever known filled me up, making me feel ugly and wrong to my core.

Take advantage. *Marietta* asked me that.

One kiss. One kiss and a hug. The only time anyone had touched me in years outside of stiff hugs from visiting relatives or strangers bumping into me in public. Even Emmet's mom acted like it was the most shameful thing she'd ever seen.

"Answer her," my father demanded.

I started to cry.

I thought things couldn't get worse, but they did. Marietta started apologizing, to me, to my parents. "I'm so sorry. I should have seen this coming, I suppose. He's strong-willed, and I knew he had a crush on Jeremey, but I thought it was harmless. I never dreamed he'd act on it."

My mother twitched. "Why did you let him do that to you? What's *wrong* with you?"

Marietta straightened, stiffening. "I think that's a little harsh—"

"He's not gay," my mom snapped. "I didn't realize your son was or that he was so poorly controlled—"

"Stop."

They turned to me all at once, and the looks on their faces—rage, surprise, wariness, disgust—made me want to run and hide, but I couldn't let them talk that way about Emmet, couldn't let them believe that about him.

Drawing a ragged breath, I forced the words out. "I *am* gay. I never told anyone because I thought I'd never find a boyfriend. Except—"

I stopped. I wanted to say *then I met Emmet*, but shame cut off the words.

My mother filled them in for me, her disgust dripping from each syllable. "Except then there was the poor retarded boy who wasn't smart enough to say no to you?"

"Emmet is not retarded," Marietta snapped, all her gentleness gone. "Nor is he stupid."

My mom waved this away. "Yes, he's an idiot savant or whatever. He's certainly not *normal*. I should never have let him associate with Jeremey in the first place. Certainly he won't any longer."

I recoiled, her casual remarks harsher than a slap across my face or a punch to my gut. They weren't going to let me *see* Emmet? Marietta began to argue more pointedly, but I saw the expression on my parents' faces, and nothing Emmet's mother could say would change their minds. As far as my mom and dad were concerned, Emmet and I were through.

I pushed off the wall and stumbled out of the room, ignoring them as they shouted after me. I took the stairs two at a time, slammed the door shut and dragged the edge of my bed over to block the door from opening. Climbing into bed, I pulled the covers over my head and stared into the darkness.

Emmet was gone. From my house and from my life. No more walks to the store or around the block. No more meeting him at the train tracks. No more texts, no more Google hangouts. No more kisses. No more touches.

No more Emmet.

I played the argument from downstairs over in my head. I should have fought for him. I should have shouted back. But I was weak and worthless. I couldn't fight. I could barely get out of bed on a good day.

Emmet deserved so much better than me. And I didn't deserve anyone or anything at all.

I sobbed quietly under the blankets, mourning my ineptitude, my impotence, my failure. But more than anything, I mourned the loss of Emmet.

Chapter Nine
Emmet

A lot of things about autism are unfair, but the worst is people on the mean have a double standard about autistic people's behavior. I have to practice facial recognition charts and controlling my anger, and when I make a mistake, I get scolded and punished. But when Gabrielle acted bitchy because she didn't like that Jeremey was gay, did anyone yell at her? Did they say, *Hey, maybe you shouldn't be such an asshole to your own son?* No, they didn't. They apologized, they sent me home, and then they acted as if I'd done something wrong. They told *me* I had to calm down, got upset with *me* when *I* couldn't control my anger.

Worse, I couldn't simply be angry. I couldn't wallow in my feelings. I couldn't put on my Dalek shirt and bang my foam hammer until it broke. I couldn't pout or sulk. I had to get myself together as soon as possible. I'd seen Jeremey before I left. He was so upset that for the first time, I couldn't see the light in his face. I couldn't always read his face, but I could read his light, and his light had gone almost completely out. I remembered what he said about the voices, about how they were always loud and negative in his head, and I worried what would happen when he had his mother's angry voice *and* his bad voices. I worried so much it made my stomach hurt. It's not logical for Jeremey's voices to make my stomach hurt, but it still happened.

I tried to go to him, to put the light back, but Althea said I had to wait for Mom. I wanted to use the sign to say I was going to stop talking, but if I did that, I couldn't explain about Jeremey.

"Althea, you have to listen to me."

"*You* have to listen to me. You're in big trouble. Mrs. Samson is really upset."

I stared at her shoulder. "Jeremey is upset. He's *very* upset, and I have to go to him. He's my boyfriend. I'm supposed to comfort him."

Althea made a funny noise, so I looked at her face to see if I could read it. Surprised face. Very surprised face. "Your—" Her mouth opened and closed several times. Then her face got complicated. "Oh, Emmet. Oh, sweetie, that's totally not okay. You can't just decide you're someone's boyfriend."

Why was everyone so dumb? "I didn't just decide. We discussed it together. We decided to be boyfriends, and then she came in and started screaming because we were cuddling. Good thing she didn't see us kissing."

Her face kept changing so fast it was hard to keep up. "Peanut, did...did Jeremey make you do something you didn't want to do?"

It took so much work not to be angry. "Jeremey wouldn't ever make me do something I didn't want to do. He couldn't. He's way too shy. He has depression, and it makes him overwhelmed. He doesn't have any modifications, either, and no medicine. He's sensitive. Much more sensitive than me. His mother makes him feel bad, and I think she's doing it now. We have to help him. *I* have to help him."

I spoke calmly and slowly, but she didn't understand. My dad didn't say anything, but he frowned at Althea a lot. I didn't know what that meant. When my mom came back, she made me almost as angry as Althea did.

"Sweetheart." She stood in front of me, looking worriedly at my face. "What's going on?"

Why was she asking me? How would I know what was going on at the Samsons'? "I need to see Jeremey. Right now. He's my boyfriend, and he's upset. I need to make him happy again."

"*Boyfriend?* Emmet—"

I didn't have time for this. "Mom, stop. I have a boyfriend. Jeremey. Why do you think I've been hanging out with him so much? But I can't talk about that right now. He's upset. I have to fix it."

I started toward the front door, but she grabbed my arm. I hate it when people grab me, and I started to swing my arm to hit, then made myself stop. I pulled away from her and made an angry face instead. "Mom, get off me."

She blocked the door with her body. "Honey, you can't go over there right now. You can be angry with me, but you cannot go to the Samsons' house. It's not safe for you. Mrs. Samson is very angry."

"Mrs. Samson is a *bitch*, Mom."

She made her lips flat, which means she didn't like what I said, but she didn't tell me it was rude not to say it. Because she knew I was right.

She shut her eyes and let out a slow breath. "You can't go over. We'll talk about this later, but right now I need to speak with your father."

"*I* need to speak with my boyfriend. I'm an adult, Mom. Stop treating me like a baby."

We argued for fifteen minutes, but I'm sorry to say I didn't win. I didn't hit, or hum, or have an episode, but in the end I still went to my room. I whaled on my bed with the foam hammer and said bad words about Mrs. Samson, loud enough they had to hear me downstairs, but nobody came up to tell me I had to stop. I called my mom a few bad names too, but it made me feel uncomfortable, so I quit.

My mom might be bossy, but she's not a bitch like Gabrielle Samson.

When I calmed down, I tried to decide what to do. All I could think about was that I needed to check on Jeremey, but they'd catch me going out the front or the back door in the house. Also, probably they were right. If I went to Jeremey's house, his parents would stop me from seeing him.

If he still had his phone, though, I could call him, or text.

I texted. His parents wouldn't hear if he had the sound muted, which he usually does.

Jeremey, this is Emmet. I am worried about you. I'm worried you're upset. I want to help you, but my aunt and parents are being strange. Please tell me if you are okay and how I can help you. If I can help you.

After only a few minutes he replied. Except I could tell by the way he answered something was wrong.

am v ovrwhlmed

Sometimes Jeremey is sloppy about spelling and punctuation, but never that bad. Usually he lies and says he's okay too, but today he admitted he felt bad. I didn't know what to do.

I want to help you. Can I come over?

His reply was quick, and it made me sad.

no bcuse mom

I felt sad. *No, because Mom.*

If I shut my eyes, I could see him on his bed, lying under the covers using all his energy just to push the buttons. Even if we used the phone, speaking would be hard. Plus, his mom would hear.

I was angry with Jeremey's mom. My brain octopus was furious, and I wanted to give in and be angry, but I pushed it aside. Anger wasn't important right now. Jeremey was.

Do you want me to keep talking to you? I know it's hard for you to type back, but do you want to keep texting? You can type Y or N.

It took a few seconds, but he typed *y*.

I relaxed and sat cross-legged on the floor on my thinking cushion. I wished I could use a keyboard—then it occurred to me that if I hooked my wireless keyboard up to my phone with Bluetooth, I could. Excited, I typed *brb*—that's shorthand for *be right back*—and I set myself up, with my keyboard on a board on my lap and my phone propped up on a bookshelf. Then I started to type.

Sorry, it took longer to get ready than I meant it to. I set my keyboard up with my phone, so I can type fast. But I have a question. I want to ask you some things, but are you too overwhelmed to answer? I can maybe make them yes/no questions, but I don't want to make you talk if your depression is feeling loud right now. So here is my first question: can I ask you some questions?

y

I smiled and started typing again. *I'm glad. But let's make a code. Y is yes and N is no. D is done, meaning you want to be done talking. If you do that, I will say goodbye and text you later. If I ask something you don't want to answer, say X. If I make you angry, type A, and I will apologize. Does that sound okay?*

It took him a few minutes to answer, and when I saw his big reply, I understood why the big pause.

y. but add S for me saying sorry, and H for I hear you but don't have anything to say. so sometimes it doesn't have to be questions.

These are good. You're good at modifications, Jeremey.

One more. T for thank you. That text came through, and then he added, *t*.

This was what Jeremey did. I was nervous for him and angry at our parents and my aunt, but he could still make me feel good.

You said I can't come over because of your mom. Is she angry at me?

y

This made me angry right back, but I made it wait. *Is she angry with you?*

y. also sad.

I wanted to ask why she was sad, but that would be too hard for him to answer. I couldn't think of another question, so I told him about Althea. *My aunt acted strange when I said we were boyfriends, and she got weirder when I said we kissed.* A thought in the back of my head came to the front, and I decided I would share it with Jeremey, though it made me sad. *I think they believe I'm too stupid to be your boyfriend. That it's not okay for me to have you for a boyfriend because I'm autistic.*

Jeremey interrupted me, he texted so fast. *n i am broken one*

I was so angry I wanted to type an A for angry instead of an answer. *You aren't broken. You have a mental illness. Mental illness doesn't mean you're broken. It means your brain is sick. Don't say you're broken. It's mean. Don't say mean things about yourself.*

There was a long pause, then he typed *h*. And then *s*.

I had a question now, but I had too many emotions about it. It took me a long time to put my words together. *Are you still okay to be boyfriends?*

I had the words typed for a long time before I could hit send. But Jeremey's answer was fast.

Y

Then, after a short pause, *RU?*

My chest had hurt while I tried to be brave enough to send, but now it was warm and happy. *Yes, I want to be your boyfriend. More than ever.*

T

I hummed for a minute, feeling happy and needing a minute to let myself feel happy because Jeremey still wanted to be with me. But I made it quick. *He* still needed to feel better. *I worry they won't let me see you now, but don't worry. I will be persistent until they let me. I'm good at being persistent.*

h

t

I rocked and hummed as I tried to get brave enough for the next question. *Can I be persistent with your mom?*

He paused, then typed *IDK.* That's shorthand for *I don't know.*

I sighed. *I don't think your mom likes me. It makes me sad. I practice my social skills every time before I come to your house, but she makes unpleasant faces at me. Do you know what I'm doing wrong?*

It took him a long time to answer. *mom wants everyone to be normal esp me*

I wished he could use full punctuation so I could understand him. *Did you mean to say your mom wants everyone to be normal, especially you?* When he typed another *Y*, I shook my head and rocked before I typed.

Jeremey, there is no such thing as normal. It's wrong of your mother to say you have to be normal. I can't be normal either. I have autism. My aunt has autism too. My dad has lactose intolerance. My mom's feet are a whole size different from each other, and her sleeves are always too short. Everyone is different. Nothing in the world is the same as anything else, so how can anyone be normal?

I worried he would type X or D, but after a long time, he said, *my mom believes in normal but I can't be normal. it makes me sad.*

I was trying to think of what to say back when he typed again.

sometimes I want to kill myself. a lot of times I do.

I hummed loud, and I had to flap my hands before I could type. *Jeremey, it makes me upset when you say that. Please don't kill yourself. I would be so sad. If you killed yourself, you wouldn't be alive.*

sometimes being alive is v hard

This was a strange thing to say. I tried to make sense of his words, but they didn't make any sense. How was being alive a hard thing? All he had to do was keep breathing, eat food and not get too hot or cold. Did he have a disability about those things too?

I'm sorry, Jeremey. I don't think I understand what you mean. How is being alive hard?

It would take him a long time to reply, so I hummed and rocked while he did. When his text came through, I held myself still and read slowly and carefully, so I could understand.

my emotions feel loud and big. its hard for me to keep hold of them. they weigh me down. make me heavy and tired and overwhelmed. sometimes I feel like everyone else is carrying a bucket of water but I'm trying to carry an ocean. its very hard. sometimes I would rather not carry my ocean, even if it meant I couldn't be alive.

I hummed loudly and rocked. I made hand signs and flapped too before I could type a reply. This is another good thing about Jeremey. He uses metaphors I can understand.

I replied.

Autism is like an ocean for me. Little things are overwhelming. Senses, touches. Everyone else can read faces, but I can't. Everyone else knows how to look people in the eye, but I can't. Only autistic people have to have special classes and facial recognition charts to understand what people mean and say. When you're autistic, everyone acts as if you're not a real human. I'm angry at my family because they said I was a real human, but when I say I'm your boyfriend, they say I can't be. So they lied. I'm not a real human.

The anger filled me up, but I told it no, I wanted to keep talking to Jeremey, not be angry.

That's my ocean. I have to pretend as best I can to be like people on the mean so people don't call me a robot. I'm not a robot. I'm real and I have feelings the same as everyone else. And I want a boyfriend. Except my ocean doesn't make me want to be dead. It makes me want to fight. I want you to fight too, Jeremey. I want us to carry our oceans together.

I gave him time to read. I'd said a lot. I reread what he'd said about oceans and what I wrote. I don't always understand analogies very well, but I liked this one. It made sense. My autism isn't wet and doesn't have any fish, but it is big and difficult to carry, and most people think it's too complicated to deal with. I could see how depression would be the same way.

I tried to imagine a bucket big enough to hold an ocean, and I realized the bucket was the earth. Which meant Jeremey and I were trying to carry the whole planet's water. It's not fair, but Dad says little about life is.

Jeremey typed back to me.

I like you a lot, Emmet. I'm glad you introduced yourself to me. I wish you could come over. But I'm too tired to fight my mom. Sorry.

I wished I could go over too, but I didn't want Jeremey any more upset than he was. He seemed better—he used whole sentences and capitalization now. But probably he should rest.

Jeremey, I'm going to stop texting now, but I will text you later. Don't feel sad and don't kill yourself. If you need me, you can text me. I will remember your codes, and if you want me to talk so you can listen, we can do that. Even if it's not on our schedules. I will change the settings on my phone so you can always go through. Even if it is during my do-not-disturb times like sleeping or appointment, I can talk to you. If it's a bad time, I will type X and text as soon as I can. And if I text when you need to rest or it's a bad time, you use the X. Do you agree with this plan, Jeremey?

Y. T.

Then he made the sign < and a 3. At first I started to do math, but then I remembered. That was code for sideways heart. It's meant to be right-side up, and Emoji will do that for you, but he doesn't have Emoji installed in his phone. I knew, though, that basically he was hearting me.

I laughed and hummed as I hearted him back.

The week after Mrs. Samson caught Jeremey and I kissing was very stressful. I wore my Dalek shirt so much I had to wash it every other night. If you wear a shirt more than two days in a row it's gross, and people say you smell. Everyone could have used a Dalek shirt, though, because everyone fought at our house. Mom and Althea fought with me. They fought with each other. My dad fought with them and took me to get so much ice cream I started to not like ice cream. We switched to watching *The Blues Brothers* instead, which made my tummy less upset.

I loved my dad before that week, but I loved him more after because he kept defending me to Mom and Althea. When I complained they weren't treating me fairly, he said he agreed with me. *How could you, Doug,* Mom said, and Althea glared, but he shook his finger in their faces.

"You can't tell him he's as normal as everyone and then act like he's retarded." Usually when my dad says the R word, I tell him he's supposed to eliminate it, but he had a red face and it wasn't a good time to interrupt.

I told him he shouldn't use the R word when we were watching the movie later. He laughed and tweaked my nose.

Jeremey and I texted, but he didn't always answer, and I could tell he was getting sadder all the time. He still said I couldn't go over, and my mom wouldn't let me go, either. Even my dad said no. It wasn't until my appointment with Dr. North that everything started to get better.

Dr. North is a medical doctor, but he's also a social worker. He was a medical doctor first, a psychiatrist, and then he went back to get his social work degree because he thought they did a better job than psychiatrists. He's been my doctor for a long time. We didn't live in the same town as him when I was younger, but when we were trying to decide where I should go to school and Mom found out Dr. North was working at the Ames hospital, Mom said this was the perfect setup.

Mom says a lot of doctors at the hospital call him a crazy old hippie, but whenever Mom says that, she smiles. I guess she enjoys crazy old hippies. I like Dr. North a lot, so I enjoy crazy old hippies too.

I see Dr. North every six weeks. I enjoy talking to him, and it's good to do maintenance on the brain. The same as changing the oil in a car, except there is no exchange of fluids. That would be gross. My last appointment had been just before Memorial Day, so I had a lot to tell him.

I told him all about how I'd rehearsed the meeting and used my social skills, and how well that had gone. I told him about Jeremey's depression, how it was bad. I talked about how I had helped him clean his room, and how we'd kissed, and then about Mrs. Samson, about Mom and Althea and Dad and the R word, and how I still couldn't see Jeremey. I talked so fast he had to tell me twice to slow down and enunciate because he couldn't understand me, and I hand-flapped the whole time.

It's okay to hand-flap with Dr. North. He says it's a flap-safe zone.

"We talk every night, but always on text or IM, and it's not the same thing. I can't kiss him in texts. I know about putting X and O, but that messes the code."

He asked about the code then, and I had to explain.

"But he's using the code all the time now. He hardly ever uses capital letters, and three or four times in a conversation I have to repeat it back with proper punctuation and grammar for confirmation so I know I understand what he said. And we don't talk long. I can't see him because his mom thinks Jeremey has to be normal. He can't be normal. Even if normal were a real thing, Jeremey has bad depression. But he doesn't have any modifications or facial charts or any behavior therapies. His mom just says *you have to be normal now* and then they both get upset. It makes me so angry. I want to see Jeremey, and Jeremey wants to see me. He's eighteen years old, and I'm nineteen. We can do what we want. We're adults."

Dr. North is a good listener. He sat still while I said all this, and when I was done, he held his beard for a minute to make sure I was finished talking. "This does sound like a serious situation, Emmet. I understand how this makes you frustrated. May I tell you that you're doing a good job keeping your emotions in check during a stressful time? I daresay you're doing better than most of the adults in your life right now."

He always said things like that, *may I tell you something nice*. It always made me laugh, which is maybe why he did it. "Yes, you can tell me that."

"You're doing a very good job, Emmet. An excellent job. The behavior and accessibility modifications you've given your friend—"

"My boyfriend." It's rude to interrupt, but I was getting tired of nobody believing we were boyfriends.

"Pardon me. You've given your boyfriend some good advice and some excellent tools of accommodation. I hope you feel proud of yourself for being such a good friend *and* boyfriend."

I smiled. "I do feel proud. Thank you."

"Jeremey's depression, as best I can understand it through your description alone, seems severe. And no, it isn't something he can snap out of. Depression often requires therapy and sometimes medication for proper management."

"We have to help him, Dr. North. We have to help Jeremey. I'm worried. He says sometimes he wants to kill himself. I don't want Jeremey to do that. I can make him laugh and smile—I'm good at it—and people who are laughing and smiling don't usually want to kill themselves. But I can't tell if he's smiling sometimes in a text."

Dr. North wore his thinking face, so I waited and let him think.

"Emmet, you remember I told you everything you say to me here is confidential, that I won't tell your mother or father or anyone else anything we've talked about?"

"Yes. I remember." I loved that part. My mother is bossy sometimes, and I enjoy keeping secrets from her.

"With your permission, Emmet, I want to request we spend some time talking with your mother today about this subject of Jeremey. For one thing, I would like to validate your independence and your right to have a boyfriend if you and Jeremey wish it, and to encourage her to follow up or facilitate your follow-up of this situation."

I smiled. My mom would *have* to listen to Dr. North. "Yes, you may tell her."

"May I give you some advice also, Emmet?" When I nodded, he said, "I would encourage you to keep texting your boyfriend and attempting to see him, with or without your family's help. You know I don't care to give you direction, that therapy is about self-exploration and discovery, but in this instance I believe it's important."

I felt confusing emotions. Proud because I'd been right about everything, but nervous because Dr. North definitely had his worried face on.

He spent twenty minutes talking to my mother. I counted the ceiling tiles, the stripes in the wainscoting, and the pages in all the magazines, and I still had to configure pi in my head when I ran out of things to count. I was too edgy to do pi for too long, though, so I murmured *The Blues Brothers* script under my breath.

I was all the way to Mr. Fabulous when Mom finally came out of Dr. North's office. She was quiet, and she kept looking at me as if I had something on my face. I didn't have anything on my face, though. I checked, and it was clean.

That night we had a family meeting, which was great. Everyone apologized to me, even Dad who apologized for using the R word. Mom told me she'd call Gabrielle and talk to her about not letting me see Jeremey and about how serious his depression was. We *all* went for ice cream at Hickory Park, which is the best place for ice cream in the world. Althea didn't eat any because she's vegan, but she came with us anyway and had a pineapple soda.

It would have been the perfect day. Except as we went to our car to go home from Hickory Park, I saw I had texts from Jeremey.

sorry

I'm so sorry

i miss you

i love you E

sorry

s

s

bye

I tried to text back, but he wouldn't answer. I started rocking and humming, and when I started flapping my hands too, Althea asked what was wrong, and I showed her the phone.

Althea read the texts, and she got a scared face. She showed my Mom.

Mom didn't have a scared face. She had the flat face she gets when she's being a doctor. She opened the dialer and pressed three numbers.

Nine, one, and one.

Chapter Ten
Jeremey

I don't think people understand about suicidal thoughts. They act as if everyone who makes an attempt is looking for attention. There aren't enough words in the English language for me to explain how untrue that is. It's using the wrong language to talk about it at all.

To start, when someone is depressed, really depressed, their thoughts are messed up. There's the dome I told Emmet about, keeping people out but sealing stimuli in. What I didn't tell him was sometimes I like the dome. Sometimes it feels good, because nobody can get you. The problem with being left alone, though, is you're in there all by yourself. You're in there with your own brain, and a depressed person's brain does some seriously crazy shit.

When I saw the Harry Potter movies and the dementors came on screen, I thought, that's how I feel all the time, except I don't have a Patronus and chocolate doesn't do much to make me feel better. In fact, when I'm especially depressed, all food tastes dull and gross, and people have to yell at me to eat at all. Depression is having a crowd of dementors live in your head twenty-four/seven. They are *always* inside the glass dome, and they can whisper bad things at you whenever they want. Sometimes I can tell them to fuck off, but a lot of times I start to get confused about what's real and what isn't. Sometimes I don't know if the whispers in my head were echoes of something I saw or heard or something the depression said. It feels *so real* to me that if I'm able to see I was wrong, sometimes I stand there and blink, freaked out over how badly I was fooled—by my own brain.

I don't know why my brain says such nasty things to me, why it's so incredibly mean, but it is. My brain is a bully who never leaves. My depression will tell me things are bad, really bad, and I can say I don't believe it for a while, but at some point it's the same as the game you play with kids, where you say "yes" and they say "no" and after a few rounds the adult switches but the child doesn't catch on and ends up saying yes because they were tricked.

Sometimes my depression tricks me. The day Emmet's mom called 911 on me, it tricked me so well that if she hadn't called, right when she did, I would be dead.

Ever since my mom yelled at Emmet and kicked him out of the house, the voices in my head had been off-the-charts bad. Emmet texted me every day, sometimes several times a day, but basically if he wasn't texting me, my personal brain bullies told me he wouldn't ever text me again. He didn't want to hang out with a loser who had a bitchy mom, a guy who couldn't stand up to her. The bullies told me I was ugly. They told me my mom was right, except Emmet was fine and it was me who was awful. I tried to fight them. I tried to listen to Emmet. But the bullies live in my head, and Emmet could only talk to me in text. I became convinced Emmet was just making me feel better, that he didn't like me, didn't want to be with me and wished I would go away and leave him the hell alone.

My brain whispered, all day, every day, how I could make alone happen for good.

The sad truth is I think about ways to kill myself the same way Emmet counts things. I don't tell anyone because they'll think I'm weird or lock me up, but it's true. Usually thinking about suicide is almost a game, like when people talk about where they'd store a body if they killed someone. They don't mean it, and neither do I. Except I think of ways I could kill myself every day. I've researched them. I know not to use an overdose of Tylenol. It's horribly painful and awful and long and impossible to correct. We don't own a gun, and I don't think I could handle the noise—which is dumb. Obviously done right I'd only have to hear it the one time. Blood squicks me out, so no wrist-cutting.

But the car in the garage. If my mom and dad knew how many nights I sat for hours in the car, the keys in my hand and my gaze fixed on the garden hose, they would have torn the garage down.

Of course, then I would have routed the exhaust into the basement and blocked the door to the upstairs so they wouldn't die with me.

I'd decided long ago when I killed myself—in my head it was so absolute that it *would* happen eventually—I would do it by funneling the exhaust from the tailpipe and asphyxiating myself. That night, I climbed into the car with the garage door shut. I got the engine running, and I put the hose in through the driver's side window. Even as I did it part of me was aware, like a match flare in the back of a dark room, that this wasn't right. You weren't supposed to kill yourself, no matter what the bastards in your head said. But I felt so miserable, and everything was so heavy, all I could think was I couldn't do this anymore, and the next thing I knew, I was in the car.

I knew this time was real before I closed the door. Not just because I'd hooked up the hose—I'd done that before too—but because I brought my phone. When I texted Emmet goodbye, told him I loved him, it was the last flare of light. I cried while I texted him. I cried so hard I had snot running down my face. When I sent the last text, I almost wanted to change my mind.

But Mom would never let me see him again, and I was too weak to fight for him, and it made me feel sick. Emmet had only put off what I'd been planning to do since graduation. He'd be better off without me. He should get a boyfriend who wasn't so fucked up.

I wished I could have had one last kiss. I gave him texts instead. Then I smashed my phone so I couldn't get any messages, and I sat back to wait for the end.

I wasn't quite asleep when the paramedics opened the door to the garage, but I was groggy enough I couldn't respond to them when they called my name. I remember being dragged out of the car and put on a stretcher with a mask on my face. I remember being wheeled out of the garage and into an ambulance.

I thought I saw Emmet getting out of his car, maybe coming up to me, but after that I don't remember anything until I was in the hospital.

I woke up feeling as if someone had made me crazy drunk. I felt flat and floating. I don't want to say it was good, since words like *good* and *bad* were too descriptive. I didn't feel as heavy as I usually did, and I didn't feel like crying. I didn't feel anything at all. When the nurse stuck a needle in my arm, I didn't care about the blood. I just watched. She could take it all, if she wanted it. For a long time they had a mask on my face too, but at some point they took that off and put this nose thing in instead.

Obviously I was on drugs, which were handy when my mom came in all hysterical and weeping. For once she didn't upset me when she did that. I was thinking how I wanted a box of this medicine to take home. But then after a few hours—I think it was hours, I wasn't sure—Emmet came in, and I hated how flat I felt. Inside I jumped for joy and smiled at him, holding out my arms, but all I could do on the outside was stare at him like a zombie and blink and sort of lift my hand.

Though in a way it was funny. I understood, maybe, what it was like to be Emmet. He'd told me he felt more than his face showed, but now I got what it was to feel things and not be able to express them.

Except I had one thing I had to express to him. One important thing. I tried to say it, but I felt like lead. I scrambled for ways to talk to him, wishing for my phone. Then remembered I had one way to use our codes.

I made the American Sign Language letter T, and then the S. I did it over and over.

Thank you.

Sorry. So sorry.

"What's he doing? What's wrong?" That was my mother, but I ignored her, just kept signing to Emmet.

He caught my hand. "Not sorry. It's okay."

"What—what is he doing to Jeremey?"

God, Mom. I dragged my gaze to her so I could glare, but I was pretty sure I was still a zombie.

Emmet answered for me. "I'm not doing anything to Jeremey. We're talking. He's trying to tell me he's sorry, but he doesn't need to apologize. I don't know why he's thanking me, though."

I thanked him because he'd helped save me, and I didn't actually want to die, especially now that he was here. Especially not on these drugs. I didn't think I wanted to feel this flat all the time, but if I could get a doggie bag of zombie meds, I was willing to stop thinking up ways to kill myself to pass the time.

Of course, the side effect of these drugs was that all I could do was blink at Emmet and keep saying *thank you* and *sorry* over and over again.

Wait. I had one more thing I could say. *Needed* to say. And I was high enough that signing *I love you* didn't make me feel so nervous I wanted to vomit.

I knew Emmet-face well enough that despite his limited facial expression and me drugged to my eyeballs, I could tell I'd moved him. Even before he signed *I love you* back and held my hand tight.

"But what does he mean he's talking to him?" my mom asked.

"We use sign." Emmet stared at my mouth. I wondered if it was because it was as close as he could get to my eyes or if he was thinking about kissing me. "It's difficult for Jeremey to talk sometimes. When we have our phones, we have shortcuts for words, but he's using ASL now because he doesn't have a phone. Also I think they drugged him too much to type."

He looked over his shoulder at the wall near my mom. "Jeremey is sick, Mrs. Samson. He needs to have modifications. You have to stop trying to make him be normal. There's no normal. You can ask Dr. North. He said I gave Jeremey good behavior and accessibility modifications. He said I was a good boyfriend. He has four degrees, Mrs. Samson. You don't have four degrees. You should listen to Dr. North."

My mom started to sputter angrily, and I laughed. Well, I would have laughed, but all I could do was smile. Right at Emmet, who smiled at me and squeezed my hand.

A nurse came and changed my IV, and everything got muddy. Time sort of floated around. There was a doctor, there was a nurse. Sometimes my mom was in the back of the room, sometimes she wasn't. Once I thought I saw Jan, but I wasn't sure.

Emmet was always right beside me, holding my hand. A few times he would lean close and tell me in his whisper which wasn't a whisper at all that he had to use the restroom, or he had to let go of my hand to eat, and a few times the nurses needed my hand, but otherwise he was always there. It felt as if he was there for days, but when it got dark, I realized it was the first time it had been dark since I'd come to the hospital.

He leaned close to my bed, focusing on my ear as he spoke.

"It's 9 p.m. I have to go home. I wish I could stay, but I can't."

I panicked. I should tell him to go home, but I didn't want him to leave. When he was with me, I was still depressed, but I had an anchor in my big ocean of emotions. I didn't want to sleep in the dark alone in the hospital on drugs. In fact, as I thought of it too much, I felt tears in my eyes.

Dragging his hand to my lips, I brushed a dry kiss against his knuckles as a tear slid down my cheek. *"Please,"* I whispered. "Stay."

He squeezed my hand tight, and he hummed, and he waved his hands in front of himself, as if he were trying to shake off water. He stared at my lips. "I have to go home. It's not okay for me to stay here overnight, and I don't think my autism would let me. I'm sorry. But I can stay another few minutes."

I wanted him to stay all night long. I *needed* him to stay, but I understood he couldn't. *Just a little more.*

A hug.

A kiss.

I motioned to Emmet. Some of the heavy drugs were wearing off now. I patted the space beside me. *Lie with me. Cuddle me.*

He frowned and rocked on his heels. "There isn't room. And you're full of IV lines."

I was too worn out to argue, so I pulled back the covers and waited.

After a little more rocking and a lot of humming, he got in. He fumbled with the rail and knocked the TV remote on the floor, and he grumbled, but he got in, nesting so close to me our bodies touched.

"They're going to arrest us," he murmured.

I draped the blanket over our bodies. I touched his face, a firm touch the way he liked, and I pressed my lips to his.

I opened my mouth over his, licked the seam of his lips. He jolted and murmured *"You licked me,"* but then he opened his mouth and let me inside.

I couldn't get an erection with all the drugs, but I felt his pressing against my groin. His kisses were clumsy and tentative, but when I was bold, he met me stroke for stroke. He gripped my shoulders and breathed heavier and heavier until he pulled away. When he spoke, his voice trembled.

"Jeremey, if you keep kissing me, I'm going to get semen in my underwear."

I smiled but didn't kiss him anymore, only nuzzled his cheek. It had the finest bit of stubble, and it felt good. "Thank you. For calling 911. For staying." *For being you.*

"It was my mom who called. But she used my phone." He nuzzled me awkwardly. He wasn't much of a nuzzler. "Please don't do that again, Jeremey."

I wished I could promise him I wouldn't. I wished I could say as long as he was with me, I wouldn't think about killing myself. That would be a lie, though, so I only brushed one last kiss across his lips, shut my eyes and snuggled against him.

When the nurse came in, she didn't yell, but she did make Emmet go. I wept silently as he left, but before the sadness could take too much hold, the nurse gave me another injection of some drug, and I drifted off to sleep.

The next morning I woke up feeling much less groggy. It turned out I'd had a much stronger reaction to the sedatives than they'd anticipated, which was why I felt so woozy so long, but now, though I still felt flat, I was able to sit up and walk and move. After checking my oxygen levels, they took me off all the tubes and IVs, and they gave me a big breakfast.

Emmet got a breakfast too, because he was back as soon as I was awake. He ate in silence, and afterward he stood over me and all but spoon-fed me to get me to eat.

The nurses seemed to think we were cute, from the looks and smiles they kept giving us. Though several knew Emmet, which he explained was because his mother saw patients at the hospital.

Shortly after we ate our breakfast, our parents arrived—all four of them, mothers and fathers both. My dad kept holding my mother's arm, rubbing it reassuringly as she dabbed at her eyes. Jan was with them, but she stood a little ways apart from them, rigid and blank. That's how she always is with our family, but when we talked on the phone or were out together by ourselves, she was different.

I got tired thinking of how awful the day would be, how bad they'd make me feel for what I'd almost done. It made me wish, for a fleeting moment, I'd succeeded in killing myself. But then Emmet took my hand, and I didn't wish for that anymore.

The lecture and scolding I'd anticipated, though, didn't happen. As everyone was starting to get awkward milling around, a doctor came into the room. Emmet stood up, beaming. "Dr. North, are you Jeremey's doctor?"

"I'm one of them, yes. Good to see you again, Emmet. Marietta, Doug—" He shook Emmet's parents' hands, then turned to mine. "Dr. Howard North. Pleasure to meet you."

My mom and dad accepted his handshake, but they acted ashamed, as if they were embarrassed they had to call a doctor for me.

Dr. North didn't notice, or if he did, he ignored them. "I'm going to have to ask you all to step out for a little while so I can talk with Jeremey alone. If you wait in the lounge, I'll have the nurses' station let you know when we're finished."

My dad stood straight, his mustache bristling as he pushed back his shoulders. "We're staying. He's our son. We have a right to hear what you ask him."

Jan rolled her eyes but said nothing.

Dr. North addressed my parents calmly. "With all due respect, Mr. Samson, your son is an adult. If he wishes for you to come for part of the interview, you may, or if he consents to a follow-up afterward, I can give you that, but Jeremey is legally allowed to make his own decisions about his health care. Even if he were a minor, I would be quite firm about this interview being conducted at least in part in private. It is meant as no disrespect to you as parents, but is out of respect for Jeremey as an individual."

This surprised me in a good way, but I immediately tensed as my dad looked at me, clearly expecting me to say yes, Dr. North could tell them everything, that I wanted them to stay. I didn't, though, so I stared down at the blanket and let the doctor shoo everyone out.

The one person I wouldn't have minded staying left without any complaint. All Emmet did was hook two fingers against my two fingers, a silent goodbye.

Then they all left, and it was only Dr. North and me in the room.

Smiling, he pulled up a chair beside my bed and assumed a relaxed but attentive position. "You're looking quite well this morning. How are you feeling?"

I flexed my hands against the blankets—I didn't want to talk about how I felt. It had dawned on me I might have screwed up so badly they would put me in an institution. The thought made me want to throw up my breakfast. "Thank you for arranging for Emmet to stay with me yesterday. I mean, I assume that was you. I appreciate it, and I think he did too."

"You're quite welcome." He let a beat pass. "Is there a reason you don't want to tell me how you're feeling?"

My fingernails scraped the blanket over and over. I stared at my legs. "I'm fine. I'm sorry I scared everyone." I started to say *it won't happen again*, but I stopped myself, fairly sure this guy would see through the lie.

"You don't have to be nervous, Jeremey. You have nothing to fear here."

I had plenty to fear. Despite the drugs, I felt a panic attack trying to claw its way out. I couldn't lose Emmet after just getting him back.

A cool, slightly weathered hand closed over mine. "Talk to me about what is making you anxious. Let me help you."

I shut my eyes and drew a deep breath, trying to push the fear down. I didn't want to tell him what I feared, but not telling him ensured a panic attack, which seemed more likely to land me in a loony bin. "I don't want to go to a mental institution."

"This interview isn't a screening for such a possibility. We're dealing with right now, Jeremey. How are you feeling *right now*?"

Confused, and scared. Also stupid. I'd felt so good before. *When Emmet was here.* "I want to see Emmet."

"You will. But first I need you to talk to me about your feelings."

I didn't want to. "I want to go home." I didn't really, but it was better than this. God only knew what this guy would find in my head if he started poking around.

Dr. North didn't touch me, but he leaned forward in a way that made me feel as if he had. "I need you to listen carefully, Jeremey. What I'm about to say might upset you, but I want you to *listen*. Can you do that?"

My stomach knotted into a ball. I nodded stiffly and stared at my lap.

"Good. Thank you. What you've done is serious. You aren't in trouble—no one is judging you or scolding you or sentencing you. But going home isn't an option right now. In fact, shortly we'll be leaving Intensive Care for the psychiatric unit, where you'll stay for a minimum of several days for observation."

He might as well have poured ice into my veins. I felt too heavy to panic, though I tried anyway. This time he did put a hand on my arm—gently, but it kept me in place as he looked me in the eye.

"This is not a punishment. This is treatment. It's important you understand this."

His eyes were blue, but so faded and soft they were almost grey. They were kind eyes, like a young grandfather's. Except even with all his kindness, I wanted to cry. "I—I can't— I *won't*—"

He kept a hand on my arm, but it was his gentle voice that held me in place. "Please understand this isn't something I decided to do to you. By attempting to harm yourself, you've triggered a powerful public health system. Your actions have dictated you are not in control of yourself, and neither you nor your family get to make decisions about where you go and what happens to you just yet. Deep breaths."

He paused and waited while I tried to obey, to stop hyperventilating. Then he continued.

"I understand this is difficult. It isn't easy for anyone. But put out of your head Hollywood visions of bleak hallways and insane asylums. You'll be going to the psychiatric ward of a private hospital. It's two floors above where we are right now. It looks much the same as this room, but with less glass and machines. You're being admitted there not to be punished but to be observed and aided."

I *was* thinking of Hollywood. In fact I was thinking of a ghost-hunting show where they toured an old asylum from the turn of the twentieth century. No ghosts had appeared, but the decayed, isolated imagery of that place still haunted my mind.

The idea that they could put me away so easily—no choice, no discussion—made me cold. It made me wish I'd done a better job of offing myself.

Except it wasn't true. I didn't want to die. Not if I got to see Emmet.

Dr. North withdrew his hand from my arm. "You aren't being moved right now. Right now, in this second, Jeremey, I am talking to you. I'm asking you how you feel. I'm your doctor and I want to know. I want to help you, because helping people who feel overwhelmed is my job."

I understood what he was trying to do, but it all was pointless if this was only going to end in me never seeing Emmet. "You're trying to see if I'm crazy. And if I'm crazy, you'll put me away. Not here. Somewhere else, for good."

"No one is putting you away. You'll have to stay here for a few days at the very least while my colleagues and I make sure you're no longer a danger to yourself. If you or your parents tried to argue with me, I would get a court order keeping you here until we determined the danger had passed. But committing someone to a mental institution is a step we don't take lightly. It isn't something I'm entertaining for you. What I would like is to begin working on your therapy so you can return to society strong enough to face what life brings you."

My nostrils flared, and I stared down at my lap. "Then you might as well send me away now. I'm never going to be strong."

"Do you mean you won't try, or you don't believe you'll succeed?"

Self-loathing curled like smoke inside me, choking out hope. "I don't *believe* I'm not strong enough for the world. I *know* I'm not. Everyone wants me to be stronger, be normal, to stop being sad and overwhelmed, but I can't be. I can't change who I am. I can't like girls, I can't be happy, I can't go into a crowded store without having a panic attack. I can't drive in heavy traffic. I can barely drive at all. I can't be strong enough for life. I can't change who I am. I should know, because I've tried."

I thought I'd put it pretty plainly, but Dr. North only smiled, his blue-gray eyes glittering as if he had a secret. "But I never said I wanted you to change who you are. I want to help you find a way to be strong. To help *you* be strong, as you are. To modify the way you approach the world and possibly the way the world approaches you, so you are able to cope with it."

Was *he* crazy? "That's not possible."

"Then this is my first job, to convince you it is." He held out his hands and raised his eyebrows. "But first. Let's have one success today. One small start. I'm going to ask you two questions, and I ask you to answer each honestly. Even one word will do. I'm going to ask how you're feeling, and what you want. Today that's being strong, answering those questions even if you don't want to or are afraid to. And remember practicing being strong is how you get to go home, not simply to leave the hospital but to have a good, happy life. Are you ready to try?"

That wasn't strong at all, answering two questions, but I nodded.

He sat forward. "How are you feeling right now, Jeremey?"

So many emotions rolled around inside me I didn't know where to start. I didn't want to say anything, because I didn't want to say the wrong thing, but he kept watching me. He'd keep me here all day until I said *something*. So I swallowed against my dry throat and said, "Scared."

"Very good, and an understandable emotion. I would feel scared too right now, if I'd undergone your ordeal of the past day. I'll tell you how I'm feeling right now: proud of you, and sad for you. I wish I could make you not scared. In fact, I'm doing my best to make it go away. But I also know I can't take it all. So I want to sit here for a second and practice feeling with you. I'm going to count to ten silently in my head, and we'll sit here together, feeling. I don't want you to try and stop your feelings, or fix them, or change them. Only sit and feel. If your feelings shift, that's fine, but try not to direct it. Give yourself ten seconds to feel. Are you ready?"

I wasn't. I nodded anyway.

"Go."

It was weird. I don't know how good a job I did of not directing my feelings, because I kept thinking about them. But sometimes I thought maybe I did what he asked and just felt. It was like sinking into water. Deep and blue and floating, but the sensation felt as if it could pull me down. Except the more times I let go, the more I wondered if I really could drown, or if I only feared I would.

"Ten seconds."

I jolted, opening my eyes and blinking at Dr. North as if surprised to find he was there. He smiled at me.

"Very, very good, Jeremey. How did you find sitting with your feelings?"

I wasn't sure how I felt about the experience yet. What did he *want* me to say? "It was okay."

I kind of hoped we did the ten-seconds-of-feeling exercise again, though. I wondered if it was okay to do it on my own. Except how would I know when ten seconds were up?

"Now for my second question. Are you ready?" He waited for me to nod. "What is it you want, Jeremey? Right now? There's no wrong answer. I'm not judging you for your answer. All I want is for you to practice identifying feelings and desires. What do you want right now?"

The question was so hard. Not because I didn't want to tell him—though I didn't—but because I didn't know. I wanted out of here, but honestly, I didn't want to go home. I wanted to go *home*, but to a place that didn't exist. Somewhere soft and safe and good. That wasn't my parents' house.

I shoved the thought away and tried again. What did I want? I didn't know. I started to panic.

He put his hand on my arm. "It doesn't have to be complicated. You can tell me you want a bowl of ice cream."

I didn't want ice cream, though. I wanted something. I could feel it, almost see it. I shut my eyes and went back into the water of feelings. It felt horribly empty to not know what it was I wanted. I let go, let myself sink into the blue—and I knew.

Dr. North asked me again, "What do you want?"

I didn't want to tell him, but down in the feeling water, it turned out, my worrying couldn't reach me. "Emmet." By speaking out loud, the spell broke, and I glanced at him nervously. "I...want to be with Emmet."

I wasn't sure what I expected from him, but it wasn't softness and a smile that made my insides feel warm. "Excellent. And much better than a bowl of ice cream, I should think." He rose, patting my arm. "Even more, it's something I can give to you. Possibly very soon."

I almost corrected him, to explain I didn't mean I wanted to see him but that I wanted *to be with him*, like, *with* him, but my censors were all back in place now, and I stayed silent.

The way he winked at me made me think he understood what I'd meant anyway.

Chapter Eleven
Emmet

They didn't let Jeremey go home from the ICU. On the second day he was in the hospital, he had to go to the psychiatric ward, which Mom says is what happens when someone tries to commit suicide. I was glad he had people to take care of him, but I was sad he had to stay there. I couldn't see him as often as the day he'd been in the ICU. In fact for the first few days, I couldn't see him at all.

I visited him on the third day, when Dr. North said Jeremey could have visitors again. He said Jeremey had been good and worked hard on his therapy and deserved a reward, and I was the reward he wanted. That made me happy. I've never been a reward before.

We met in a small white room with a couch and a window. Dr. North said if we needed him, we could flip the red light switch on the wall, which would send in a nurse. Otherwise he would come get me when our time was up.

Jeremey waited at the window when I arrived. He was wearing regular clothes, but no shoes. He turned to smile at me when I came in, and I smiled back. I even looked him in the eye for a few seconds because I wanted to show him how much I cared.

We hugged, but we didn't kiss. Dr. North was still in the room.

"You have an hour," he told us with a smile, and then he was gone.

"It's so good to see you, Jeremey." I flapped my hands a little because I was too excited not to. "Dr. North is a good doctor. My mom says he's the best in the whole Midwest. Is he a good doctor for you?"

Jeremey made the embarrassed face. "Yes. I—" He bit his lip, glanced at me, then looked away again. "I'm...sorry. For what I did."

I was confused. I didn't know what he'd done. I hadn't seen him for three days. "What did you do?"

His whole face went red. This means someone is *very* embarrassed. "I tried to kill myself and got myself locked up in here. That's not...being a good boyfriend."

I liked it when Jeremey talked about being my boyfriend. "You're sick. It's okay. It has nothing to do with being boyfriends." I wanted to hold his hand, but that made me nervous so I flapped once instead. "Let's sit on the couch and talk. I have paper and pencil in my pocket if you need to use code. But I had to leave my phone with Dr. North."

We sat next to each other. I could smell and feel him, but I had room to rock. Since we sat side by side, I couldn't look at him, so I didn't have to feel bad about not meeting his gaze.

"What do you want to talk about?" I asked him.

He fidgeted his fingers in his lap. "I...don't know."

I laughed. "But you said you wanted to see me. That I was your reward for hard work. What work have you been doing?"

This was an okay thing to ask. Althea and I practice acceptable social questions all the time, so I was sure, but Jeremey's shoulders hunched and he got embarrassed again. "It probably sounds silly. Basically my emotions make me feel like a big baby Dr. North has to retrain."

I frowned. "I'm sorry, I don't understand what you said."

He tugged at the hem of his shirt. "We talk about how I feel all the time. I have to practice feeling. Talking about what I feel and rehearse sitting with it. And explaining them out loud."

I brightened. This I understood. "At home I have shirts for feelings. If I wear different clothes, it means I'm sitting with my specific feelings. It used to be only for anger and sadness, but now I have shirts for anything that feels too big for me to explain."

He sighed. "You always make it sound so easy. I wish it could be that way for me so I didn't have to end up in the hospital. I don't want to be in the locked ward."

"The locked ward is scary at first, but they take good care of you, and they're good at patterns, which is comforting. I haven't been to this locked ward, but Mom says they're all pretty much the same."

He stopped hunching and looked at me with a face I couldn't understand. "You...you've been to the psych ward? As a patient?"

"Yes. When I was twelve."

Now he had a surprised expression. Almost scared or upset. "When you were *twelve*? They locked you up?"

"No, they admitted me to the psychiatric ward. It was when I'd just started speaking again, and I got angry a lot. That was also when I had the bad therapy, and I had to go to the hospital until I could get control of myself."

He kept looking at me with a complicated expression. "You say it like it's no big deal. Wait—what do you mean you'd just started speaking?"

"I didn't talk for a long time." I could feel him staring at me, and I started to feel uncomfortable, so I rocked and flapped. "I could write, and I knew *how* to talk, but I wouldn't. My brain octopus wouldn't let me. I stopped talking when I was nine and didn't start again until I was almost thirteen. But I enjoyed math. I did a lot of math."

"I don't understand. Why wouldn't you talk?"

I tried to think of how to explain, and I had to hum a little first before I could. "It was a long time ago, and I don't remember well, but I was angry and overwhelmed. I was still in regular school then, and the other students made me feel uncomfortable. It was a private school, but it wasn't a good fit. The academics were good, but the students were not. When I started homeschooling, it was better, but I wanted to be quiet for a long time after I left. It made everyone upset. Then we had the bad therapy, and then I went to the hospital."

"What do you mean, bad therapy?"

"I had a therapist who tried to fix me, like I was broken. It made me angry, and I hit her. It was a scary time. But then they put me in the hospital, and it was a good hospital. The Mayo Clinic in Minnesota. We lived in Iowa City then, but Minnesota is the best psychiatric hospital in the region. Dr. North worked there. He helped me the same way he's going to help you."

I rocked and smiled, remembering how Dr. North made the bad therapy go away. "He's an important doctor in psychiatry, so I bet things will be the same here as they were at Mayo because he's in charge. The ward at Mayo was good. Everything was clean and organized and punctual. I felt safe. We talked about me maybe living there for a while, but everyone said I should try to go home. So I did, and I practiced coping strategies. It was good. This is why we have to listen to doctors. Sometimes our brains make bad decisions, and we need to borrow the doctors' brains."

Now I felt nervous too. It made me uneasy to see how surprised Jeremey was I hadn't spoken for four years.

When he spoke, though, he seemed less nervous. "I...I had no idea how much you understood."

"I do understand." I considered a moment. "Not about killing myself, though."

He hunched. "I'm sorry."

"You're sick. It's okay. You don't have to apologize. You have to do your work so you can get better and we can be together again."

Jeremey didn't say anything to that. But he took my hand, and he squeezed it.

It was a hard touch, so it was okay. Also, I've decided I like holding Jeremey's hand. Touching him is always okay.

Originally Jeremey was only supposed to stay in the hospital for a few days, but he and Dr. North decided thirty days would be better. It upset Jeremey's mom a lot when she found out. My mom tried to talk to her, but she didn't want to discuss it, so we left her alone. Also I think my mom was still angry with Gabrielle, so she didn't try very hard.

The good news was though Jeremey didn't get discharged, I got to see him several times a week. Sometimes it was to visit, but a few times Jeremey and I had group therapy together. I hadn't done group therapy in a long time, and normally I don't like it. But Dr. North thought I might enjoy having group with Jeremey. It turned out he was right. The first time was a little rough, but for Jeremey, not for me.

The other times I'd done group, I'd been in a big room with five other clients at Mayo, but group this time was only Jeremey, Dr. North and me, and we met in the same room where Jeremey and I got to visit. Jeremey sat on the couch, so I sat in a chair.

Dr. North sat in a chair too. "Jeremey, Emmet. Good to see you both."

"It's good to see you too, Dr. North," I said. Jeremey didn't say anything, only looked down at his hands.

Dr. North watched him. "Jeremey, is something wrong?" When Jeremey said nothing and hunched forward, Dr. North sat forward in his chair. "Talk to us, Jeremey. Tell us what you're feeling."

Jeremey wouldn't look up, and he wouldn't talk.

"Do you need a notebook?" I asked him. Sometimes he had to use a notebook at our visits, and I always brought one with me now. But I saw Dr. North had one too.

"I feel stupid," Jeremey murmured.

He was in trouble now. Dr. North didn't like that word.

Dr. North used his *I'm serious* voice. "Use a different word to describe your feelings. Why do you feel foolish? What are the feelings that word is hiding behind?"

It took several tries before he could get Jeremey to talk, eventually only on the notepad, and I counted the ceiling tiles while I waited. I'd counted them before, but there were a lot and I enjoyed counting them every time. Plus several were replacement panels and were a slightly different color. Three hundred and twenty-six total tiles, seventy-three yellowed. I got so absorbed in counting I didn't realize they'd been trying to talk to me until they called my name twice.

"I'm sorry. I was counting."

"I assumed so." Dr. North nodded at Jeremey. "Could you tell us why you chose to sit in the chair you're in?"

It was a good question, but it surprised me he asked. Usually people don't care. "There were only four straight-backed chairs. You hadn't sat down, and you didn't care which one you had, and Jeremey took the couch, so I took the chair I wanted, which was the chair where I could see out the window. Also two of the other ones are uneven and that bothers me."

"Why didn't you choose to sit beside Jeremey, the way you do when you visit him outside of a therapy session?"

That was a strange question, but I answered it anyway. "This is group therapy. I should have my own chair. Plus I don't like to sit on a couch when I'm supposed to pay attention. It makes me sleepy, and I can't focus."

"Oh." Jeremey's face went complicated, and he stared at the floor. "Now I feel stupid."

"You need to stop using that word," I told Jeremey. "Dr. North hates it, and you'll get in trouble. I don't like it when you use it about yourself, either. I think it's your R word. Why do you feel that way?"

Jeremey glanced at Dr. North, but he stayed quiet. Jeremey couldn't look at me. "I thought you didn't sit with me because you were upset with me."

"But why would I be upset with you? You haven't done anything."

Jeremey got quiet, and after a long pause, Dr. North spoke for him. "Jeremey worries a great deal about people being angry with him. He often assumes he's done something wrong."

I frowned at Jeremey. "You haven't done anything wrong. I'm not angry with you. I'm excited to be here. If I were angry with you, I'd tell you."

Dr. North raised an eyebrow at me. "This is true. Emmet is a good test for your tendency toward negative thoughts, Jeremey. He doesn't come with the same kind of artifice you're accustomed to from people. And, Emmet, Jeremey is a good challenge for you. To understand him and what he's feeling, you must pay extra attention to his emotions and his cues. He told you he was upset by your choice of seating, but you missed his silent message because reading those kinds of cues are more difficult for you."

Now I was confused, and worried. "Was it wrong of me to sit in this chair?"

"Not at all. No one has done anything wrong, but this moment is a good opportunity for you both. Jeremey, you've learned when you worry you've upset Emmet, you can ask him if it's true, and he will tell you. Emmet, you've learned you must watch Jeremey extra closely to read his emotions and his body language. I want you to practice right now in fact. Study

Jeremey, Emmet, and tell me what emotions you think he's feeling. Guesses are okay, but tell me if you're guessing. If you're deducting, tell me how you're doing that. Jeremey, when he's done, you tell him if he was accurate."

I studied Jeremey carefully. Reading someone's emotions is something I will never be good at, but I know my adaptations. I studied Jeremey, noticing how he sat and how he held his body and his face. He was very close together, all his arms and legs and body parts tucked in close, as if he were a bug someone had flipped over. His shoulders were round, and he didn't look at me. His face didn't match any of my expressions pictures, so I looked at each part of his face like Dr. North told me. His mouth was flat, but his lips weren't pressed together. His eyes were flat. Sometimes he'd glance up, and sometimes his lips would press for a moment, but that was it. He also moved his fingers in a way that reminded me of when I wanted to flap.

I wasn't sure how he felt. I had ideas, but that was all. I started to flap my hands.

"Try to guess," Dr. North told me. "Let's start with big emotions. You tell me yes or no. Does he seem happy?"

No, he didn't. "Not happy." I rocked in my chair. "But not sad or angry."

"What are your other options?"

I tried to think. How did Jeremey usually feel? "Nervous, maybe." I brightened. "Yes—nervous. Not a guess."

"Jeremey, is that correct?"

"Yes, mostly."

"Excellent. Good job, Emmet. Can you tell us how you knew?"

I smiled a big smile, proud I'd gotten it right. "Because of his hands. His face is too complicated for me to tell what he's feeling, but he keeps fidgeting his hands. That's like when I want to flap. It's kind of the same thing, except hand-flaps are bigger and make people stare at me."

127

"Can you talk to us, Emmet, about why you flap your hands?"

Normally I was fine talking about hand-flapping with Dr. North, but I worried about Jeremey. I rocked a little.

"Honest feelings, Emmet. Tell us about flapping your hands. Jeremey confessed about his hurt feelings, made himself vulnerable for you. Now it's your turn. Do you feel Jeremey is a safe space to talk about flapping?"

"I want him to be." I rocked a little more. "But most people don't like it. They think I'm the R word."

"I don't think you're the R word," Jeremey said.

Dr. North winked at me. "Talk about both things. Explain why you flap your hands and how it makes you feel when people misunderstand."

This is what I like about Dr. North. He's good at asking questions.

I thought about it for a moment, then explained as best I could. "Hand-flapping feels good. Sometimes I flap when I'm excited, but sometimes because I'm nervous. It's different for each feeling. Excited flaps let off energy. I have so much inside me I have to let it out. But if I'm nervous, it draws in energy. In my head it feels as if I'm making a wall. The happy-flapping takes down the wall, giving my energy to other people." The idea of sharing my happiness with people that way made me feel good, and in my head I could see it, bright blue-white light going from my hands to other people. But then I remembered how most people reacted to my flapping, and the happy feeling ended. "People make bad faces at me and stop talking to me. Or they talk to me like I'm a baby instead of a person."

Dr. North was in his listening position, sitting straight but not too straight, with his hands resting on his legs. "How does it make you feel when people react badly to your hand-flapping?"

"Sad, and sometimes angry."

"Can you elaborate? What does the sadness and anger feel like inside?"

I considered Dr. North's question. "Gray-blue."

"Thank you, Emmet." Dr. North smiled at me before turning to Jeremey. "Jeremey, I have a few questions for you. One, do you mind when Emmet flaps his hands?"

I was so nervous waiting for the answer, I had to hum.

"No." Jeremey didn't hesitate at all. "I don't mind when he hums or rocks or flaps his hands, though I've never seen him flap his hands much, really. I know that's how Emmet is."

"Maybe that can be something to work toward, Emmet, letting Jeremey in far enough for you to flap in his presence. Now I have a second question for you, Jeremey. How did it make you feel to hear Emmet speak so easily about his feelings?"

Jeremey sighed. "Jealous."

I sat up, frowning. "But why would you be jealous of that?"

"It's so difficult for me to say what I'm feeling. You said it as if it's no big deal."

I wasn't sure what to say, but Dr. North asked me a question. "Jeremey says it's challenging for him to express his feelings. He has a difficult time identifying what those feelings are. This is part of his depression. Acknowledging feelings seems dangerous to his mind, so he has to practice. What's something challenging for you to do, Emmet? What do you have to practice because of your autism?"

This was an easy question. "Faces. Faces are impossible."

"Talk more about that. Explain why they're difficult, so Jeremey can understand."

"I can't read faces the way people without autism can. I can't see a face and know if someone is happy or sad. Which is bad because people assume I can, and they get angry when I don't notice how they feel."

"Do you care how other people feel?"

"Yes. But I don't always remember to check for it. Sometimes I'm busy worrying about my own feelings and I forget."

"Talk about how you check for other people's emotions. I think Jeremey might find it illuminating."

He did? I glanced at Jeremey but couldn't meet his gaze, so I stared at the arm of the couch. "I have charts. I look at the charts to learn what each emotion is like on a face. Sometimes Althea practices with me. I know a lot of emotions now because I've memorized them, but it's always good to have a refresher."

I glanced at their faces now—Dr. North wore his listening face, but Jeremey was too complex to read. I was starting to call the face he made the depression face, and I didn't care for it.

"I don't think they make practice charts for figuring out what emotions you have," Jeremey said.

Dr. North didn't say anything, so I did. "Why not? They would be the same. You could use my charts. You could have a mirror and look at your face."

"It doesn't always show on my face, how I feel."

The idea was alarming. How could I read what Jeremey felt like if it didn't show on his face? "Is this part of depression? Does it keep the emotion from showing?"

Jeremey's face became annoyed. Almost angry. He turned to Dr. North. "I don't want to practice identifying my emotions. I want to go home. I want to be normal. I want to go to college. I want to have a job and a house and a car."

Dr. North calmed him down, telling Jeremey what he'd told me, about how there is no normal, about how modifications help us integrate with society. I listened, but I thought about what Jeremey had said too. About the things he wanted.

Independence, that's what he was talking about. I had some—I was in college, and I could get a job when I was done, but no one talked about me moving into an apartment, and obviously I wasn't getting a car. Mom had said she was looking for somewhere for Jeremey and me to live together, but she hadn't mentioned anything about it for a while now.

Maybe there was no normal. But there were a lot of things most people could do which everyone assumed I couldn't. Jeremey too.

At the end of every therapy session, Dr. North has us set goals. I gave one, but it wasn't my real goal. Because as of that session, I had a new one. A secret one, one I wanted very much to make real.

I wanted to be independent. Maybe I couldn't be normal, but I could be like everybody else. Maybe not all the way. But my goal, my wish for myself, was to see how far toward everybody else I could get.

What I didn't know, though, was how close that kind of independence was for me—and for Jeremey too.

Chapter Twelve
Jeremey

Sometimes it bothered me they could keep me at the hospital for as long as they wanted. Technically I agreed with Dr. North that I should stay, but it still scared me that my freedom rested in the hands of another person. Even if the person was Dr. North.

Worse, I was stuck in the psych ward until I could learn how to manage my emotions better, and right now I couldn't be counted on to report what I was feeling. Not that Dr. North didn't try to teach me. Every day in therapy he asked, "What are you feeling right now? This very second?"

Finally one day I gave up and said what I always thought. "Stupid." I tugged at a thread until it came loose. "Ashamed. Sorry. Embarrassed."

I thought he'd scold me for saying *stupid*, but he smiled. "That's good, Jeremey, how you can identify those negative feelings so easily. Do you feel any other emotions? Any positive ones? You mentioned gratitude in an earlier session. Is it still present?"

I considered his question. Answering quickly, I would have said I only felt negative, but it was like someone pointing out an image in one of those Magic Eye paintings. Suddenly there was more. "I'm grateful, yes. To you. To Emmet. I feel stupid that I'm here, that I can't manage myself, but I'm grateful to Emmet for stopping me and to you for helping me. I'm glad his mom is helping my mom."

I stopped talking. All I could think about was how my mom was always upset every time I saw her.

Dr. North didn't miss a trick. "What are you thinking about, Jeremey? What else are you feeling?"

I fidgeted in my chair. "I'm anxious about my mom." I took a deep breath before saying the next part. We'd talked about it a lot, but it scared me every time. "I'm nervous about going home."

"You're doing an excellent job, sitting with your feelings. It's perfectly fine to feel nervous. Can you talk about why? No judgments on you or your mom. Let's outline what you're feeling."

I stared at the tile on the floor in front of me. "She wants me to be someone I'm not. I feel as if I'm starting to accept that I'm different from other people. I worry she'll drag me back into bad feelings."

"Are you ready yet to have a group session with her?"

He asked this every day, and every day I said no. Today was no different. I shook my head. "Yesterday she started complaining about Emmet again. She said she'd help me find a normal boyfriend if I wanted one so badly."

"How did you feel when she said that?"

"Angry. Upset. Hurt." The emotions flowed so easily inside me, it almost alarmed me. Once I lifted the lid, it wasn't a soup of feelings. It was a raging sea. "I love being with Emmet. He's the best part of my day. But she makes me feel guilty, like maybe I shouldn't call him my boyfriend. That we shouldn't be boyfriends."

"Is there some reason you and Emmet shouldn't be romantically involved?"

I snorted. "My mom has plenty of reasons. She calls Emmet retarded. It makes me so angry, and it hurts. Which is dumb, because she's insulting him, not me."

"You strike me as a young man who feels deeply. I'm not surprised a slight against your boyfriend wounds you." Dr. North leaned forward. "I notice you've referred to yourself in a

133

derogatory way several times now. And in none of those instances would I have agreed with your self-assessment even on a minor level. Is this common for you, to see yourself as deeply flawed?"

Was it common? It was how I lived and breathed. I glanced at him sideways, sensing a trap. "Yes," I said nervously.

"Do you think about killing yourself when you feel this way?"

This had to be a trap. I clutched at the bedding, trying to wait him out, but it was clear this man had limitless patience. He asked this sometimes, but he hadn't in a week. "What...what happens if I say yes? If I fail the test?"

"Am I giving you tests?"

They always answered questions with questions. "Yes. You're trying to decide how crazy I am."

Instead of telling me he wasn't, he withdrew a small tablet from his jacket pocket, poking at the screen a few moments before presenting it to Jeremey. The tablet showed a 3-D drawing of a human brain. "This is a picture of a healthy human brain in a normal state." He flipped to another picture, which was 2-D and top down. "This is a brain under normal activity. All the blobs of yellow you see indicate brain activity." He flipped the screen again. The brain looked similar, but had fewer blobs. Less than half as the other one.

"This is a depressed brain, isn't it?"

He nodded and flipped to another screen, this one showing whole bodies. "These are thermal images of humans experiencing different emotions. Notice how anxiety heats in the chest but leaves the other parts cold. Notice how love heats everything."

I couldn't look away from the depressed human, who was totally blue, cold as ice. It made me feel sad. Without thinking, I touched the screen.

Dr. North didn't pull the tablet away. "Depression is a serious mental illness. We don't understand it as much as we'd like, but what we do know is a person suffering from depression cannot make the same decisions and shepherd their emotions the same way brains that are not depressed can. Our brains are not who we are, but they must be dealt with, like it or not."

"But how do I deal with it?" I'd been trying to be normal for years, but nothing worked.

"The drugs you're taking might help. But so will active therapy. Most of the help, though, will come directly from you. Like Emmet, you'll have to work harder to adapt. But you *can* adapt. I'm not attempting to commit you. I want to understand the background of your decision to attempt to end your life. I'm asking you to try to determine if this was a singular event based on heightened emotions and a rare feeling of despair or if you often experience this level of dangerous depression."

I let out a shaking breath. "But we're having a tough time finding the right drugs." One had given me weird electrical shocks in my brain, and the next made me cry all the time. The one I was on now was better, but I worried it wouldn't be right and I'd have to start all over again.

"SSRIs and SNRIs, since they are powerful drugs working on a fragile organ, must be treated with care. Which is what we're doing right now. Part of checking to see if the drugs are working are your answers to my questions."

I drew in a long, slow breath. "I think about killing myself all the time. Less since I've been here, but it's almost a bad habit. Sometimes it's because I'm upset. Sometimes it's just there, like an option. I try not to think about it, but it's not easy. It makes me feel safe, to know where the door is. Except that's crazy."

He held up a hand. "I would prefer you refrain from using both that word and the word stupid."

"I am, though. Aren't I? Crazy. I'm mentally ill."

Heidi Cullinan

"Mental illness is no different than a heart condition. In the same way a faulty valve can cause harm to the body and require medication and care, so does a malfunctioning brain. Insanity is a crude, culturally loaded term setting the sufferer apart in a way which will not aid the patient's recovery. The way we regard those whose brains hinder them with fault or injury is a prejudice, not a diagnosis."

Where was this guy when I was fourteen, fifteen, sixteen? All I remembered from back then was my parents yelling. Maybe I should have attempted suicide long ago. Except, of course, what if I'd succeeded?

"So what happens when we find the right drugs? Will I not be depressed anymore?"

"Unfortunately, no medicine exists which can permanently or fully stop the thoughts and feelings depression and anxiety cause. We don't understand enough yet what is going on, which makes the conditions difficult to treat. The best analogy I can give you for what SNRIs and SSRIs do is to say they're a crutch, or a set of leg braces. You still need to walk and fight the limitations your brain gives you. But the medications, when carefully selected and administered, can become something to lean on and keep you from falling down so often."

The mental picture was clear. "But I wouldn't ever run a marathon, and I'd walk a little jerky?"

"You would walk, more regularly then you possibly ever have, and on good days you might even run a little ways. But no. With the levels of depression you're describing, you will likely struggle with the tide of your emotions every day of your life. With proper care and assistance, this life can be a long and happy one."

I asked the question that in its way was more frightening than being committed, because in a way the questions felt linked. "What if my parents won't let me take the drugs? What if I go home and my mom says I have to quit them?"

136

Dr. North's smile glinted. "Your parents do not make this decision. Your health care is private business between the two of us."

Hope fluttered in my chest. How was that possible? "I want to take the drugs. I want to try to be normal."

He raised a finger at me. "That's another word I want you to eradicate from your vocabulary. There is no normal. There is not an invisible bar you must meet to be acceptable to society."

Yes there was. "I don't want to be the moody guy who cries all the time and has panic attacks if the grocery store is loud."

"There's nothing wrong with being that guy. There's nothing wrong with learning to manage yourself so you may react differently to stimuli, to control your environment, but being that man is being yourself. You are the young man your parents are eager to protect, the one Emmet is so fond of. I'm sure I don't have to tell you how difficult it is to impress him."

I appreciated what he said, but I felt he was deliberately misunderstanding me. "Dr. North, I want to go on dates and go to school and go shopping and...everything. I don't want to live with my parents. I want to be the same as everyone else who graduates high school. I don't want to feel this way."

"You *can* go on dates and go to school and go shopping, and everything. But you must do it as Jeremey Samson. You can no more erase your anxiety and intense emotional responses than I can become a sixty-year-old professional basketball player. What you *can* do is learn to manage your emotions. To learn how to tell yourself your feelings are not facts. That they seem real, *are* real, but that does not make them laws and truths."

I had felt so hopeful, and now I felt such despair. "So you're saying I have to be a loser for the rest of my life? The guy everyone laughs at? The guy no one wants to be friends with? The kid his parents wish hadn't been born?"

"I have said none of those things. What I am saying is you can be yourself. Your best self. And your first step toward it is accepting and loving who you are."

"Then I'll need to have Emmet around all the time. He's the only one who makes me feel okay."

"When managing depression and anxiety, you must do the work, and you must do it yourself. It's perfectly fine to feel stronger or better with Emmet or any friend or loved one. But you must never let them be the *only* way you're stable. People are good medicine, but they can't be your foundation of functionality. You must build that yourself."

Tears welled up so fast I could barely hold them back. "But I can't. You don't understand how impossible it is for me."

"This will be a challenge, yes. But you'll get there, and I will help you. I promise."

I didn't see how he could make that promise, but I didn't argue, because I wanted to hope.

The most difficult part about being in the hospital wasn't the meds, or the loss of freedom, or the scariness of what would happen when I got out. It was my mom.

She came every day, though honestly I wished she wouldn't. I don't mean to say unkind things about her or make her sound like a bad person. She loves me, and I know this. But sometimes I think she loves the boy she wishes I were a little more than she does the one she actually has.

Mom always wants to fuss, but in the hospital she was unbearable. She took issue with the light in my room, saying there wasn't enough. She didn't like the bare walls. That I never got to go outside made her crazy—she lectured Dr. North and the nurses about fresh air. She criticized the food—and honestly, this I was down with. I didn't tell her Althea brought me in amazing vegan dishes. She made me eat a lot of kale, which was only okay, but she also gave me these fruit salads with cashew cream and sometimes, if I'd been good, vegan and gluten-free cupcakes from the co-op, the same ones Carol had given us the day I'd had a panic attack outside of Wheatsfield. They were sweetened with maple syrup and were so good I thought I might die.

I never made the joke out loud, though. I figured I'd kind of used everything up on that subject for a while.

Mom wouldn't have understood about Althea's food, because basically the food I should be eating was the food she made at home. I should *be* at home.

"When will they let you out?" That was always her first question when she came to visit. Not *how are you doing?* She made no remark about how I was looking so much healthier and happier. She always seemed sad, as if she were about to cry. She'd cover her mouth with her hand, or press her lips flat and shake her head, and ask me when I'd be able to go home. Go back to normal.

I didn't know how to tell her she was the reason I *wasn't* going home. I'd admitted to Dr. North the greatest threat to my mental health was her attempts to nag me out of my funks. He agreed with me. But this was my stumbling block: how to tell her. And, honestly, what to do instead of going home.

As my tension over my inability to confront her grew, Emmet noticed. Of course, *he* had no problem asking me what was wrong.

"Is it your meds?" He looked over my head as he sat beside me on the couch. "Are you dizzy?"

"No. My meds are good. I feel a little foggy, but calmer. The world isn't as sharp-edged." I rubbed the butt of my palm nervously against my jeans. "The problem is my mom. I need to tell her she's too intense, that she's part of the problem. But I'm nervous. I don't think it's going to go well. And until I confront her, I can't go home."

Emmet smiled, but it was a wicked smile that made my insides jumble up. "I don't think you should go home. You should come live in an apartment with me."

I blinked, several times. "Live—in an *apartment*? Are you crazy? I thought you said you couldn't handle that?"

"No, I'm not crazy. You shouldn't use that word." He rocked back and forth, but I could tell it was happy Emmet, not nervous Emmet. "I can't live in a regular apartment, but Mom found a special kind of place for us to live. You know the old elementary school on the street north of our houses?"

I did—Roosevelt School was an old brick schoolhouse which had closed before I went to kindergarten. People had a huge fit about it closing, and four times people tried to reopen it, but it never did. There had been a lot of construction around it lately. "What about it?"

"They're turning it into apartments. It's called The Roosevelt now. It'll be open soon. I asked to see the blueprints. I didn't know about how blueprints worked exactly, but I read a book and did some research, and I think they did a good job." He smiled his mischievous smile. "The Roosevelt was full, but Mom talked the owner into letting us have a room they were using for one of the social workers. They'll share an apartment so we can have a place in the new building. We could move in there. Together. We could *both* be independent."

The idea was wonderful and terrible all at once. I didn't know how to respond. "I don't have any money, or a job. And neither do you."

"My mom and dad have a lot of money. They'll pay for you if they have to. It's a good idea. It's a two-room apartment. We could each have our own space. But we're close to our parents if we need help. Wheatsfield is still within walking distance, and so is the bus stop."

"But, Emmet, I don't have any money. And *my* parents will never pay."

"Dr. North can help you find an appropriate job. Sitting around isn't healthy. You need to stimulate your brain. Just carefully so you don't get overwhelmed."

He made it all sound so easy. He didn't address at all the boyfriend issue, which to me was the bigger obstacle. It couldn't be okay to move in together after basically admitting we liked each other for a few weeks. Except who else could I possibly live with? Nobody else would understand me the way Emmet could.

Also, if we lived in the same apartment, we could have sex. The drugs dulled the yearning a little bit, but only when Emmet wasn't in the room. When he was with me, like right now, talking and planning and being so bright, all I wanted to do was kiss him and touch him.

He touched me now, taking my hand and squeezing it. "Say yes, Jeremey. Say you want to move in with me."

Yes. I want to move in with you. "We...we have to talk to Dr. North."

"We will. At group." He fixed his gaze on my hairline and touched my cheek. "But it isn't time for therapy yet."

Oh, it was—my *favorite* kind of therapy. We sat there on the couch, Emmet holding my hand and kissing me sweetly...then not so sweetly.

Our kisses were never movie kisses with suave bending-you-over, full-body clinches. Sometimes our kisses were awkward. But they were always passionate, and they always made me feel good. They made me *feel.* For as much trouble as I had with Dr. North's *I want* statements, when Emmet and I kissed, I knew everything I wanted, and I wanted so much it rattled around in my head. I wanted to kiss him. Touch him. Take off his clothes. Explore all the things about sex I'd read about or watched. I wanted to touch his cock. Maybe put it in my mouth. *Do things.*

Kissing him now, when he'd filled my head with ideas about living on my own—oh, it couldn't happen, but being able

141

to dream about not having to go home was better than a whole bag of SNRIs.

To my surprise, when we went to group and Emmet told Dr. North his idea about the apartment, our therapist was in *favor* of the plan. "I was already looking into group home situations for you, Jeremey, but this could work out far better."

I couldn't believe this. "But—I don't have any money. And there's no way my mom will go along with this."

"She might surprise you. Even if she didn't, you can supplement your half of expenses with disability payments, though I'd like to see you begin part-time work. I'd entertain college if it's what you wanted, but given what you've told me about school, a break might not be a bad idea."

I didn't want to go to college. I didn't want anything to do with school ever again. "But...how can it be okay for us to live on our own?"

"You're both over eighteen," Dr. North pointed out. "You're legal adults, and there's nothing wrong with living on your own, provided you're given assistance. Your families will help, but you both need case workers as well. Someone to help you learn how to go shopping, pay bills, do laundry. Live your life. And handily, The Roosevelt has *two* social workers on staff."

I didn't know what to say. All I could think was how this couldn't be real. "Are you saying we can do this, just like that?" *Even if we're boyfriends?* We hadn't even had a date yet. How could we possibly move in together?

Dr. North smiled sadly. "No. It won't be quite so easy. But it's a good idea, one worth exploring."

We did explore it—two days later I had my first outing in almost a month, and it was to get in Althea's car and drive to The Roosevelt. There was still a lot of construction outside, which made me nervous to go in, but when they saw us, they took a break, and the building's owner gave us a personal tour.

Emmet seemed to know him well already. "Did you get the fire ladders, Bob?"

Bob smiled at Emmet. "I did. You can come see them for yourself." He grinned. "Is this your friend?"

"My boyfriend." Emmet stared at the wall between us. "Jeremey, this is Bob Loris, the owner of The Roosevelt. Bob, this is Jeremey Samson. We're going to move into your building."

"That's what I keep hearing. I like it." Bob extended his hand to me. "Good to meet you, son."

Bob showed us the whole building. It was weird, how you could see how it used to be a school, and yet it looked totally different at the same time. We went into one of the apartments upstairs—number six, which was the one Emmet said he wanted.

"It has a view of the train tracks, so I can count the cars and engines. Bob put in fire ladders for safety. If you jumped out of these windows, you'd break your neck, or your legs, or maybe both. But now we have the ladders, so it's fine."

I had to admit, I liked the apartment. A lot. I couldn't tell what it had been before—maybe two classrooms? It had two bedrooms with a bathroom between them, a small laundry in the closet off the kitchen, and a kitchen and dining room that opened into the living room. The ceilings were so much higher than I'd ever have guessed they'd be. Each room had a ceiling fan, which Emmet would appreciate, because he loved them. The one in his bedroom at home had a remote, and he loved to slow it down, wait until it stopped, then start it up again. I had a feeling he'd be talking Bob into remote-controlled fans, if he hadn't already.

Emmet kept rocking, and sometimes he flapped his hands. He'd done it around me only a few times, but I was surprised he did it in front of Bob. I glanced between the two of them, worried Bob would stop being so friendly toward him, but it never happened. On the way to the hospital, I found out why.

"Bob is a good guy. He built this place because of his son, who was in a bad car accident and can't move from his neck down, except for a little bit of his right hand. He wants somewhere for David to live where he can be on his own but still have help."

The comment made me balk. What, this was the special ed building? But I supposed that's what I was now. Special ed. Special needs.

Better the special needs house than your home.

As I lay in bed that night, the room dark and quiet, the nurses and aides moving through the hallway, the guy next door to me crying because that was what he did at night—I thought about The Roosevelt.

It still stung a little that it wasn't a regular apartment building. I wondered who else would live there, what kind of disabilities they'd have. I hated the idea that this was who I was, someone with a disability. That even if I wanted to go to college, I'd have to have adaptations like Emmet did. And I still didn't understand why everyone was so *whatever* about us moving in together so fast. It wasn't that I didn't want to. I just...worried maybe it was too soon.

During the day those truths had burned, but as I lay there in the dark, I closed my eyes and imagined living in The Roosevelt. I imagined looking out at the train tracks with Emmet, enjoying his silence as he counted. Walking down the street to the co-op to buy food. Making dinner in the cozy kitchen.

Having my own room, but sometimes sharing my bed with Emmet.

I thought about having a job. The idea scared me, but excited me too. I loved the idea of getting my own money and making my own choices.

When I imagined telling this to my mother, I got cold inside. But for the first time, the cold feeling wasn't stronger than the warm one that came with the alternative of living on my own.

Chapter Thirteen
Emmet

I had lied a little to Jeremey when I acted like my parents didn't care if we lived together as boyfriends. It was true, Mom had found The Roosevelt for me, but she was nervous about me living on my own, even assisted. There were other issues too, and they were about finances. It's not clear whether or not I quality for SSI, which is Supplemental Security Income provided by the government, and health insurance. My mom has always worked for the State of Iowa so they have to pay for me, and until I'm twenty-one they still have to. But once I'm an adult that changes.

Dad pointed out it wouldn't hurt to have me try living on my own and start the SSI paperwork for me as an adult. Mom said if living on my own didn't work, I could go home to their house.

I was going to make living on my own work. And I was going to make it work with Jeremey living with me.

The other tricky issue was that my mom was fine about us living together when she thought we were just friends, but now that she knew we were dating, she said she wasn't sure.

"It's not that I don't think you should be boyfriends," she said when I started to get angry. "It's different when you're dating someone, and I'm not yet convinced you fully understand what dating someone means."

Yes, I did. "It means you take care of them like friends, but you also have sex with them. Duh."

Mom got still and quiet, which with her means she's working not to overreact. "Emmet...have you had sex with Jeremey?"

"How could I? The vent in my room means you hear everything, and his room was too messy until the day his mom got upset, and since then I haven't been with him except at the hospital. You can't have sex in a hospital. You get arrested."

She was still nervous about it, though, so we agreed we'd talk about it with Dr. North.

It had been a long time since Mom and I had gone to therapy together, and this time was a lot nicer than the last time, because she wasn't crying. But I hadn't stopped talking for four years either, so I suppose that makes sense.

My dad came too, which he'd never done before, and I was glad he did, since he was one hundred percent on my side.

"Here's how I see it," Dad said after Mom had told Dr. North the same things she'd told me about how I don't understand dating. "Emmet is a lot better put together than most nineteen-year-olds I know. I understand Mari's reservations, but I know my boy. If he's made up his mind about this, it's already as good as done. I'd rather he didn't move in alone, and I know it's going to be tough for him to room with anyone. The only person I can possibly see working in that scenario is Jeremey. So what if they might fool around? We raised him right. He knows how to be safe. It's not as if putting them across the hall from one another is going to change anything. Plus I think the Samson kid could use this almost more than Emmet."

Mom did *not* care for that. "Doug, you're entirely missing the point."

I wasn't going to let her undo what Dad had said, because I thought it was the best argument anybody had ever made. "*You're* missing the point, Mom. You're being as bad as Gabrielle." Mom gasped and made an angry face, but I kept talking. "You always tell me it doesn't matter that I'm autistic, but now you're telling me that it does. If I were on the mean and wanted to move in with my boyfriend—"

"If you were on the mean and wanted to move in with your boyfriend, I'd still say no."

Dad held up a hand, which meant we both should be quiet. "Stop it. Both of you. Emmet, you will respect your mother. She's not trying to keep you from good things. She's trying to protect you."

"Jeremey *is* a good thing."

"Yes, but that doesn't mean you *have* to live with him, and not this second. I still think it could work, but she's not saying she's nervous about it because you're autistic. In fact it's exactly the opposite. You're her little boy, and you're saying you want to grow up right now. She's nervous for you, and she's sad for herself."

Mom started to cry then after all, the cry where she shuts her eyes and puts her hand over her mouth. Dad put his hand on her back and rubbed small circles and said quiet things to her. I watched, wanting to keep arguing because I wanted them to say I could live in The Roosevelt with Jeremey, but I didn't want Mom to cry.

Dr. North looked over the top of his glasses at me. "Emmet, tell me why you think you and Jeremey should live in The Roosevelt together. Explain why it's okay even though you're in a new relationship. Show me you understand why that element is significant."

I hummed as I stared at the floor, rocking and flapping gently as I thought. I *didn't* understand why that element was significant. Well, I did, but not the way my mom thought it was. She made it sound like a problem. To me, the fact that we were boyfriends made this better. It made me uncertain that I understood that and no one else did. It made me worry that maybe I was wrong, maybe this was a bad idea.

But how could it be a bad idea when it felt like the most important thing in the world?

Dr. North's quiet voice drifted into my thoughts. "We've discussed in sessions with Jeremey how important it is to watch our feelings when we're in a new relationship. You remember the euphoria?"

I frowned. Yes, I did remember. Was he telling me this was euphoria?

Dr. North is so good, sometimes he can read minds. "I'm not telling you I agree with you or your mother, Emmet. I'm pointing out things you should consider, and urging you to make a logical argument to defend your choice to your parents. Also to yourself."

It helped, knowing he wasn't judging me. I shut my eyes and concentrated, rocking and flapping gently as I recalled the conversation we'd had a few days ago, Dr. North and Jeremey and me. About how the endorphins released during a new relationship, friendship or romantic, were the same kind of high as heroin. It makes our brains do crazy things, which is where the phrase *crazy in love* comes from. Dr. North talked about how we had to be cautious about any decisions we make early on in any relationship, because we're caught up in the high. Was I caught up in the high? Yes, probably. But it didn't mean my decisions were all bad. It just meant I had to be extra careful.

I thought about living in The Roosevelt, let the euphoria rise inside me, and then I put it in a box and set it aside so I could rationally analyze the situation. It was such a good choice for both of us. We would have assistance but not babysitting. It was real life but with backup. Like the bumpers in bowling. No bad neighbors—or rather, no neighbors who wouldn't understand autism. Not far from my parents' house. We could still walk to Wheatsfield. Even the hospital wasn't far away. Downtown was close, so was the bus. Everything was good.

So why was my mom nervous? Because of Jeremey and me being boyfriends? I didn't understand how that could be negative. I opened my eyes and told Dr. North this.

Dr. North turned to Mom. "Well, Marietta? Can you be more clear to Emmet why you think his living with Jeremey might be negative?"

"Yes, I can. Their relationship might not work, and then they're stuck together."

"If our relationship didn't work," I said, "we would stop being boyfriends and just be roommates, or one of us would move out. But it will work. We'll work on it every day. The same as facial recognition charts. It's more homework, is all."

"What if there's no space for one of you to move out? We can't buy an extra apartment in case."

"If that happened, I'd move home and let Jeremey have it. His home isn't good, but mine is." I flapped angrily. "But we're not breaking up. Stop saying we are."

"I'm not saying you are. I'm saying you *might*. You can't *know* everything will be okay."

"I know that. Our house might burn down and I'd lose all my things. They'd burn in the fire and cry. You might die, and then I would cry. But I'm not going to live my life worrying about bad things happening, Mom. You shouldn't either."

Mom's shoulders slumped, and Dad grinned. "Like I said. More put together than most nineteen-year-olds." He rested his elbows on his knees and looked me in the eye. "Kiddo. I believe you can do this. I think, though, you and Jeremey and everybody's parents need to meet first, have a big fat family meeting. So your mom feels better. Jeremey might need the meeting too."

I considered this. "It would be okay if we met with Jeremey, but his parents will be awful."

My dad smiled his John Belushi smile. "That might help your mom even more."

It took another week, but the meeting got set up, and in the meantime, we started filling out the application for The Roosevelt—me and Jeremey both. My parents usually do this kind of thing, but I helped because that's part of Bob's process of making us independent. It was exciting. I got my own checking account, which I'd never had, and a debit card. Bob's friend Sally, who is one of the social workers who would live at The Roosevelt with us in the downstairs apartment, showed me how to keep track of my balance. It wasn't hard, but I didn't like the paper version, so I showed her the online software I found with an app to use on my phone to enter purchases. It was buggy, though, so I made a new one which worked better and gave it to her. She said I was a genius.

I said "thank you" instead of "I know." It's rude to tell people you know you're smart, I guess, which makes no sense, but Althea said I had to just go along with that one.

It's hard work to be independent. I had to make a budget in a spreadsheet about how much I would spend and where I would spend it, but the problem is I can't always know what I'll need in advance. I had to save money in case I needed something extra, but when I used my savings, I had to decide if the something extra was worth it. Managing my money overwhelmed me. It was so much easier to ask Mom if I could buy something. Sally said it would get easier, but I understood now why everyone was so nervous about me being on my own. I was glad they would only be down the street and Dad would watch my checking account carefully.

But the checkbook wasn't the hard part about being independent at The Roosevelt. The hard part was Mrs. Samson.

It was good my dad suggested the family meeting, because Jeremey was so worried about telling her that even when Dr. North pointed out we'd all be there with him, he was still nervous. Originally Mom had wanted it to be about discussing us living together, but Dr. North said this needed to be Jeremey's meeting before it was anything else. The therapy session would be Jeremey, me, Dr. North, my mom and dad, Althea, and the Samsons. Mom said Mrs. Samson was going to feel ganged up on, but Dr. North said better she felt uneasy than Jeremey felt cornered.

Mom also said this still wasn't a for-sure thing, the two of us living together as boyfriends so quickly, but whenever she said that, Dad winked at me, so I kept my mouth shut. When Dad winks, good things are coming.

Mrs. Samson had a pinched face when we all went into the group therapy room at the hospital. Mr. Samson's face was hard to read with his mustache and eyebrows, but she looked like the angry pictures and the nervous pictures at the same time. I told this to Mom, and she said this emotion was *tension*.

We sat in a circle on hard chairs, and I worked not to fidget because my rocking and humming upset the Samsons. Absolutely I didn't flap. I wasn't sure I could do eye contact, but I would try. I wanted Jeremey to live with me at The Roosevelt more than I wanted anything else in the world.

Dr. North smiled at everyone and sat with open posture. "Good to see you all here. Thank you for coming. I wanted to go over a few things first, to clarify any misconceptions we might have about the meeting. The first rule is that this is Jeremey's meeting, and everyone here is present at his invitation as he discusses his recovery and the next stage of his life. Everyone here is important to him and part of that process. Is that understood?"

My parents and Althea nodded, and I said yes I did, but Jeremey's parents only sat stiff and rigid. I think they understood but didn't like it.

Dr. North gave Jeremey his patient smile. "Whenever you're ready."

Jeremey didn't look ready. His shoulders were hunched, and he took shallow breaths. I sat beside him, so I could see everything clearly. I could hear him breathing hard. He tightened his hands into little balls in his lap, so tight his knuckles were white.

"Take your time," Dr. North told Jeremey. He also touched Jeremey's shoulder.

That was the thing about Jeremey. He enjoyed touch, a lot. I worried because I didn't. I thought, as we sat there, how Jeremey might like it right now if I touched him. Except touch is tricky, and I wasn't sure how to do it. Dr. North made it look so easy.

Could I do it? Put my hand on Jeremey's shoulder? It seemed like no big deal, but what was simple when other people did it didn't work the same for me.

Jeremey let out a hard breath. "I'm going to move out on my own, into my own apartment. With Emmet."

Mr. and Mrs. Samson both started talking at once in angry voices, and I jerked in my seat. I was surprised and uncomfortable. Jeremey drew back too. I watched him because it was easier than paying attention to his parents. Jeremey looked so scared and nervous. I almost touched him, but then I wondered if it wouldn't be better to take his hand. That was a more boyfriend thing to do. Except his hand was far away. I wished it were next to me, that we were sitting on the couch and I could sort of sneak over and grab it.

"Please hear Dr. North out," my mom said, and Mr. Samson got so angry his face was red.

"So you're behind this? You knew about this crazy plan? Knowing your family, you probably gave him the idea."

My dad stood up and aimed a finger at Mr. Samson, who stood up too and twitched his mustache so much he looked like an angry walrus. But then Dr. North rose as well. He went between them and held out a hand at each of our fathers.

"Gentlemen. We're here to have a discussion, not toss out accusations. As for whose idea this is—you may blame me. It is my professional opinion Jeremey would recover better in an independent environment, with monitored responsibilities. I would also like to see him take part-time employment. I have several positions in mind, in fact."

"He can't get a job and go to school," Mrs. Samson said.

"I don't want to go to school," Jeremey said, and everyone started yelling.

This kept happening. Jeremey or Dr. North would explain something about what Jeremey was going to do, and his parents would get upset. I understood now why Jeremey was so nervous to tell them. Even with everyone in the room, they got angry. They make me very stressed.

I imagined Jeremey living with that stressed feeling all the time, and I thought maybe this was why he was so depressed and anxious. Though probably it's more complicated than that.

"What I need you to understand," Dr. North said finally when everyone had calmed down, "is decisions about his future are Jeremey's to make, and his alone. I'm giving him my advice on what I think he should do, but he's making his own judgment calls about his health."

"So you expect us to pay for whatever he decides is all right?" Mr. Samson asked. His mustache kept twitching. "To pay to let him shack up with this kid he thinks he's dating?"

"We've started disability paperwork for Jeremey, which will mean he's eligible for SSI funding—"

"*Disability?*" Mrs. Samson's face pinched, and Jeremey hunched forward more.

My mom had looked for a while as if she wanted to say something, and now she did. "Gabrielle, I understand about the labeling of your child feeling limiting. I understand more than you can possibly know. But denying it doesn't change Jeremey's situation and in fact hurts his chances of getting help and feeling normalized within society."

Mr. and Mrs. Samson started yelling then, so much that I wanted to make the sign to my mom that I needed to leave. I thought about seeing if Jeremey wanted to leave too, but he couldn't leave his own therapy session. The yelling made me feel anxious, probably Jeremey too, but I worried if I left, maybe Jeremey and I couldn't live at The Roosevelt together.

Jeremey didn't have a phone, but I did. I pulled it out of my pocket, opened Notes and typed, then passed the phone over.

The yelling is bad. I wish we could leave.

He read my note and typed one back. *Yes. I'm sorry. You can go if you want.*

When he gave me my phone, I added an E before my text and a J before his, and when I replied, I added my initial so it was organized. *E: I don't want to leave unless you leave too.*

Jeremey let out a small sigh when he read my comment. *J: I don't think I can. But isn't the yelling bothering you? It's hard to tell because you're so calm. You're not even humming or rocking.*

I wasn't, and it was stressful not to, with the yelling *and* having to sit still. *E: I'm trying to be good so your parents don't call me the R word.*

That was all I wrote, but Jeremey stared at my text for a long time, like I'd written a whole paragraph. He held my phone tight, not looking up. In the background our parents yelled at each other, and Dr. North used his quiet voice to get them to calm down.

Then Jeremey yelled, "*Stop.*"

I startled. His voice was loud and angry, and a hum escaped before I could stop it. I rocked a few times too, but I stopped when Jeremey put a hand on my shoulder. It was just the right touch. Okay because it was from him, heavy but not too hard, not so light it made my skin tingly.

"Sorry," he said, his voice much more gentle. "I didn't mean to scare you."

I gave one tiny rock, but I didn't shake off his hand. "There's a lot of yelling."

There wasn't yelling now, though. Everyone was quiet, watching me. I wanted to hum, rock, flap. The more they stared, the more I wanted to relieve the stress, but the Samsons would think I was stupid. Retarded. My grades and scores wouldn't matter when I was humming and rocking and flapping.

I needed to leave, but I felt I would wreck our chances if I did. Another hum escaped, and a rock.

Jeremey took my hand. He didn't yell, but he spoke to his parents with a stern voice I hadn't heard him use before.

"I'm tired of this. I don't care anymore what you guys think. I'm living on my own. You can pack up my things. Or—get rid of them. I don't care. It's bad enough admitting I have mental illness so severe I have to go on disability. But this I don't have to put up with, everyone yelling and making me and my boyfriend feel like shit."

His hand tightened on mine. "He *is* my boyfriend. I don't know why he wants to live with such a hot mess as me, but I'm glad he does, because he's the only good thing in my life right now. The thought of being with him at The Roosevelt makes me work harder to get up in the morning. I don't want to have to stay at the hospital until it opens. I wanted to go home and have a smooth, careful transition. I wanted to tell you about it, but I was so nervous I thought this might be better, having Emmet's family here too, and Emmet. But you're embarrassing me and upsetting Emmet, and me. So we're done. We're just done. I'll stay at the hospital or under a bridge before I go home to you."

The Samsons started yelling, and I couldn't do it anymore. I let go of Jeremey's hand and made the sign to my mom that I had to leave or I would melt down. Jeremey wanted to talk to me, wanted me to stay, but I couldn't. I held back until I left the room, but then I hummed, rocked and flapped as I faced the wall. The halls were quiet, but everything felt loud and sharp in my head.

Mom talked me down. She didn't touch me, but she stood beside me and spoke quietly, told me how my dad was getting the car and we'd go out a side door to the parking lot. Althea stood on the other side, not saying anything, like a guard. It felt good.

We left through the authorized-personnel-only door, which normally isn't okay, but my mom is a doctor and doctors can do what they want in hospitals.

At home they wanted me to rest, but I wanted to code. I worked for a long time with my door closed, but eventually Mom knocked.

"I'm fine," I said.

"I need to talk to you and make sure. Also, you need to eat and drink something. It's been six hours."

I glanced at my clock and saw this was true. But I still didn't want to stop. "I'm almost finished. I'm making a design."

"Okay. I'll wait. But I'm coming in."

I didn't mind that she came into the room. Mom is good at being quiet. I finished the lines of computer code, then checked them. "I'm going to run it and see if it works or if I made a mistake."

"Is it okay if I watch?"

"Yes."

I ran the program. It wasn't difficult, but it looked complicated because I'd written in a lot of patterns.

"That's pretty. I like the changing colors. Does it do anything else?"

She was making a joke. My programs always do something else. "The patterns are numerical representations of a comment feed. I assigned people different colors and pattern variations, and how long their responses go determine the length of the pattern's run. I was going to code for common words, but I decided I didn't want to bother."

"What was the comment feed?"

"A thread on Reddit."

"Oh, honey. You know I hate it when you go there. And today of all days."

I watched the pattern weave by, let the numbers calm me. I'd set it to go slow enough I could remember the code for each part, could remember how I'd written it. "It was an ugly conversation. I made it pretty."

"What was the conversation about?"

I watched the code some more. "A post where a parent talked about curing his son's autism."

"*Emmet.*" She put a hand on my shoulder. "Please tell me you didn't listen to any of it. We've discussed this. You're not broken. You don't need to be fixed."

"I'm not the same as everyone else. As *anyone* else." The code made swirls now, because it was the part of the thread where people had written lots of short things, and some of the comments had been deleted. I'd made the pattern movement change direction whenever a post was deleted. It changed direction a lot. "Mom, sometimes I think you're wrong. There is so a normal. There's a kind of person everyone else can be, and then there's me."

She crouched beside me and turned my chair so I faced her, held my face so I had to work to not look her in the eye. Her face was serious, her eyes wet. "Emmet David Washington, you're beautiful, brilliant and perfect as you are. I don't ever want you to be normal. I can't think of anything sadder on this earth than losing you to the pool of lemmings."

I understood she was making a metaphor, but I was distracted for a minute by the image of an empty swimming pool with lemmings running around the bottom. I couldn't understand how in the world this would explain anything except that her imagination was really weird.

I shook my head to clear out the lemmings and pushed her hands away. "I don't want to be special. I want to belong the way other people do." The fear that had lurked in the back of my mind while I wrote code found its way out. "I messed up the meeting, and now I won't be able to live with Jeremey. And I want to, Mom. More than anything."

"You didn't mess up anything. In fact, I think you gave Jeremey exactly what he needed: someone to protect. He was so nervous until he saw you needed rescuing, and that gave him his courage. You helped *him* belong. You were better medicine for him than anything Dr. North could prescribe."

"Really?"

"Really." She smiled, but she looked sad at the same time. "Your dad is right. This is important for Jeremey, and for you too. Just promise me you'll be careful. That you'll practice being a good boyfriend as much as you do learning emotions and conversation prompts."

"I will." This was good, but she hadn't said everything was settled. I worried about what would happen to Jeremey if his parents wouldn't help him. I hoped Dr. North would get him SSI money. But what if he couldn't? "Mom, can Jeremey come live with us here if his parents kick him out? I don't want him to live under a bridge."

"His parents aren't going to kick him out, and he won't live under a bridge. Your dad went over to talk to Mr. Samson. Mrs. Samson got upset and went to her room crying and hasn't come out all afternoon. I think her husband is ready to listen to a little reason."

"Mom, if mental illness can run in families, she might be depressed too."

"She might be." She rubbed my arms. "Don't worry about it. It's all going to work out."

I hoped she was right. "I wish I could make Mrs. Samson like me. I wish she thought I didn't need to be fixed."

"This isn't about you, hon. This is about her processing what's going on with Jeremey. She's only seeing the outside of you, not the inside. She's only looking at what makes you different and not at what makes you special. She sees safety in normal. But remember normal doesn't mean *right*. It means average. Conforming. Why would you want to do that?"

"Because I want to drive a car and have a boyfriend."

"You have a boyfriend. He called earlier to make sure you were okay and to ask if you were still visiting tomorrow. Remember, too, conforming to the way most people are means giving up a lot of what makes you *you*. If you conformed, you couldn't see numbers the way you do. You couldn't shut the world out with a little rocking and humming. You wouldn't be you, Emmet. You'd be someone else."

She was right, I didn't want to be someone else. But sometimes it was so hard to be me.

Dr. North called in the morning and asked if I could come to a group session with Jeremey in the afternoon. I didn't want to. I still felt bad about the meeting from the day before, but I did want to see Jeremey, so I said yes. I was glad I went. Jeremey's smile made his whole face light up when I came into the room, and he hugged me.

"I'm glad you're okay. I'm sorry for my parents."

I nodded. I didn't know what else to do.

"There's good that came of it, though. My dad came this morning and told me they'd be okay with me moving to The Roosevelt, that they'd help pay what my job couldn't cover until the SSI comes through. Dr. North still thinks I should move to the residential group home near the hospital first, though, instead of going home until our apartment is ready. My mom is pretty upset, and my dad says it might be best for everyone if we take it slow."

I couldn't believe it. I wanted to laugh, be happy, but I felt like if I did that, I'd find out this was a dream.

Jeremey's smile fell. "Emmet, aren't you glad?"

I tried to say yes, but I was so frozen. In the end all I could do was hug him. I held him tight, so tight it was almost too much, but I couldn't stop.

Jeremey kissed my cheek and hugged me too. This time when he kissed my cheek, it was a longer kiss, and it made my skin tingle.

Dr. North wasn't in the room, and I wanted to kiss Jeremey for real. I turned my head so our mouths met, and we kissed, mouths together, lips moving over lips while the electricity built up in my body. It was the same as being on his bed, the kiss before the hospital, except we were standing up. It was a good kiss, and everything felt right.

I belonged. I wasn't normal, but I belonged—to Jeremey. We could stay boyfriends, and we'd get to live in The Roosevelt together, just like we wanted.

I smiled against Jeremey's mouth, and he smiled back.

Chapter Fourteen
Jeremey

I'd been tempted to move back with my parents after being discharged from the hospital, and when my mom and dad started accepting my condition after the disaster of a family meeting, at first I considered giving a return home a try. Dr. North made me wait to finalize my decision, and he asked me a lot of questions about why I wanted to go home. "Do you think you'll be kicked out of the hospital?"

Well, not *kicked*, exactly, but yeah, I didn't think I could hang out until The Roosevelt was finished. I wasn't sure what would have happened if my parents had disowned me, but I figured now that they hadn't, I *had* to go home. "I can't move in with Emmet yet, so where else would I go?"

That was when he told me about the group home.

In my head I called it the halfway house, which I know the term is for people with drug additions, but it fit me too. I wasn't ready for living on my own, and honestly, I worried if I went home, Mom especially would try to make everything the way it used to be. I didn't know if I could be strong enough for that yet, and just thinking about it, Dr. North pointed out, increased my anxiety. The Icarus House was meant to be a bridge, he told me, between an institution and total independence.

I was confused. "Isn't that what The Roosevelt is?"

"It is, in a way. The Roosevelt won't have such a formal daily structure. Essentially there will be a common area for laundry and socialization, plus social workers will live on site and be available in case of trouble. Beyond that, though, the residents will be responsible for rent, utilities, everything but building maintenance. If you don't clean your apartment, it won't get clean. But if the social workers are concerned about how unsafe the room is, they might say something. And Bob will probably make occasional inspections to make sure someone hasn't set up something that would harm the residents. At Icarus the residents are much more monitored. Many live there permanently or in similar facilities, and The Roosevelt is wildly beyond their reach. Some are like you, simply needing one more leg of recovery or a stop-gap between situations."

I'd had no idea group homes existed—which was how most of my life felt right now. I felt like Alice, lost in an alternate world that didn't always make sense or at least followed a logic pattern I'd never considered.

I went home for an afternoon the day I moved into Icarus. Mom wanted me to stay a night at the house, but she didn't push when I said I didn't want to. That was good, but things were still tense as I packed.

It felt weird to be home, even for a few hours. Everything was familiar, which was nice, but the house felt heavy too. It would be easy to slide into my room, to let my mom nag me to send clothes down the chute, to empty the dishwasher, and then go back to shutting out the world.

That wouldn't be the case at Icarus. Dr. North had told me I'd have chores, house meetings in the morning and group therapy meetings in the afternoon. I'd made my peace with this and told myself it would be temporary, a bridge between the hospital and getting my own place with Emmet. However, when I arrived with Mom and Dad to check in, I became immediately aware of a challenge I hadn't considered: the other residents.

To be blunt, the other men and women at Icarus were a mess, and it shocked me to think these were my peers. Sometimes their disabilities were starkly, physically obvious, from vacant stares and odd postures to loud noises and inappropriate gestures and comments. Some of them appeared normal until you tried to talk to them. One woman had severe schizophrenia and carried on whole conversations with people only she could see. One boy made noises that could have been the soundtrack to a horror movie—screams, moans and other elements of cacophony that made my skin tingle. A middle-aged woman had Down's syndrome—she was my favorite because she didn't make loud noises, and she always smiled.

Three residents were autistic, a condition I thought I was familiar with, but I quickly learned wherever Emmet was on the spectrum, it wasn't *anything* close to these guys. They were a mixed bag of strange behaviors: one guy never moved, always sitting at a small table by the window watching the street, maybe rocking back and forth a little, sometimes humming. He only got up to go to the restroom, to eat and to sleep. Another guy was his polar opposite, talking nonstop and always moving. He had his own room, and it was a cluttered mess of clothes, books and broken things. He had a strict idea of how the house should be run, and something as simple as his cup not being in the right spot in the cupboard could send him into a frenzy.

The third autistic boy played solitaire and watched YouTube videos on an iPad, and he talked to the people in the videos. He wouldn't speak to anyone directly, but if his videos were playing, sometimes he'd tell the people in the videos if he wanted oatmeal or pancakes for breakfast, stuff like that.

My parents flipped out.

"Are you sure you want to stay here, honey?" Mom kept asking me this as we set up my room. I could tell she was working not to shout or be angry and barely making it. "I understand you're...sick, but you're not like *this*. This isn't the place for you. Come home. It'll be so much better now."

I wanted to believe her, but here's the thing—Jan was with me too. While Mom made promises about how everything was different, Jan stood behind her, shaking her head and mouthing the word *no* over and over. The reason Jan had come all the way from Chicago to help move me in was to make sure I *did* move in. When my parents left, she lingered and drove the point home.

"I know this place looks freaky, Germ, but let me tell you how much better it is than Home Farm. You'll get one good night, and then she'll start undermining every decision you've made. You want to know what's spread all over the kitchen table? Apartment brochures. Regular apartments close to campus. She still wants you to go to school, to be a real boy." She ruffled my hair and kissed my forehead. "Except you *are* a real boy. You can do this. If your therapist said this is the place for you to be, then it is."

I stayed, but the first night was horrible. My roommate was the YouTube-watching autistic boy, Darren, and I lay awake late into the morning listening to him snore as he tossed and turned in his sleep.

It was difficult to believe I belonged here. If I didn't have my parents or The Roosevelt as a backup, I'd *have* to live here, or somewhere like Icarus, and the idea terrified me.

I told this to Dr. North when we had our session back at the hospital the next morning. "I don't belong there. Or if I do, I don't *want* to."

"Tell me what upsets you specifically."

Specifically? Where did I start? "Everyone is so broken. I'm not that bad, am I?" I sighed. "I guess I thought Icarus House would be a warm, safe place. It's not. It's not a *home* at all. It's stark, cold and weird. We're all the rejects nobody knows what to do with."

I thought this might make him mad, but he only smiled a little sadly. "You will find, I'm sorry to say, this population is rarely given priority or much attention by our culture. Caring for adults with special needs is challenging on the best of days and always costs a great deal of money. Staff are paid poorly and often move to different jobs. Housing is rarely kept up. Food is government issued and not often prepared with the care one might expect at home. No, group homes are rarely homes at all, despite the best efforts by those who care for the residents. But they are better than institutions. In decades past, many of these people would have been institutionalized at birth."

The idea of Emmet in an institution—of *me* in an institution—was beyond thinking about. "I guess I'm nervous about what happens if I can't make it work at The Roosevelt and I have to live there."

"Perhaps it would be better to focus on working to be sure you *are* successful."

That would be smart, yes, but I'm rarely able to focus on the positive. I'm so conscious of the negative ready to pounce.

I tried, though. I didn't have it in me to actively make friends, but as I sat in the living room watching daytime TV talk shows while Darren watched YouTube with headphones, I made an effort to notice the good things, not the bad. The room was threadbare and the furnishings tired, yes, but the room was actually quite clean. This, it turned out, was because of Carrie, the woman with Down's syndrome. It was her job to clean up, and she loved her work. In fact she came through once in the morning with a dust mop and a cloth and again in the afternoon. No food or drink was allowed in the living room, so there were no wrappers. If someone got out a puzzle or a game, they had to pick it up when they were done.

The staff was also great. Sure, they spoke to most residents as if they were children, but honestly? Mentally a lot of them were. I noticed Darren got different vocal tones than Carrie. In fact the female staff member working that first day seemed to quietly favor Darren. As I watched the two of them interact, I thought maybe he felt the same way. His face didn't change much, but his mouth almost smiled when she was nearby. I'd learned with Emmet that autistic facial changes are subtle and difficult to catch—but they're always there.

I wanted to connect with Darren. Partly I was curious—I was about to live with someone with autism, so some recon couldn't be bad, right? Also, there was something so comforting about him. While he wasn't really like Emmet, he kind of was. Sitting on the couch next to Darren made me feel calm and okay. I still didn't know how to interact with him, or if I should, but wanting to felt like a good start.

I admit, though, that while I could focus on the positive, I still couldn't wait to move into The Roosevelt.

Emmet came to Icarus House the afternoon of my second day there. At first I worried it would upset him, because it was sometimes so loud, but he surprised me by being almost cheerful about the visit. In fact he knew several residents, including my roommate.

He also taught me the trick of how to talk to Darren.

When Emmet came into the living room and saw Darren sitting on the couch with his tablet watching YouTube, he smiled what for him was a pretty impressive smile. He didn't say anything, however. He sat on the far end of the couch and remained still. Then, when Darren's video finished, Emmet lifted his hands and began to sign. Not spelling the way we sometimes did, no ASL that Emmet had taught me, but complicated gestures I couldn't understand.

For the first time since I'd met him, Darren put down his tablet. He signed back.

This went on for several minutes, and it was the damnedest thing because neither Emmet nor Darren looked at each other, but they seemed to see anyway. I, however, couldn't stop staring. Every so often one of them would laugh, and sometimes Darren made one of his semi-articulate sounds. Eventually Emmet made one last sign and stood up. He took my hand, which made my heart flutter, and led me out back to sit in the garden on one of the benches.

"I didn't know your roommate was Darren. He's nice. We were friends in Iowa City. I didn't know he was here in Ames now. That was a nice surprise."

I blinked. "How did you know he was my roommate? I hadn't had a chance to tell you yet."

"Darren told me."

"So you were using sign language?"

"Darren language. Some of it is ASL, but mostly he made up his own language. It's simpler. He says he works at the library sorting books. He's good at that kind of thing."

He'd learned more about my roommate in ten minutes than I'd learned in a day. "How could you read what he said with his hands without looking at him? And the same for him with you?"

"We both have camera eyes. It's easy."

"You have *what*?"

"Camera eyes. A lot of autistic people can see things like camera pictures. We use our peripheral vision to see things, and we can remember what we see. It's why sometimes we get overwhelmed in busy places. We take too many pictures."

This potentially explained so much about Emmet. "Are you telling me right now, though you're not looking at me, you're looking at me? I mean, even though your eyes aren't focused on me, for you they are?" Every time I said it, the words didn't make sense.

Emmet smiled, understanding anyway. "Yes. I can show you. We'll play a game. Hold up a number with your fingers and I'll tell you. You can try to hide it a little to make it challenging."

I did try, and he never, not once, failed to know exactly how many fingers I held up. I went into the house and got a book to hold up, and as soon as I held it close enough, he could read it from the side as well as he could in the front. In fact, it wasn't as close as I'd have had to have the book reading it the usual way.

"That's amazing." I put the book down and shook my head. "You're Superman or something."

He smiled, but it was a subtle smile. "I am. Super Emmet."

"Are you this way with everything? Can you hear like that too?"

"Yes."

I never thought I'd be jealous of an autistic person, but I was. A veil had been lifted between us, and while I'd admired him before, I was besotted with Emmet now. "Everything about you is more powerful, isn't it? When you smile, it's big to you. And to you your voice isn't flat at all. I'm the stupid one."

"Not stupid. You can't use the S word." He rocked on the seat. "Sometimes autism is bad. Sometimes I don't have control. I'm lucky. It's not as severe for me, and most of the therapy worked to help me modify myself. Some autistic people have a difficult time. We have trouble sleeping, and our digestive systems can be sensitive. Darren can't make his mouth work the way he wants. He thinks a lot, but he can't make his mouth work right. He says people are too loud too, so he watches YouTube."

"Is that why you sat so far from him? So you wouldn't be loud for him?"

"Yes."

Huh. I watched Emmet rock for a second. "How can I be a friend to Darren? I don't know his sign language."

"I can be an interpreter. Also, he can use his tablet to make it talk, when he wants to. But he doesn't usually want to."

The idea of being able to bond more with my roommate excited me. "Can we go talk to him now?"

"In a minute. I want to kiss you first."

Emmet always announced our make-out sessions, and it thrilled me every time. There was something delicious about him giving the order. Emmet always arranged us, initiated the kiss and introduced any new elements.

Today it was tongue.

We'd kissed at the hospital, and some of those kisses had felt pretty steamy to me, but they'd only been teases of lips, maybe a little nibbling and gentle suckling. Emmet liked to play with the sensory aspects of a kiss, sometimes stopping to comment on the feelings they elicited. I loved that.

I didn't often say much, but sometimes I did. I could tell him anything: how hard he made me, how my chest felt tight, how I loved the way I could feel his mouth on my lips for an hour after. He always smiled when I said that and paid more attention to my lips.

That first day in the garden, though, he parted my lips with his tongue. Surprised, I opened my mouth. His tongue slipped inside and touched mine.

I gasped. Emmet smiled and pulled back, touching my face. "That felt like a fish."

I laughed and leaned into his hands. It had, kind of. "Bumpy. Like wet sandpaper."

Emmet's fingers stroked my cheeks. "I want to do it again. Open your mouth and let me kiss you with my tongue."

The shiver that went through me was so intense I had to shut my eyes. "Emmet, you make me so hard when you talk like that."

"Let me touch my tongue on yours again, and I'll make you harder."

He did. I'd stopped asking him where he learned to kiss—it was the Internet, always. Sometimes he watched videos, sometimes he read things, and sometimes he found message boards. There wasn't a corner of the Internet he didn't know how to find, I swear.

I loved being the recipient of his kissing research, and kissing with tongues was no exception. His tongue stroked along mine, exploring my mouth. He was hesitant and uncertain, but not for long. I made my own explorations too, but mostly I went quiet and let Emmet lead me, because it was the way I liked it. When he kissed me and touched me, everything went away except for Emmet.

The only problem today was that Frenching Emmet made me so hard it drove me crazy not to touch myself. I wanted to touch *him*. I broke the kiss to nuzzle his nose with a careful amount of pressure. "Emmet, I want to do more than kiss you."

His fingers in my hair tightened. "Yes. When we get our apartment, we can have sex."

I wasn't sure I wanted to go *that* far, but I didn't want to spoil the moment. I also didn't want to wait that long to do more than kiss. "We could go to my room here, now."

"No. Darren might come in."

I rested my head on his shoulder. "I don't want to wait. Moving into our room together is another month and a half away."

I swear I could *feel* him smile. "I forgot to tell you. Bob said we're a special case, and we can move in two more weeks."

I lifted my head and caught him grinning. He *hadn't* forgotten. He was playing one of his Emmet jokes on me. I didn't care, I was so glad. Everything in me got loud and hot, but in a good way.

"I want you to kiss me again," I said. But when he leaned forward, I put fingers over his lips. My stomach flipped in nerves and anticipation as I made my next request. "Can you kiss me hard, Emmet? With your tongue too?"

His face didn't change much, and his voice was flat, but I could hear his smile anyway. "Yes," he said.

And he did.

Chapter Fifteen
Emmet

I was so excited about moving into The Roosevelt. We had all my things packed up in boxes, which was a little disconcerting, but soon I'd be opening the boxes at my own apartment. My apartment with my boyfriend.

We went shopping at Target for our own dishes and pots and pans. I did most of the shopping. The one time Jeremey went, it didn't go well.

It took us three tries to get to the store, to start. The first day we had an appointment to go, Icarus House called my mom to cancel. "Jeremey is having a bad day," the aide told her.

I got upset and insisted Mom take me over, but they wouldn't let us go upstairs. I paced in the living room and hummed and flapped while my mom argued—and then Darren signed to me.

Are you here for Jeremey?

Yes, I signed back. *Why won't they let me see my boyfriend?*

Because he's very sick today. In bed. Sometimes he cries.

That made my octopus go crazy. I signed to my mom I was not okay.

"Please—you need to let my son see his friend, if only so he can see Jeremey is safe," she told the aide. "If you don't, I can promise you you're about to witness a very angry autistic young man."

They argued a few more minutes, and Darren talked to me some more.

He might have a cold, or the flu.

I shook my head. *He has depression. I'm scared, Darren. I don't want him to try to kill himself again.*

It would be hard to do that from his bed. He won't get out of it.

It actually would be easy to use his bed, if he had somewhere he could string up the sheets. I hummed loudly and flapped my hands so hard they hurt. I hadn't banged my head against the wall for a long time, but I wanted to do it then.

Mom calmed me down, and a few minutes later we were able to go upstairs to see Jeremey.

Looking at him scared me. He was in his bed, the sheets over his head, and when I called his name, he didn't respond. I pulled the sheets back, and my stomach felt funny when I saw his face. He looked flat. I knew he was alive because he blinked, but he didn't look like my Jeremey.

I felt nervous and upset. I didn't know what to do.

Mom came up behind me and put a heavy hand on my arm. "Jeremey's depression is bad today. They've given him some medicine to help."

He looked like he had the day he'd first gone to the hospital. "Did his mom make him upset?"

"No. Nothing in particular made him upset, as far as the nurse could tell. That's how depression works, jujube. Sometimes you're sad for no reason at all."

"But we were supposed to shop for our apartment stuff today. That's a happy thing."

"Depression likes to eat happy things, sometimes."

Right now depression was eating my boyfriend. He looked almost scary. I knew it was the drugs, but I wondered what was going on inside his head.

"I hate depression, Mom. It sucks. It's a bad disease."

"Yes, sweetheart. It really is." She tugged my arm. "Let's let him rest."

I pulled my arm away. "No. I'm not leaving him."

Mom sighed. "Emmet, you can't—"

"*Not leaving him.*" I sat on the floor and clamped a hand on to the metal frame of his bed. "Not until I know the depression won't hurt him."

Mom crouched beside me. "Sweetheart, he's not going to attempt suicide again."

"How do you know? Besides, it's not him who wants to do it. It's his bad octopus. What if the drugs—?"

I stopped talking because something was tickling my hair. When I turned, Jeremey was looking at me.

His eyes were dull and strange. I could see his light, but it was all messed up. I hummed. I was scared. Was Jeremey okay?

He petted my hair, and he smiled. It was a tiny smile, but it was a smile.

The touch was too soft, but I didn't care. "Jeremey, don't listen to the bad voices. You can't kill yourself."

"Honey, it doesn't work like that—" Mom started to say this, but I put my hand over my ear and she stopped.

Jeremey kept petting my hair. He looked like he wanted to talk, but it took him several seconds to get started, and when he spoke, his words were slurry and quiet. "Not...going to. Just a...bad day. Sorry."

"I want to make it better," I told him.

"You can't." Mom stopped trying to pull me away, but she stayed beside me on the floor. "Jeremey has medicine—not his usual antidepressant. This is something else. A sedative. To calm him and help his brain unplug. He's still having an intense depressive episode, but the drug is helping him separate from it. It makes him very tired, though."

"It's making him drool."

Jeremey blinked long and slow, and on the last blink, his eyes stayed closed. I hummed, worried.

Mom kept talking. "He's fine. Yes, the side effects of the drugs aren't fantastic. But sometimes we need a day off from our brains. He'll be better later. We need to leave, so he can rest."

Why didn't she understand I *couldn't* leave? "Someone has to sit with him. Someone has to make sure it doesn't get too dark for him."

Mom started to tell me I couldn't stay, but a sharp sound, like a bark, stopped her. I smiled and turned enough that I could see Darren with my camera eyes.

"Hi, Darren."

Darren typed into his tablet, then held it up. A computer voice spoke. "Emmet, I will stay and watch your boyfriend for you. You can go home."

Without moving my eyes, I looked at Jeremey, then at Darren, then at my mom. I wanted to stay—but I didn't. I wanted to make sure Jeremey didn't hurt himself or wasn't lonely. But it scared me to see him all drugged like this. I didn't want to think of Jeremey like that.

"Will you text me and let me know how he's doing?" I asked Darren.

He tapped into his tablet again. "Yes, if you give me your phone number."

I gave it to him. "Thank you, Darren."

"No problem. Jeremey is my friend too."

Darren did text me, several times, until in the evening Jeremey was able to. He didn't talk much, just enough to tell me he was okay and feeling better but was still tired. I went to see him the next morning, and he wasn't quite so drugged out, but he wasn't himself, either. He cried a few times, and when I asked why, he said there was no reason. He started to apologize, but I told him to stop, and he did. We hugged a little, but he wanted to sleep again, so I hung out with Darren until Jeremey was awake from his nap.

"Sorry," he said when we sat on his bed that evening. He wouldn't look at me. "I don't know what happened. I just felt all panicky, and then all heavy, and then it was just...bad. Very dark."

"But you didn't want to kill yourself?" Mom had told me not to ask, but I couldn't help it. It worried me a lot.

He shook his head. "Not...really. I mean, I always do a little, but it's not because I don't want to be with you. It's because it feels so *hard* to be alive. This time I hurt all over. I felt like I was sick. But I didn't have a fever, or anything. Just depression."

"Is it gone now?"

"No. But it's quieter."

That seemed better. "When you're ready, we can still go shopping for the apartment."

His hand tightened against his leg. "Okay. I'll try. Hopefully I don't have a panic attack."

It took another couple of days before he was ready. He said he wanted to try the next day, but when Mom came to pick him up, he said he was sorry, but it wasn't the right time. The day after, though, he got in the van, and we drove over to Target.

We went at a time it wasn't busy, but we didn't make it five minutes before he stopped in the middle of the cleaning products section, like he'd bumped into something. His body became rigid, his shoulders hunched, and he shut his eyes as his breath started coming fast. He didn't say a word, but I knew this was a panic attack.

Mom knew too. She led him to the pharmacy area, where they had a bench, and made him sit down. The pharmacist came out, looking concerned, but Mom told her everything was fine. Mom never took her focus off Jeremey, and whenever she spoke, to him or anyone else, she kept her voice soft and gentle.

"Shh. You're okay. Put your head between your knees if you need to."

Jeremey didn't, only shut his eyes tighter and tucked his chin to his chest as his breath came faster and faster. "I'm sorry."

"Nothing to be sorry about." Mom stroked his shoulder, moving her hand to his back. I could tell she was trying to nudge his head down without making him do it.

Normally I worry when Jeremey has panic attacks, but my mom is a doctor, and she'd take care of him. I counted the different kinds of shoe insoles on the wall behind the bench while I waited. Beside me, my dad stood quietly, waiting to see if my mom would tell him to do anything. She did—she told him to go get a bottle of room-temperature mineral water from the shelf in the food section. The pharmacist brought out a cool hand towel, and my mom draped it over Jeremey's neck. He'd put his head between his knees twice now, and his breathing was normal. But his eyes were full of water, and sometimes tears leaked out.

Six tears by my count, though one was large and might have been three or four tears in one.

"I tried so hard." His voice was a whisper, all ragged and uncomfortable. "I thought maybe with you guys it would be better."

"You've been through a lot lately." Mom kept rubbing his back. It would have made me crazy, that much touching, but Jeremey loved it. "Do you want to keep trying, or do you need to rest?"

"Rest," he said, no hesitation at all.

"That's okay. We'll try again once you've settled into your new place and are feeling confident."

Jeremey didn't say anything else, and after my dad returned with the mineral water, we walked them both to the food court area, which is mostly a Starbucks and an ICEE machine. My dad offered to take Jeremey to Icarus, or to drive him around in the car, but Jeremey said no.

"I can sit here and not freak out." He sounded angry when he said it, which confused me, but Mom didn't argue with him, just told my dad to text her if they needed anything.

We picked our cart back up, and once we were away from the food court, I texted her.

Mom, this is Emmet. Why is Jeremey angry? Why won't he go to the car so he doesn't have a panic attack?

She read her text, then glanced at me. "Can I answer you out loud, or do I need to text too?"

I glanced around us and shook my head before I texted. *Too many people can listen. I don't want them listening to Jeremey's business.*

Mom texted me. *This is Mom. Jeremey is angry with himself. He wants to stay in the food court because he knows he's lost the war, but he wants to win a battle.*

I read her text three times. Finally I said, *Mom, you don't make any sense. Jeremey is not at war with anyone.*

She made a winking Emoji. *He knows he can't shop with you, but he wants to challenge himself to simply stay in the store. That will make him feel as if he accomplished something.*

That made sense. I wished he could have shopped with us. Doing it alone meant I would pick everything, which I enjoyed, except I wanted Jeremey to pick some things too. I tried to think of how we could modify shopping so he could participate.

"Maybe we can give him some choices," I suggested. "We could take them to the food court."

"That's a good idea, but you told me he gets nervous when people make him pick."

This was true. I frowned.

"Maybe you could take photos of things you thought he might like and send them to him for approval. He'll probably say yes every time, but it will make him feel more a part of things. You could also ask him what his favorite color is and use it to make choices, and ask if he prefers big towels or regular-sized towels for himself. Things that won't make him feel as if he has to guess the right answer."

I thought it was a good idea, and it worked pretty well. I texted a lot of pictures to Jeremey, and like Mom said, he said they all looked good, but it included him. I already knew his favorite color, but I asked him anyway so he could still participate. Eventually I put my headphones in and called him, and I told him about the things I was looking at for our apartment. It wasn't the same as having him there, but it was better than nothing.

We did more than shopping to get ready to move into The Roosevelt, though, and Jeremey was able to participate in all the other preparations. Althea and Mom gave us cooking lessons, and my dad showed me how to keep a spreadsheet for my bills. We made a lot of checklists so I wouldn't forget to do anything, and we devised a new schedule which included doing laundry and going grocery shopping. Usually new things and change upset me, but this was an exciting shift.

I think Jeremey was excited too, but he was also nervous. His mom was definitely nervous, and she still didn't like me. His dad's mustache twitched all the time.

The day we moved in I had *move in* on my schedule for nine in the morning. We were there on the dot, and so was Bob, smiling and holding up two sets of keys. He'd aired out the apartment so it didn't smell like paint anymore, but the leftover smell worried me a little, because it wasn't the right smell of my house. It got better as we brought the boxes in, and my clothes.

I set up my bedroom first. We'd bought a new bed so I could still have my other bed at home. My new bed was a double bed, so I could have sex in it if I wanted. I told this to

179

Mom, but she told me not to tell her those kinds of things. I told her she doesn't make sense, and she said she understood but still didn't want to hear about me having sex.

I'd asked Jeremey how we should set up the main living areas, but he said he didn't care so long as he could sit on the couch and see the TV, and that there was a couch and a TV. He said I cared about setup more, so go ahead and take over. If anything bothered him, he'd tell me, but he said he doubted it would. So I positioned everything up exactly the way I wanted it.

All the floors were hardwood. Bob preferred them for dust control, and they were mostly the same hardwood floors the school had when it was a school. The kitchen had heavy tile, durable and easy to clean or replace. I put a soft rug down in front of the couch and between the TV because it was good for yoga. It was exactly four inches from the TV and four from the couch. The couch would move, since hardwood floors are slippery, but we put a heavy table behind it and anti-slip pads underneath. We had small end tables on each side of the couch, which was blue-green and soft to the touch. The fat stuffed chair matched it.

We bought all these things new. Mrs. Samson had said she would give us her living room furniture and get replacements for herself, but my mom explained I'm sensitive to fabrics, so she bought them all. Also Mrs. Samson's furniture is ugly, but Mom said I couldn't say that.

The living room had one not-new thing: a rocker. It was the rocker from my room, but I wanted it in my living room now, by the window so I could watch the trains. We put our new dishes in the cupboards and our pans under the sink. These were some new dishes and some old, some from my house and some from his.

We went shopping at the co-op and filled our pantry and our fridge and had fruit on the counter. We had our own TV and DVR and Roku box, and I had my computer set up in my room. Everything was clean and amazing and wonderful.

Jeremey's face was difficult to read. He carried boxes into his room, and he helped his dad set up his bed, which was his from his parents' house. It was a double bed, like my new one. Except he wouldn't have one at his house now, so if he got nervous and wanted to go home for a night, he'd have to sleep somewhere other than his room. That would make me sad, but I couldn't tell if it made Jeremey sad.

I stayed away from Jeremey's mom, which wasn't hard since she barely looked at me, and when she did, her lips went flat like she was holding back angry words. Dad and Althea left as soon as things were unpacked, but Mom didn't leave until the Samsons said goodbye. She was there in case Gabrielle was weird. Except some day Mrs. Samson would come over when my mom or Althea wasn't around. I decided when that happened I would go to my room and put on headphones and write code.

Eventually the parents were all gone, and it was only Jeremey and me. He stood in the kitchen, leaning on the counter, and I stood by the window in case a train came. It had started to drizzle, so if a train came, it would be perfect—but I was more interested in watching Jeremey at that moment. He had his arms wrapped over his belly, but his face was flat, and his eyes behind his glasses were too complicated to read. I wondered if we were going to stand there until it was time to reheat the dinner my mom had put in the fridge.

I wondered if we would have sex today.

"So." Jeremey's shoulders hunched forward. "What do we do now?"

I wanted to suggest sex or kissing, but I was nervous. If he said no, it would be awkward, and I didn't want anything to be awkward on our first day. "Dinner isn't for two hours. But we could have a snack."

"I'm not really hungry."

I wasn't either. I was horny, but still scared. "We could watch a movie, or we could play a game. On the computer in my room or on the Xbox in the living room." We'd brought my Xbox from home.

I still couldn't read anything on his face. "How about you show me your room?"

I did. We stood in the middle, and I pointed everything out. My bed, my dresser, my desk and computer, and another rocker in case I wanted to rock in here, though sometimes I used the floor and made my body the rocker. I didn't tell Jeremey about how the bed was new and big for sex because I was still nervous. Except now that we were in the room, sex was all I could think about.

Jeremey didn't seem to be thinking about making out. He put his hands in his pockets and turned around, looking at everything. Even the ceiling. But not me. "It's nice. A lot like your old room, but different."

That didn't make sense, but I was too overwhelmed to point it out. All I could think about was how I wanted to ask him if he wanted to have sex, except I was too nervous to talk out loud. I wondered if I could write it.

Then I realized I could sign it.

"Jeremey, I want to teach you some more ASL."

He stopped looking at the ceiling and turned to face me. "Okay."

"Four words." I made my hand flat and moved my fingers from my mouth to my cheek. I did it several times so he could learn it. "That one is *kiss*."

His cheeks got red. "Okay."

I felt embarrassed too, but I pushed the feeling away and focused on the lesson. "Next word." I held out my hands, palms up, with my fingers open. I pulled them to my body, tightening my fingers a little. "Want. That sign means *want*."

Jeremey nodded. His face was redder still, but he didn't look upset.

"Third word." I put my hands together like I was praying but placed them beside my ear and tilted my head. "That's *bed*."

He smiled. "I think I sort of knew that."

"Last word." I made the sign for the letter X with my right hand and moved it from my cheek to my mouth and back again. I did it several times. "That word is *sex*."

Now I could tell Jeremey was nervous. Neither one of us could talk out loud, and he didn't know enough sign. "Jeremey, go to your room and log in to IM chat."

He blinked. "Why?"

"Because I want to talk to you."

Jeremey laughed. "But we're here, in the same apartment. We're talking right now."

"It will be better for this conversation if we have space. Go log in to IM. I'll wait."

He left, looking uncertain, but I ignored this and sat at my computer, where I was already logged in to iMessage. He still used an IBM computer, but Dad had helped him set up a Yahoo! account, and I had his account plugged into my iMessage. When I saw him come online, I sent him a message.

Hi Jeremey. This is Emmet.

He typed back. *I know. This is weird when we're in the same house.*

I can't tell you what I want to tell you to your face. We're both too nervous, and you're embarrassed.

It took him a second to write back. *Are we going to talk about sex now?*

Yes.

He paused. *You're right. This is probably better. Though I still feel silly.*

Jeremey always felt silly, so I ignored that. *Jeremey, I want to kiss you. I want to have sex with you. In my bed. Now. But when I said the word* sex, *you got nervous. Do you want to have sex with me?*

I hummed and rocked while I waited for him to reply. I could hear him clicking.

I do, but I'm scared. Not of you but of sex. I'm afraid it will hurt.

I frowned at his IM, not understanding what he meant, but then I remembered the boards I had read. *Oh. You're talking about anal sex.*

Yes.

That was interesting. I hadn't been thinking about that. *I meant more touching cocks and maybe rubbing them.* I wasn't sure about oral sex. Sometimes cocks smell.

You're supposed to call them cocks, not penises, when it's about sex. I'm not sure why, but it appears to be the rule. But whatever you call them, they're sweaty.

I wasn't thinking about anal sex with Jeremey until he wrote that in the chat, because an anus is where poop comes out, and that's kind of gross to put a penis there, even if the guys in porn like it. Except when Jeremey said he thought it might hurt, he meant anal sex with my penis in his anus.

My cock got hard thinking about it.

Emmet, you're too quiet, and now I'm more nervous.

Sorry. I sent it fast so he didn't worry. *I was thinking about my cock in your anus, and it distracted me.*

I heard him laugh from his room. *Okay that's a pretty good excuse.* He clicked some more. *It distracts me too, but it scares me.*

I have to research anal sex before we can do it. We could look it up together, maybe.

More clicking. *I assume when you say research that's not a sneaky way to get me to watch porn with you.*

I frowned. *I don't understand.* Then I added, *Watching porn would be fun with you though.*

He laughed again. *What kind of sex did you mean, if not anal sex?*

He wanted me to list it? I tried to think of everything I wanted to do to him.

I want to kiss you for a long time, on the bed. I want us to not wear shirts or pants while we do it. Not even underwear, sometimes. I want to masturbate with you. I want to touch your penis and maybe rub ours together. If we take a shower first, maybe we can try oral, but let's go slow there. But nipples could be good to suck on. One message board said if you suck on a guy's neck, he melts in your arms. I know they don't mean literally melt, but I wondered what that would be like. I also want to touch your ass. Not the inside but the outside. You have a nice ass, and I want to see it naked. Maybe I'd kiss it after a shower. I watched a video where a guy fucked the tight space between his boyfriend's legs, and they both enjoyed it, but maybe that's too far for today.

I considered a moment, then decided that was most of the sex I'd thought about. I hit send.

I didn't hear any typing, but Jeremey's desk chair creaked. He walked into my room and stood in the door. His face was red, but he looked at me the way he looked when he wanted me to kiss him. He didn't speak with his mouth, but he used his hands to sign ASL.

I want you kiss bed sex.

It didn't make a lot of sense, but I understood what he meant. I stood. My pants were tight because my cock was very hard now. When I stood and undid my jeans button, Jeremey watched. He looked excited and nervous, and when I thought about taking my clothes off, I got nervous too.

Jeremey stepped away from the door and undid his pants.

We pushed them to the floor at the same time. I wore briefs and so did Jeremey, except mine were boxer briefs and his were standard ones. His were white with a black band at the top. I could see his cock in the pouch, poking toward his leg. It was long. So were his legs. Long and a little skinny, and pale.

"Sh-shirts too?" Jeremey asked.

I thought about Jeremey standing in front of me in only his underwear. "Shirts too." I pulled mine off, then watched as he did the same.

His nipples were erect. I wanted to touch them.

I walked over to him, and I did touch. I pressed my thumb against the red bead. Jeremey shivered and put a hand on my hip.

"W-we're still wearing socks," he whispered as I kept rubbing.

"And underwear." His nipple got harder and harder the more I touched it, and in his briefs his cock got bigger and bigger. "Should we take them off?"

He had his eyes shut and breathed rough and fast. "I...I don't know. M-maybe not—*oh*—today."

I wasn't disappointed. Underwear was sexy too. "When I have an orgasm, I have to take my penis out because I don't want to make a mess. But it's okay. I have cum rags by the bed."

Eyes still shut, Jeremey moved closer to me. He kissed my naked shoulder, then ran his tongue on the skin. It made me so hard it almost hurt.

"Jeremey, I want to lie on the bed with you and kiss you and touch your cock inside your underwear."

He gasped and kissed my neck. "Yes."

It's true. A guy does melt if his boyfriend sucks on his neck. The veins stay in place because there's definitely blood flow, but the muscles all relax like they've spent too long in the sun.

I've thought about sex for a long time. My parents let me watch some porn, but we had to talk about it after was the rule, since they said porn was unrealistic. We talked about condoms and sexually transmitted diseases and how they spread. Jeremey was a virgin and so was I, but I promised my mom we would get tested anyway, so Dr. North took the samples and took care of that before we moved in. We were negative. It was fine. I had done research about positions and how to not accidentally hurt someone. I knew a lot about sex.

But I learned the day I first had sex with Jeremey that it's one of those things that is different in real life no matter how much you study it.

I was supposed to pay attention to my partner and his needs, but even with our underwear on, touching and kissing Jeremey made me so excited I felt as if I could masturbate ten times in a row, though the male refractory period means that's not ever possible. I was torn. I wanted to get my cock out and shoot right away, but I wanted to kiss and touch him more, and once I had an orgasm, my body wouldn't care about sex even if my brain did. The Internet said to think about baseball statistics, but I don't care about baseball. I configured pi for a few minutes, but then I switched to remembering code. I tried to turn the feelings Jeremey gave me into code in my head, and that worked.

Sometimes funny things work on brains, and it's better not to ask why and go with it.

We breathed really hard while we kissed, and we wiggled. Jeremey liked it when I pressed him into things while we kissed. It's the same as the weighted blanket I use sometimes when I sleep. He enjoys the pressure of being held down, and he liked it when our cocks rubbed together through our underwear. I tried out a few things, moving my hips in circles, and that made him cry out and make all kinds of noises, but he also said, *"Don't stop."*

You know, everything I read said noises were okay in sex, but if autistic people make noises because things are too intense and it's not sex, everyone acts as if it's a big scandal. People make less sense than my mom or brains.

I loved Jeremey's noises. Sometimes I made noises with him, and he liked that. He didn't care if I hummed or grunted or anything. It was all good so long as I touched his cock. He wanted me to kiss him almost rough and rub his cock at the same time. The code in my head got intense.

"Stop," Jeremey said when I broke the kiss. He sounded as if he'd run up all the stairs in The Roosevelt. "I'm going to come."

I rubbed the tip of his cock with my thumb through his underwear. "I want to watch you masturbate. I want to see your cock."

Jeremey bit his lip, then pressed his cock into my hand. "How...how about you masturbate me."

That sounded good. "Let me take off your underwear."

He let me do that, but he got nervous when I pulled them all the way to his ankles and opened his legs so I could see his cock and his balls. They were red. His cock stood up like a pole in the middle of his groin, waving around a little bit.

"I want to take off my underwear also," I told him. He nodded, but when he tried to close his knees, I stopped him. "No, leave them open. I like to look at your naked cock and balls."

His cock twitched more. "Okay."

I moved my underwear down to my feet and stepped out of them, but I left my socks on. His were on too. "I want to masturbate us together. Push my balls against you and stroke both our cocks at the same time."

Jeremey's knees wobbled. "Okay."

I knelt on the bed and brought our bodies together. His skin was hot, but his balls and cock were warmer. He sucked in a breath when our cocks touched. When I put my hand over his cock, he made a kind of hissing noise.

"Emmet, I'm going to come really fast."

I was too. "Think of something boring. Count."

He shook his head and moved his hips so our balls banged together. His eyes were closed tight. "I can't. All I want to do is shut my head off and hump you like an animal. But I'll come so fast it'll be embarrassing."

My hips were moving too, slow at first but faster and faster. I liked how hard Jeremey breathed. I wanted to do what he said he wanted: to watch him shut his head off. "I'll count for you. I'll count to twenty. It's not that long, but it's long enough we can enjoy it. You can't come until I get to twenty, but you can be an animal until then."

Jeremey's whole throat moved when he swallowed. His hips kept moving faster, and his cock was leaking out the tip. "Okay. I'll try to hold on."

"Just listen to me and enjoy the feeling. Our first time having sex. This is called frotting." I jerked our cocks and rolled my hips in a circle so our balls were snuggled tight. "Do you like frotting?"

Jeremey made gasping noises as if he didn't have enough air. "Please start counting."

I counted. I didn't count fast, but I let my hips move quickly. I moved our cocks together, both the tips leaking. Jeremey made amazing noises, and his hips pressed tight to mine. I gave him firm pressure because he enjoys it, and he also likes it when I move my hips sharp and fast, not gentle. He flailed his hands all over, kind of flapping with his whole arms. At fifteen he gave a long, loud cry that made my balls tingle and almost made me shoot. I started counting faster, and then it was twenty and everything went crazy.

Jeremey made a loud, loud noise and arched his whole body—his semen went like a fountain, and I got so distracted I watched. I hadn't come yet, but my cock got so excited watching him I let go and jerked myself fast so I shot too. My semen landed on Jeremey's chest, some of it on his mouth. I wouldn't have enjoyed the sensation. Semen gets cold quickly, but Jeremey lay there with his chest heaving, his eyes closed, his mouth open with semen on his lips, as if he wanted more.

He was so pretty my cock shot a little bit a second time.

I was tired and wanted to lie beside him, but I got the cum rag first and cleaned up. I called it a cum rag because that's what the Internet called it, but I actually use baby wipes so I don't have to be sticky. Jeremey's belly twitched when I touched him with the wipe, though they were warm since I have a wipe warmer and I'd turned it on before we got in bed. I think he twitched because his sensations were as high as a person with autism.

My sensations were high too, but I didn't want to be by myself yet. I wanted to hold Jeremey and kiss him and see if he enjoyed the sex. I hurried with cleanup, and then we got under the covers. Jeremey snuggled against me, his penis along my leg. It was getting soft, but it was still happy from sex.

"We've had sex now." I stared at the ceiling, all my feelings so loud their colors swirled in clouds above me. "It was good. I want to do it again after we rest."

Jeremey's hands moved on my skin, but when I jerked at the touch, he stilled. "I'm sorry. I forgot you don't like light touch."

"Everything is loud right now," I told him.

"Is it okay if I stay here with you, or do you need to be alone?"

That was a tricky question. I thought maybe I did need to be by myself, but Jeremey didn't want to be alone, and anyway my research said cuddling was important to bonding. "I want you to stay," I told him. "But everything is very loud."

"How can I stay and not make it so loud for you?"

I thought about it for a minute. Jeremey needed touch, and I thought maybe I did too. But I needed stillness. I wondered if maybe I could touch him and it would be okay.

I ended up holding him with his back to my front. It made him feel close, but I felt as if I had enough space to find myself again. Once he went to sleep, I would get up and go rock in the living room to process and enjoy the rain pelting against the window. I told myself I could wait, that my brain could count to twenty for a different reason this time.

My plan worked, and my brain octopus didn't have a fit. It was happy to wait, and then once Jeremey was asleep, it liked sitting in the chair, rocking and humming and flapping and counting train cars during a rainstorm. I felt proud of myself. Not many people would understand how difficult that had been for me, but that is what being an adult is. Doing hard things and nobody knowing or helping.

I lived independently, I had a checking account, I had sex, and I made my own modifications. Though I had been legally an adult for a while now, that day was the first time I knew I really was one.

Chapter Sixteen
Jeremey

The Roosevelt had thirteen apartments, and one of them was occupied by Tammy and Sally, who lived rent-free and got a stipend for being our live-in backup. Originally they were supposed to have their own apartments, but they shared because of Emmet and me. That made me feel guilty, but Tammy and Sally both said never worry about it, they were glad we'd come.

The day after we moved in, Tammy was our first houseguest. While I was in the shower, she texted Emmet and me both, and when I came out from getting dressed, Emmet asked me if he could schedule her at ten. I had exactly nothing on my schedule, so I said sure.

Emmet had plenty on his schedule. I'd seen peeks of his iCalendar before, but by living with him I found out firsthand how rigidly every second of his day was mapped out. He'd had a small fight with his mother the day before. She'd wanted to come by and verify he was doing okay without her monitoring his schedule, but he was adamant he was an adult and could manage his own life. Their compromise had been that he'd text her often to let her know how he was doing.

As I watched Emmet go through his morning routine, I understood why his mother had been so hesitant. For all his confidence and determination, he could be undone by the strangest things. Like the toaster.

He had special gluten-free bread his mother made him. This meant he had his own toaster, which had been purchased new for the apartment so he'd still have one at his parents' house. Emmet had been practicing home skills, especially cooking, for a month. But when Emmet made his toast, it came out burned.

It sent him into *orbit.*

"The toast is burned. *Burned.* I can't eat this." Emmet threw the toast at the wall, made a strangled scream, and for a terrible second I thought he would throw the toaster.

He didn't. Instead, he stormed into his room, then slammed and locked the door.

I didn't know what to do.

I stared at the closed door for a few minutes, holding my breath, fearing he'd come out angry. I didn't think he'd hurt me, but I was pretty sure he'd break something. I thought of the thousands of dollars worth of equipment in his room, and my stomach went queasy. But I didn't hear any crashes. There were some loud thumps, but that was all. Then it was quiet, but Emmet didn't return to the kitchen.

I cleaned up the burned toast—which wasn't really burned at all, only a little extra brown—and put his bread away. I didn't know how he liked his toast, or I would have remade it. I was no longer hungry for my own breakfast, and the cozy apartment which had been so comforting now felt empty and dangerous. Unsure of what else to do, I went to my own room and crawled under my covers.

We were both still in our rooms when a knock came on our front door. Blearily, I glanced at the clock and saw it was ten. Tammy was here.

She smiled at me cheerfully when I opened the door, holding out her hand. "Hi there. Jeremey, right? I'm Tammy. Good to see you again. Everything going okay?"

I shook her hand, or rather let hers envelop mine. "Um, okay," I lied.

I'd been bristly at the idea of having a minder, but I couldn't help loving Tammy on sight. She reminded me of the counselor in middle school I'd loved, both in looks and demeanor. She was both warm and easy and a wall nobody could climb. She was heavy-set in a way that made her both soft and strong at the same time. Her hair was natty and stuck out like a dark-brown halo around her head except for where a thick red plastic headband pushed it away from her forehead. She wore glasses with leopard-print sides and gold bling that matched the huge gold hoops in her ears. When she entered the room, she moved like water, rolling as if every step were a sensual dance.

"Nice place you got here." She grinned and chuckled as she pointed at the rocker by the window. "There it is, my boy Emmet's chair. But where he at?"

I glanced at the counter, where the offending appliance loomed. "There was...an issue. With toast."

Tammy rolled her eyes knowingly, not unkindly but as if she knew all about devil toasters, the bastards. "I got this, sweetheart, don't worry." She sashayed to the door of Emmet's room and knocked five times. "Emmet, honey, it's Tammy. I want to hear all about this toaster."

It took her ten minutes to get him to open the door, and that was when I learned two things: Tammy had read some kind of Emmet manual, and she had the patience of Job. She never raised her voice, never scolded, only kept pointing out he had an appointment with her and he was keeping her waiting. She offered to help him fix the toaster and to talk with him about what went wrong, but mostly she kept repeating, over and over, that he needed to open the door. When he finally did, he pulled her inside and shut them both in.

This is when I had my own toaster moment.

There is this thing I do which I can't stop. I've talked about it some with Dr. North, and my dad has scolded me for it, but basically I feel like everything that happens, everywhere, is my fault. I understand it doesn't make any logical sense, but I can't stop feeling that way. Emmet talks about seeing emotions in the air like colors, but I swear I can *feel* all of them. If I'm in the store and someone drops a jar, I feel embarrassed for them, and I am always sure I must have somehow made them drop it. If someone is upset, I'm sure I must have done something to make them feel that way, even if I don't know them. Sometimes I can tell myself the feelings are wrong, but a lot of times that makes me so tired I just want to go to bed.

When Tammy closed the door to Emmet's room, I was overwhelmed with the conviction I had broken Emmet's toaster, or I'd failed to help him or should have gone to comfort him or all of the above. I felt stupid and worthless, and the cloud that always hangs over my head descended in full until I could barely breathe. I didn't want to go into my room. I didn't want to wait for Tammy. I didn't want to break anything. I wanted to lie down somewhere far away in the dark and wait to die.

I didn't lie down, and I didn't try to kill myself, but I did start crying. It never takes much for me to get teary, but this was going to be a bad cry, I knew, and the thought of them coming out and seeing me this way filled me with so much shame my face was hot. Shame turned to fear, fear turned to panic. I knew I could go under the dome and feel heavy and trapped like I had before we went shopping, but I didn't want to do that on my first day after moving into a new place. Yet I couldn't choose not to feel the panic and sense of despair. I wanted away from it, but I didn't know how to escape.

Without consciously making the decision to do so, I left the apartment.

I left without shoes, which I noticed only when I got outside and the gravel hurt my feet. The sun hurt my eyes too, and the city bus passing on the street sounded like a dinosaur roaring. My chest was tight, my head dizzy. I couldn't see for tears and the saltwater spots on my glasses. I couldn't run without shoes, and every rock felt like a knife on my skin. I couldn't go inside. I was too mortified. So I sobbed as I crossed the parking lot and curled up beneath a tall tree facing an old wooden playground.

It was a good spot. The tree had a divot worn out at the base, like it had grown for the sole purpose of shielding a human body into its trunk. I couldn't hear the street traffic, a soft breeze blew, and I could stare out at the play structure, sad for its lack of children but beautiful in a melancholic way. It was an ornate monster of playground equipment, with turrets and swinging bridges and tunnels made out of old tires. If I were smaller, I would have totally hidden in its depths. If I weren't so tired, I would have tried right now.

It didn't surprise me that Tammy found me. I heard her approach, heavy feet on gravel, and I smelled her perfume as she crouched beside me and put a gentle hand on my shoulder. "Hey, tiger. You want to tell me what just happened?"

No. I shut my eyes and burrowed deeper into the tree. They'd send me to the hospital, or Icarus House. I was such a mess I couldn't live in an apartment for twenty-four hours.

Her heavy hand massaged me. The touch felt so good. "Sweetheart, it's okay. Everybody's okay. Nobody's in trouble. Nobody's angry. But I think everybody's nervous right now because it's the first day." She made sweet, cooing noises and ran her fingers through my hair like I was her baby. "Oh, sugar. You're breaking my heart, you know that?"

"I'm sorry," I said around sobs, then sobbed harder.

She was launching into another round of hushes and soothing noises when more footsteps came up, these in Emmet's halting gait.

"Why is Jeremey crying?"

I tried to hide from him, too ashamed, but I could only fix my gaze more firmly on the tree roots.

Tammy answered for me. "I don't know yet, honey, but it's going to be okay. Everybody's going to be okay." She kept rubbing my back. "This might be a good time to ask for an Ativan, Jeremey. You got yourself a little too wound up. It's okay to ask for help coming down."

She was right, I did need medicine. The wheels of shame and failure crushed me over and over again like the never-ending wheels of a train. "I'm sorry."

"Why are you sorry? You didn't do anything wrong."

That was Emmet, and he was right beside me now. He didn't touch me, but I could feel his presence. It comforted me even as it made me sad, as if he were fruit forever out of my reach.

"I think we need to have everybody take a break," Tammy said, "and we're going to try this again. Jeremey, let's get you tucked somewhere safe until you can calm down. Emmet, you can—"

"I want to stay with Jeremey."

I looked up at him through my fog. How did he always part it for me? "I'm sorry about the toast."

Emmet frowned. "But you didn't burn my toast."

"I'm sorry that it burned. I'm sorry it made you so upset."

I understood then why Emmet was so comforting to me. He regarded me with more open consternation than anyone did when my emotions didn't make sense, but nowhere in his expression was the wariness or silent judgment that told me *something is wrong with you.* He only looked at me as he would any contradiction, as if I were a simple, honest puzzle he hadn't solved yet. "You're upset because I was upset?"

That made it sound like I was angry at him, which, holy panic, Batman. "I feel bad when people are upset. I feel with them. I'm sorry. I can't turn it off."

Emmet stared at me—or near me, above my head—then touched my face with his fingers. "You don't have to turn it off. But you can't run away."

Some of the shadows in my mind lifted. "Okay."

He pulled his hand from my face but stayed close to me. "I'm sorry I got angry about the toaster. I wanted my first day of being independent to go well. I didn't mean to make you feel my anger so loudly."

I nodded, feeling better all the time. Except I still felt heavy and foggy and more than a little on edge.

"You two." Tammy's voice was beautiful, like a song, every word a note. "I want to hug you to pieces. But I think instead we're going to go inside, I'm going to make you breakfast, get Jeremey his Ativan, and we're going to have a casual get-to-know-you chat. We're going to be good friends, the three of us. I can already tell."

A month ago I would have felt this speech was pandering, social worker garbage for babies. Right then and there, I felt more helpless than a baby, and I didn't mind her soothing tone at all. In fact, Tammy seemed like a lifeline I'd been seeking my whole life.

The first week at The Roosevelt was very much a roller coaster, but whenever Dr. North asked how I was doing, I told him I was good, and I meant it. It was scary to be on my own, even with Tammy and Sally downstairs, but it really was okay. Living in an apartment was like being in my room all the time, except my mom never bugged me, there was more space and a fridge.

And Emmet.

Emmet had a harder time adjusting to independent living. While I'd appreciated how particular he was since I'd met him, I learned that first week at The Roosevelt it was something else entirely to live in the same space with Emmet's fussiness. He had so many odd little rules about how the handles should turn on mugs in the cupboard, what went on what shelf in the fridge and where I could leave my shoes. I couldn't possibly remember everything, which made me panic. But we couldn't melt down, because Tammy caught us before we figured out we were falling.

"Emmet," she began at one of our morning meetings, "we need to talk about how many rules you're giving Jeremey to remember about the apartment."

The way she said it made it sound as if I'd complained to her, and I freaked out. "It's fine. His rules are fine."

She caught my hand and laced our fingers together, soothing me. Tammy touched me all the time, hugging me and smiling. It always mesmerized me, and it did now too.

Emmet rocked slightly in his seat as he stared at the tabletop. "Rules are important. Consistency is important."

"I know, honey, but you have to remember Jeremey's brain isn't the same as yours. He overwhelms easily, and he's not going to tell you when it's too much. Jeremey is working on vocalizing his needs, but for now I'm going to be his voice. He doesn't have a camera brain for information. He reads emotion. Which means while he can't remember the angle you wanted him to leave the couch at, he can relay all the emotions you had yesterday and the day before."

I read emotion? I thought about what she said. I couldn't remember what I'd eaten for breakfast, but yes, I knew Emmet had woken up slightly grumpy, got happy when the train passed, got horny when he asked me to come into his room for sex. He was relaxed after, but too keyed up until I went to take a shower so he could be alone.

I blinked. Wow. Yeah. I totally read emotions.

Right now I was pretty sure anybody in the world could read Emmet—he was highly agitated. "I need order and rules."

"I can try to learn them." I hated how upset I was making him. I couldn't learn, though, and I hunched my shoulders.

Tammy rubbed the one she could reach from her chair. "We need to find a modification that works for the two of you."

"I could write down the rules." Emmet's rocking turned softer, more controlled. He was focusing, thinking. "I could make a manual."

"That's a good start, but you're still thinking as if his brain is like yours. You're assuming once it's written down and Jeremey sees the words, he'll remember forever."

I started to object, but I stopped as I read Emmet's face, realizing yes, he did assume that. Holy crap. Is that what *he* could do?

Tammy tapped the top of the table gently with a fingertip. "Come on, Emmet. You're a smart guy. If Jeremey needs to see your rules, needs to be able to remember them, how do we teach memory? How can you modify a rule book so he doesn't have to remember?"

Emmet clearly had no idea, and honestly neither did I. I have a horrible memory for stuff like that. I mean, maybe if it was on a hook over the top of my head, dangling in my face. But even then it would have to turn itself to the right page. I wondered if Google glasses did that. What if you could look through your glasses at the cupboard, and it would write on the cupboard door that Emmet wanted the mugs to be a certain way?

I sat upright, gasping as it all clicked in my head. "*Oh.*" When Tammy and Emmet glanced at me—well, Emmet glanced near me—I explained. "We could write the instructions on the door of the cupboard. And on the fridge, and the bathroom mirror. And by the front door. That way I wouldn't have to remember. I could just read."

Emmet grinned. His gaze was on my shoulder, but I knew he was looking right at me, so it made me feel warm and good. "That's a smart idea. I could make the signs. I could type them and print them up. You could pick the font so it's nice to your eyes." He rocked back and forth, humming for a second before continuing. "I can use different colored paper depending on how important the rule is."

Tammy's laugh was warm like honey. "Look at the two of you when you work together. What an excellent couple you are."

We were a *great* couple. We worked together on the signs—Emmet made me pick the font, which at first I said didn't matter. He insisted it mattered a lot. "You'll read the notes all the time. Pick a font that makes you happy." He had a huge font collection on his computer, several he'd designed himself, though those were all very mathematical.

I ended up choosing one called Aire Roman Pro, and Emmet changed it somehow so some of the letters swirled and curled. He printed the signs carefully, posted them in all the appropriate places, and he was right, I loved seeing the notes with that font. I smiled at the mugs as I adjusted them, felt easy and less stressed as I moved the couch inside of the tape lines Emmet had put on the floor. I didn't have to remember, and I didn't accidentally upset Emmet.

Emmet has a sense of humor, though, and he can also get a little carried away. He started putting notes *everywhere*, and sometimes they were deliberately silly. I found *Time to smile* inside my box of cereal one morning, the T all swirly and pretty. I tucked that note into my pocket, and I smiled every time I touched the paper. I also kept the one that said *Emmet and Jeremey Forever* with half the letters all swirled and beautiful. He left notes inside my towel, my shoes and inside my favorite DVDs. Usually they were reminders of how he wanted the apartment kept and nudges to be happy.

Every now and again, though, they were something else.

We had sex every day, often in the morning. He woke early, at breakfast, watched a train, did some coding, and then he would wake me up, send me to brush my teeth, and then we'd have sex. Usually there would be a note about it on the bathroom mirror. *Come to my room and take off your pants, sexy* was one he reused a lot. Sometimes he got a little steamy. *Meet me in your room, naked. I want to touch your body.*

Three days into the note adventure, though, he added a new request to his repertoire. *Come suck my cock.*

Emmet had been unsure about oral sex. "Penises are too sweaty," he kept saying. I couldn't understand his objection. I liked the smell of his cock, especially when he was aroused. I wanted his cock in my mouth. So one day I got brave enough to tell him I wanted to try. He sat on his bed, legs spread, and I knelt and took it in my mouth. He jerked, cried out, but he put his hand on the back of my head, holding on tight to my hair. I sucked harder, my skin breaking out in goose bumps as he pulled. When he thrust into my mouth, something inside me unbuckled. I forgot to be self-conscious and nervous, and I focused on sucking and drowning in the feel of his cock sliding over my tongue. When he jerked and shot, I was surprised. It tasted a little funny, but the idea that he'd come in my mouth made me so crazy I moaned as I swallowed.

I was self-conscious after, my head laying on his leg, my own cock hard, his semen dripping out of my mouth. He held still for a while, his hand on my hair.

Then he nudged me onto my back, spread my legs and kissed my chest.

I have a thing about my nipples being played with, and Emmet knows all about it. I started to object he needed alone time after coming, but then he sucked on my right nipple, and I cried out instead. He says he loves it when I make noise, so I don't ever hold back. Usually when we have sex, he starts with my nipples to make me really crazy. *He* likes best when I go all soft for him, he says. He loves that I let him do whatever he wants with my body. It's true, I do. I love being able to just feel.

That day he worked me up the way he always does, until I felt like I was only feeling and breathing. He teased my cock with one hand, toying with a nipple with the other. I gripped the bed, trying to lie quiet for him, knowing he was going to make me crazier before he was done, and I couldn't wait.

When his mouth closed over the tip of my cock, I gasped and almost sat up.

He pushed me down and sucked my cock in deeper.

I don't know that we were incredible at blow jobs compared to the mainstream gay population, but I don't think either one of us gave a shit. It felt so good, so hot and wet. I kept wanting to push up into his mouth, but he held my hips down so I couldn't, and honestly that was almost as good as his mouth. He didn't swallow me the way I did him, but that he blew me at all was more than I ever expected from him. When he could tell I was close, he pulled off and finished me with his hand.

I ended up napping for a bit after, but that night as we cuddled on the couch after dinner, I worked up the courage to ask him about it.

"I was surprised you did that. Blew me, I mean."

I had my head on his shoulder, so I couldn't see his face, but I could feel his smile. "It felt good. I wanted to try, for you, so you could feel it too. It wasn't as sweaty as I thought. I like the taste of your skin after a shower, and your cock feels good in my mouth."

It did feel good. I got stiff thinking about it. I stroked his leg meaningfully—but with a careful amount of pressure. "I'd do it anytime. Suck you, I mean. Or...anything."

Emmet turned my face up to his and kissed me—and moved my hand to his groin.

I ended up sucking him off then. We started in the living room, but Emmet gets fussy about sex anywhere but a bedroom, so we moved to my room. I blew him again, he teased my nipples, kissed me—we played around, mostly. That's how sex always was with us. Nobody penetrated anybody anywhere with anything, which sometimes disappointed me, but it was kind of a relief too, that we were taking sex slowly. I wanted to do everything with Emmet, but I wanted to do it right.

I don't think most people believed we actually were having sex, or if they did, they thought we were cute while we did it or something. People saw us walking down the street to the grocery store or wandering the aisles of Wheatsfield and acted as if we were escapees from the Island of Adorable, puppies dressed up in people clothes. Like we weren't really boyfriends, like we were fake.

No wonder I feel alienated. They're the ones telling me I'm not like everyone else. It doesn't matter how normal I am, somebody's ready to tell me I'm different.

Maybe I'm different, but I have custom font invitations on my bathroom mirror to have good-morning sex. I bet all the people who think Emmet and I are trained dogs don't have anything as awesome as that.

Chapter Seventeen
Emmet

Jeremey and I were the first residents to move into The Roosevelt, which was nice because we had the place to ourselves. It took me a little while to get used to the new rhythm, but once we had the notes set up, everything was fine with Jeremey and me. It was better for me too once the regular school year started again, as I like a schedule. Living at The Roosevelt actually meant I was closer to the bus stop, which was nice.

In our apartment, Jeremey and I had a good pattern. The notes helped us with organization, and our Saturday morning meetings with Sally and Tammy helped us learn how to make sure we didn't have any problems we needed to work out. We made a schedule of what days we would go shopping, when we'd do laundry. Jeremey went with me to Wheatsfield, but he still wasn't ready to go to Target. Sometimes he could go to the small drugstore downtown, but sometimes they announced things over the PA system and startled him too much.

Jeremey was happy, he said, but he was having a harder time than me. He was frustrated and sad sometimes, because he couldn't find a job that was right for him. Sally had made a list of possible places for him to work, and so far three of them hadn't been very good. Wheatsfield was okay until a customer cornered him by the green peppers and demanded to know what the differences in the mushrooms were. The produce manager rescued him quickly, but Jeremey still had a panic attack and had to come home and didn't want to work there after. The library was slightly better, and Darren watched out for him, but Jeremey had the same problem with patrons asking him questions in a rude way.

Dr. North suggested Jeremey help around The Roosevelt once the others moved in, assisting the first-floor residents with laundry, and cooking with Tammy and Sally. I thought it sounded like a good idea, but Jeremey got sad that night. Instead of having sex, I held him on the bed. He told me when I held him it was better than any medicine he took to fight depression.

I didn't like how sad Jeremey was, but I was feeling pretty proud of how well I could comfort him. I was doing well all over the place, actually. I'd made the transition to independent living pretty easily, *and* I lived with my boyfriend. All I needed now was to finish college, get a job, and I'd be all set.

Then on September first the other residents moved in, and I wasn't doing so well anymore.

Mom had warned me, but I learned I absolutely didn't enjoy living with lots of people at once. Our apartment was soundproofed, but sometimes I could still hear people talking in the halls, people I didn't know, and it upset me. Bob did his best to make things easy for me and everyone at The Roosevelt. All the autistic people lived on the top floor, except for a girl who didn't like being up high, and she lived near Sally and Tammy's apartment. The first floor was for people who needed extra care—most lived in more of a dorm situation, and they ate meals in the community area. They were loud, the first-floor people, but they weren't jerks. One of the guys named Stuart played a lot of Pharrell Williams music, but he was nice and would put on headphones if you asked. The first-floor people yelled instead of talked. Yelling *was* talking for them. I understood they couldn't help it and this was their disability, but it bothered *my* disability.

The loud people and the strangers weren't the real issue for me, though. There was one more resident on the first floor. David Loris. Bob's son.

I hated David.

David wasn't mentally challenged at all, and in fact most of his life he would have been the last guy in the world to live in a place like The Roosevelt. But then he was in a car accident, and now he was the most disabled person in the building. I should have liked David more since he was the reason Bob had bought The Roosevelt and converted it into an assisted living establishment. But David *wasn't* a person like me, or even Jeremey.

Carly Fleischmann talks about being a prisoner in her body. David was definitely more of a prisoner of his physical body than me, but I still think I'm more like Carly than he is, since both our brains keep us from interacting the way we want. Not David. His spine might have been injured, but his brain is perfectly fine. His mouth works *too* well, and whenever I saw him, he reminded me a lot of the guys on campus who teased me. His body wasn't buff and bulky anymore, since it had been two years since his accident, but I could tell he *used* to be a bruiser. He looked like his dad, big and strong. David talked about playing football and having girlfriends. He couldn't walk, could only move his head and a little bit of his left arm, but he drove his chair around the same way annoying bullies drove their cars.

I was the only person who didn't like him, though. The day he moved in, everyone acted as if a movie star had come to stay. Even Stuart, who never talked to anybody, came out of his room to see Bob's son arrive. There were eleven of us living at The Roosevelt, and he was the last to move in, number twelve.

He rolled up the ramp wearing sunglasses and a black T-shirt that said *ATTITUDE PROBLEM*. Bob and his wife were with him, and a tall black man. Bob waved to us, and the black man smiled and waved when some of the residents greeted him. Stuart asked the man who he was.

"Jimmy." The man smiled at Stuart and stuck out his hand, but Stuart didn't take it because he doesn't care for touch at all. Jimmy pulled his hand back. "I'm one of David's aides. What's your name?"

Stuart hummed and turned away to face the wall. That was pretty much Stuart.

David murmured something we weren't supposed to hear, but I did. He said, "Welcome to the freak house."

Bob introduced everyone to David and Jimmy, and his wife, Andi, and his two daughters, Caitlin and Trina. I hadn't met the daughters before. They didn't smile and stayed close to their mother. I could tell David and his sisters and his mom weren't like Bob. They were afraid of autistic people and thought we were retarded. I put on my best behavior, remembering all my social interactions and cues as best I could, but they still treated me differently than they did Jeremey. All Jeremey had to do was smile, and they relaxed.

David didn't like anyone. He told his dad he wanted to go to his cell, which made Bob angry. They went inside David's room, all of his family, and his aide stood in the hall looking as if he wanted to flap until Tammy and Sally came over and talked to him.

When David and his family stayed inside his room for a long time, some of the residents went to their rooms or the lounge, but Jeremey and I stayed. David made me nervous, and I wanted to learn more about him. It's important to know your enemies.

Jeremey leaned in close to whisper in my ear. "Can you hear them through the door?"

I nodded and kept listening.

Jeremey got out his phone and wrote in a notepad, *Anything good?*

I put my hand over my ear, and he let me listen without interrupting.

Jeremey waited patiently while I listened, recording the conversation with my computer brain until I could tell they'd started talking about boring things. Taking Jeremey's hand, I led him to our apartment and sat with him on the couch. Jeremey didn't say anything, only sat patiently, waiting for me to tell what I'd heard.

I'd heard a lot.

"David doesn't want to be at The Roosevelt. He thinks we're a bunch of R-word freaks, and he's angry his father put him in here. Bob told him everyone at The Roosevelt needs somewhere special to live, how some of the families cried when they found out about it because they were so grateful. There was nowhere else for their loved ones to go with as much support and independence. He told David this included him, and David got angry. He said his dad should just let him die. *How can my life be worth anything now?* he said."

Jeremey sat up straighter. I couldn't read the complicated emotion on his face. "Oh. That's not good."

"Then his mom started crying, saying *Don't you dare give up, David.* She talked about how good the facilities here were, how great Sally and Tammy are, how this is better than the care she could give him at home. She said she hoped he understood she wasn't kicking him out but that The Roosevelt could give him more than she could."

"What did he say then?"

"That she shouldn't give him anything but a clean way off this bus. I don't know what that means. They didn't ride a bus here, but the stop is close. Does he think it will be too loud? It's usually a Cybrid, a hybrid bus, and they're remarkably quiet."

Jeremey's expression was still too complicated for me to read. His lips were flat, his eyes big and round like *sad*, but his lips were tight like *determination*. "He's making a metaphor.

He's feeling suicidal. I suppose that's to be expected, after such an intense change of how you think your life will go. That's sad, though, that he feels this way after two years, and with such amazing parents helping him. I can barely get my parents to pay my rent, but Bob built an entire independent living center for David."

"David is a bully and a jerk. He's going to be trouble."

Jeremey frowned and shook his head. "I bet it's more complicated than that. But I agree, I don't think he's going to fit in easily here."

We stayed in the rest of that first night, so we didn't find out anything more about David. I had class early the next morning, so after sex with Jeremey, I got on the bus and went to class. I saw David that afternoon when I came home and went to find Jeremey. Jeremey was sitting under his favorite tree, and David was with his aide not far away.

His face was easy to read that day and every day: he was angry, and he hated The Roosevelt as much as I loved it. I tried to avoid him and not make trouble, but David was mean, and he was bored. If something wasn't trouble, he made it that way.

One day when I got off the bus, Jeremey was there waiting for me, smiling and excited. "I'm so glad you're home." He took my hand and pointed toward the railroad tracks. "I was afraid you'd miss it. We saw it coming on our walk, and I came to meet you so you could hurry to see it too."

He pulled me faster than I would have liked, but when I came around the corner and saw what was coming down the tracks, I was glad he'd pulled too hard.

It was a train, but it was a train different than anything that had ever gone down that track since I'd been watching it. It was a big black steam engine, and when it came close to the track, it pulled its whistle. My skin got goose bumps from the sound. It was so strange and beautiful, and so was the engine. All the cars talk to me, but this one was old and amazing. I wished the train would stop so I could touch it and learn everything about it.

Almost better than the steam engine, though, were the cars behind it. *Passenger* cars. Old-fashioned passenger cars, with people inside hanging out the windows, waving.

Half the residents from The Roosevelt were at the end of the street, facing the tracks, waving and watching. David was there too, but I ignored him and everyone else because this was the most wonderful thing I'd ever seen on my train tracks. I couldn't stop myself from humming and rocking and flapping in happiness as I stared, counting and memorizing the number of windows and wheels and identifying markers on each car. When the train was gone, I'd go look it up online to see what it was and why it was here, but right now it was in front of me, and I was so happy I felt like electricity.

I was so happy I forgot other people were present.

Jeremey was fine. He smiled a big, bright smile at me when the caboose passed out of sight and the train was gone. Sally and Tammy did too. The autistic boy, Mark, who lived next door to us, didn't look at me, but from the way he'd watched the train, I knew he'd enjoyed it as much as me. In fact, all the residents had.

Except for one. David hadn't watched the train. He'd watched me.

He stared at me from his chair, and I wished his face were more complicated. I could tell exactly what he thought of me. To him I was a freak. Probably he'd think that even more if he knew how much I'd been counting. But he'd seen me flap and rock and heard me hum.

He looked at me the way the jerks on campus did.

Bob Loris was a nice man, but his son was not. Sally and Tammy called David *that poor boy* when he wasn't around. So did my mom. Even Jeremey felt sorry for him.

I didn't. He might be in a wheelchair and have a damaged spine, but I didn't like him at all. I didn't wish he were dead, but if he found somewhere else to live, that would be okay with me.

Chapter Eighteen
Jeremey

I should have been happier about my life.

I had a boyfriend who I fell in love with more every day. I hadn't said the word to him yet—I had said I loved him when I was trying to kill myself, but that was more of a goodbye than a confession. I told him in the hospital too, that first day, but that was possibly drugs. If I had loved him then, I loved him more now, but I couldn't tell him because I was too scared. I knew, though, someday I'd tell him. I had good medication that kept me even-keeled, enough that with regular sessions with Dr. North, I felt better than I could ever remember feeling. Some days depression made it so I had to stay in bed, but not often, and I never felt as overwhelmed as I used to feel.

My parents were still weird, but they were paying my bills and not trying to mold me into somebody I couldn't be. I had an incredible place to live, and after my stay at the group home, I knew exactly how precious The Roosevelt was, how lucky I was to have it.

I had so many things to be happy about, and in a way, I was. Except not all the way. I'd never feel the same kind of easiness other people did. Happiness and peace would always be something I worked hard to have, even if my external life looked like a 1950s sitcom. I understood this, but that knowledge still made me sad and lonely thinking about it. I was sure my life could be more. I *wanted* more.

One of the things I wanted, really wanted, was a job. At first I'd wanted to continue staying in our apartment watching TV all day, but Dr. North pointed out that discontented feeling wouldn't go away with another *Cake Boss* marathon. I started looking at options for employment, and without consciously meaning to, I became fixated on the idea of a good job making that last piece of disquiet fall away. The trouble was, I couldn't find a good job. I couldn't find *any* job that I could work at for more than a few days.

Something was broken in me. I swear I wasn't this way when I started my senior year of high school, but I was certainly a mess now. And then Dr. North pointed out something that made everything worse.

"While your depression was more pronounced before, it seems your anxiety has taken over, at least temporarily, as the more predominant force."

I straightened. "So what, they can switch around whenever they want?"

"You will always have both, but yes, you'll have times where one is more dominant than the other. It's perfectly natural."

Easy for him to say. I felt as if he'd pulled up a cloth on the table, revealing that instead of a thousand-piece puzzle to solve, I suddenly had ten thousand pieces, all of them gray. "Basically you're telling me, while I'm calming one down, the other goes out of control."

"No. Not at all. Think of it as managing dual currents. Sometimes one is stronger than the other. Sometimes they both are. You can't maintain a perfect calm, but you can accept and control these two elements."

I sagged in my chair. "It's all so impossible. I want to be better. I want to be *fixed*."

"*Fixed* is a dangerous term. This isn't a little box we're ticking so I can give you a different colored pill. This isn't an infection we're eradicating. We've been treating *you* and finding solutions for *your* situation since the day we had our first session. These are life-long conditions. Right now the condition most difficult for you to manage is anxiety. So let's talk about what's making you anxious."

We talked about what made me anxious every single day we met after that. A lot of things made me anxious, but *everything* overwhelmed me when I was working. It was something to do with possibly letting my employer down. It didn't matter how nice and understanding they were—certainly the library staff had seen everything, between clientele and staff members like Darren, but none of that mattered in my head. It was like living in the aisles of Target every day at work. All I wanted to do was scream or curl into a ball, and usually that's where I ended up by the end of the day.

I was so ashamed of myself, so embarrassed. Sally and Tammy told me not to be—so did Dr. North, Marietta, even Althea. Emmet told me not to worry about it, that I could work at The Roosevelt, helping. It was true, I could do that. Sally and Tammy always needed another pair of hands. But I worried what would happen when I screwed that up too. I worried, a lot, about what happened to somebody so worthless he couldn't keep any job, anywhere.

Sally and Tammy gave me tasks to do, but not many, and I could tell they were jobs that didn't need doing, that if I melted down, nothing serious would come of my failure. They were also solitary jobs: folding laundry, doing dishes, cleaning out bathrooms. Ashamed as I was that this was all I could do, I did feel better for doing them. In fact, I felt more anxious and disconnected when I *wasn't* working, and I started finding staff to ask for jobs so I didn't sit on our couch and go nuts until Emmet came home from school.

One afternoon when I went to find Sally, she was in the hall with David, having an argument while down the hall Stuart wailed bloody murder about God only knew what. I hung off to the side, trying to be polite and wait my turn for her attention, but David didn't look ready to relinquish her anytime soon. His left arm jerked in time to his anger as he angled his head to the side and shouted at Sally.

"I'm going outside. Nobody has to go with me. I'm going to sit under the fucking tree and stare at the goddamned clouds, all right? I don't need a babysitter for that."

"I understand your frustration, but you haven't been here long enough for us to learn how far your independence can go, and I don't have the call button for your chair yet. Missy will be back in fifteen minutes. You can wait that long."

Missy was one of David's many aides. I got the idea David didn't like her as well as he did Jimmy.

"She texted and said she'd be late because one of the prescriptions wasn't called in. If I wait for her, it'll be time for my evening shitshow." He waved his right arm at her. It was so strange to watch, like a club attached at his shoulder, awkward and uncooperative as he screwed up his face in anger. "I want some fucking time to myself outside. I'm not gonna die sitting underneath a tree."

Sally was just as angry, but when she waved her arms, they worked fine. "I have twelve other residents to take care of, and one of them is waiting for me right now while I argue with you."

"So go to him already, *Jesus.*"

"*David.* I cannot leave you unattended yet, not out there without your call button. What if your chair fell over? What if—"

"I don't give a shit. If I die, I fucking die—"

"You're not going out unaccompanied right now, and that's final."

David's face got red, and he started to sputter, unable to swear anymore, he was so angry. Except it wasn't just that. He was *frustrated.* Helpless, furious, completely unable to control his life enough to go sit outside alone. I understood why Sally couldn't take him—people down the block had to be able to hear Stuart howling—but I felt awful David had to ask

216

permission and have a chaperone for something as simple as going outside to sit in the shade.

A thought occurred to me, and almost as quickly it tumbled out of my mouth. "I could go with him."

I hadn't spoken loudly, but David turned his head toward me in the same lopsided way he'd done to Sally. I held still, nervous and unsure as he looked me up and down. "Jeremey, right? You live with Train Man?"

I winced at the nickname, remembering how much Emmet hated David. I wondered if I shouldn't do this because of that. But how could it hurt to sit outside with David for a few minutes?

I glanced away, self-conscious. "I wouldn't mind going outside with you. I don't know if I'm strong enough to help you if your chair fell over, but I could go *get* help. Plus, I have a phone. I could call Sally or even an ambulance. I mean—that's probably too much. But I can help. If that would be okay with you."

David grinned, and I blushed. He was handsome enough most of the time, but when he smiled, he looked like a young Hugh Jackman. The smile evaporated as he tilted his head toward Sally. "Go help Stuart. My new best friend Jeremey's going to take me outside."

Sally glanced from David to me and back again. "Jeremey, you're sure?"

I nodded. I wasn't sure, but I did want to help. "It's fine." I was pretty sure I could sit under a tree with a quadriplegic without having a panic attack. Though if it turned out I couldn't manage *that* much, I was going to ask Dr. North to up my prescription on something.

"Okay." Sally pointed a finger at David. "Behave." She lowered her finger as she addressed me. "I'll be in Stuart's room if you need me. If he gets hurt, don't bother finding me. Call 911 first."

"Fucking Christ." David rolled his eyes as she hurried down the hall.

I didn't know what to say to that, so I said nothing. I wasn't so sure of myself now, alone with David. I wished Emmet wasn't at school so he could come too. Though as much as Emmet hated David, that probably wouldn't have happened anyway. "Wh-what do you want me to do?"

It wouldn't have surprised me if he'd said *nothing* or made a sarcastic remark about how he didn't need help, but instead he said, politely, "If you could hold the door open, that would be great. I know it's automatic, but it doesn't stay open long enough for me. Dad says he's going to fix it, but the repair guy can't come until next week."

"Sure. No problem." I hurried to the door, held it open wide and waited patiently as he navigated his chair through. It did take him a long time, largely because he kept overshooting his angle, heading for the frames instead of the center.

"Sorry." His cheeks reddened and he glowered as he tried again to make the approach. "I suck at driving when I'm pissed."

"It's okay. I'm not in a hurry." I remembered he said he wouldn't have much time outside and added, "If there's something I can do to help, let me know. But don't rush on my account."

It might have been my imagination, but he relaxed a little after that, and it wasn't long before he found the correct angle and went sailing through...to the next set of doors. I hurried around to open them too. They both opened out, which was great for this direction, but he'd have to drive off to the side on the return trip while I opened the inner door. I frowned. Doors kind of sucked, for wheelchairs.

"No worries." David breezed through the last barrier between him and the outside, and he sped up as he headed down the ramp, letting out a lusty sigh at the bottom. "Damn. I feel as if I got a reprieve from prison. Thanks, bro. Owe you one."

I hadn't ever been anyone's *bro* before. Folding my arms over my belly, I came hesitantly around the side of his chair. What was I supposed to say? I felt panic start to spiral, but I set my teeth and didn't let it take hold. No. All I had to do was stand here and be his live-action help button. If he wanted to talk to me, he'd talk. If not, I didn't mind enjoying the moment of quiet.

He enjoyed it too, shutting his eyes and tipping his head back in the chair's headrest so his chin stuck up toward the sky. "Perfect fall day."

There wasn't much to say to that, so I said nothing and continued to study him. He was handsome. Dark brown hair cut close to his head, a smart goatee—though I could see the rough spots under his chin where he hadn't been shaved properly. He would have to be shaved too, since his hands clearly didn't work well enough for him to do it himself. He wore a bright green shirt with yellow and white geometrics across the front, and a pair of jeans. I wanted to stare at his still torso and legs, mesmerized by how little he moved. His legs were smaller than seemed right too—atrophy. I didn't get around much, but I did enough movement to build basic muscle. The only way his muscles moved was if someone moved them for him.

When I glanced up at his face, he was watching me. I blushed, ready to stammer an apology for ogling him, but he spoke before I could.

"Are you seriously dating Train Man?"

I wasn't expecting that question, and I glanced around awkwardly. "Yes. I'm dating Emmet." My face heated as I got ready for him to make fun of me, and panic encroached as I realized I couldn't leave if he got insulting.

"Like—*dating* him. You're not playing along? You're straight-up boyfriends?"

He didn't sound as if he were making fun, more earnestly asking a question, but I still felt uneasy. "Yes."

"How did that happen?" He turned his chair so it faced me more fully. "I mean—I thought they were all no-touchy and isolated."

They being autistic people. I began to understand why Emmet hated him so much. I didn't know what to say, so I looked away and hoped he'd give up.

No such luck, though he did ease up a little. "Sorry. That was crass." He stared off into the playground. "I'm asking because it's what I want back the most. Being able to date somebody. I'd figured I was out of the scene, now that I'm glued to this chair and live in the Special Snowflake House. But you're dating someone. For real. Not a game. That's what I'm asking about. How you got it. What it's like. If you don't mind talking about it."

I leaned against the tree, hunching my shoulders as I put my hands in my shorts pockets. "We met at a picnic earlier this year. He introduced himself to me. We hung out, and..." I averted my gaze to the ground, thinking of the right turn my summer had taken.

"What are you in for again?" David's voice was light, but not teasing. "You seem so normal."

"I'm so far from normal I can't see it anymore." I couldn't bring myself to look him in the eye, so I stared at the handle of his chair. "I have major depressive disorder." I thought of what Dr. North had said and added, my lips pursed, "And clinical anxiety."

"That doesn't sound so bad."

I grimaced. "I was in the hospital until a few weeks ago because I tried to kill myself."

"Oh. Okay. Yeah. That's bad." He got uncharacteristically quiet, and when I dared to glance at his face, all his bravado had fallen. *He* couldn't meet me in the eye now. "That's the thing about being a C4 quad. You need an assistant for suicide."

His confession hung in the air a few seconds, and I remembered what Emmet had overheard the day David moved in. "Do you still wish you could? Kill yourself?" Then it hit me how that sounded and added, "I'm not offering or anything. Just wondering."

His shoulders rose clumsily—that was a shrug. "Sometimes. I'm not as serious about it as I used to be. I used to lie awake in my bed trying to figure out how I could get it done. The realization I couldn't made me more suicidal." He jerked his head at the building. "That's when Dad started The Roosevelt. I told him I didn't want it, but my therapist pointed out I'm so busy being angry at him now for spending all his money on this that I don't wish myself dead anymore. So I guess it's good for something."

"I'm glad your dad set up The Roosevelt. Otherwise I'd be living in a group home."

He frowned. "But why? Depressives don't *have* to live in a clinical setting, right?" When I glanced away, feeling awkward again, he continued. "Sorry. I'm not trying to be a jerk."

"I'm embarrassed I'm such a mess."

David snorted. "Somebody has to reach into my rectum with a finger and pull out my turds every night after dinner. I'm pretty sure anything you have to confess isn't any grosser than that."

I blinked at him, and I'm embarrassed to say my mouth fell open. I thought for sure he had to be kidding, but he wasn't. Holy crap.

Pardon the pun.

He raised an eyebrow at me. "So. You were telling me about why you have to live here or in a group home."

"I get anxious and panicky, and I'm easily overwhelmed. I have a difficult time keeping things put away, and sometimes thinking about what to make for dinner exhausts me. Emmet kind of handles all that. I mean, I cook with him, but he decides what we're eating. He asks me, but mostly I agree with whatever he says." I rubbed my toe in the dirt in front of me. "I can't live at home. My parents think I should get over it, but I can't. They make me worse. I love living here, but I can't keep a job. I've filled out Social Security paperwork, but I need to work too. For money, but also because it's not good to sit there watching TV all day until Emmet gets home from school. I can't even shelve books at the library, though."

"Why not? What happens?"

I shrugged, the shock of his poop story wearing off, leaving me feeling like a freak again. "In public places I panic. Not all places, not all the time, but it's always a danger. I didn't use to be this bad, but I keep getting worse. Dr. North says it's okay, that this is how I'm finding safe spaces or something, but I feel like a big loser. Everybody else has a job."

"Hello. I have to have a babysitter to sit under a fucking tree. You think I have a job?"

"No, but people don't *expect* you to. Everyone thinks I'm normal. They can't see the mess in my head, so they get annoyed I don't behave the way regular people do. You at least have the chair to make them leave you alone."

"Huh." He tipped his head to the side, looking thoughtful. "I'll be damned. So I feel normal but look like a mess, and you look normal and feel like a mess. We need to get together more often, dude." He straightened his head, and his eyes went wide. "Hold it. *Hold* it. That's it. That's *totally it.*" He rolled closer, his expression excited and intense. "You should work for me."

"Work for you?" I thought about the turd removal and got nervous. "What...would I do?"

"All kinds of shit. Open doors for me. Help me do my hair in a way that doesn't make me look dorky. Feed me my lunch without treating me like a baby. Hang out with me in the shade. Anything. Everything."

It sounded simple, wonderful even, but I was sure there had to be a catch. "I'm not a nurse or an aide. I barely got through high school."

"I don't want you to be a nurse. A companion or whatever. Someone to help me get to class, if I ever get the guts to go back to college."

How did agreeing to sit with him outside for a few minutes turn into this? "You want to pay me to hang out with you?"

He made another clumsy shrug. "Not like that, no. But hanging out with me is work." He grinned. "Come on. Say you'll do it. I don't have to ask my dad. I know he'll go for it."

I wanted to. It surprised me, but it was true. And since I wanted it so much, I tried to tear it down. "I'll screw it up. I screw everything up."

"You won't."

"You don't know me enough to know that."

"You're right. But, dude, I want to try. You have no idea how crazy I get, sitting inside this head by myself. I'm a rolling sob story to most people. Not to *you*, though. I don't care if you melt down every few feet or can't figure out what you want for dinner. You've treated me more like a man than anybody has in a long time. I'd pay you to sit and talk to me."

I felt warm, and hopeful—and nervous. "I don't know."

"I'll talk to my dad. He'll convince you."

The back door to The Roosevelt opened, and a short, round, smiling woman came down the ramp toward us. "There you are. David, are you ready to go have dinner?"

Missy *did* talk to him as if he were an infant. I think it was probably how she'd talk to anybody she was taking care of, not something personal to David, but I understood how frustrating that would be, to have everyone treat you that way all day long. I still wasn't sure I'd be right for the job he was talking about, but I wished I could be.

David ignored his nurse, still looking at me expectantly.

"I'll think about it," I told him, and he grinned.

David ended up calling his dad then and there, and when Bob heard the idea, he came right over.

"So we'd hire you as an informal aide?" Bob's eyes had the same intensity as David's. "Kind of a modern-day companion. He'd still need a professional nurse's aide for day-to-day care, but you could help him with simpler things, ordering and eating lunch, getting on a bus."

I balked at that. "I get anxious in public. I'm not sure how well that would work. I wouldn't be any good if something really bad went wrong."

Bob waved this objection away. "Oh, I'm sure we'll find some things work and some don't. But if you were with him on a bus and something went south, you could call me or his mom, or an ambulance. From what I understand, David wants you to help be his hands and legs. We wouldn't want to put you in a situation that triggered your own issues, but from where I sit, there's a lot of room between those and what David's looking for." He beamed. "This is a great idea. I'm one hundred percent on board if you decide to do it, Jeremey."

David huffed. "I'll convince him."

I drifted to my apartment in a giddy haze. I'd told them I'd think about it and get back to them, but I wanted to do it. I *would* do it. I'd try, at least.

I was nervous but excited too. I felt good about myself, and I loved the idea of getting up to go hang out with David as my job instead of moping around feeling useless and worthless. When Emmet came home, I still felt good, and as I looked at him, handsome and familiar and smiling at me, all the good feelings swirled like a tornado, and I went soft inside, wanting him.

This was what I'd been missing. A sense of purpose, an idea that I wasn't a waste of space. Normally I'd try to tear down all my own potential, but every time I tried, I saw David staring at me with so much yearning and hope, wanting, *needing* me to help him. To help him not feel like a waste of space, either.

I could do this, I thought. I really could do this. The thought made me feel as if I could fly.

Emmet's gaze didn't meet mine, but he smiled. "You're happy. That's good. You usually aren't happy."

"I am." I wasn't just happy. I was giddy, bouncy.

Horny.

Feeling brave, I gave the sign for *sex.*

He paused, still holding the strap of his backpack. His gaze moved closer to me. "Right now? I haven't had a snack yet."

Once upon a time that comment would have made me self-conscious, but this wasn't a rejection from Emmet, only him processing a potential alteration in his schedule. Smiling, I made the sign again.

I grinned wider as he put down his backpack and took me by the hand, leading me toward his bedroom as he said, "We'll have a snack after."

The sex was better than usual too. I was electrically charged even before Emmet told me to get undressed, but when he kissed me and rubbed our bodies together, I felt like I was full of bubbling orange soda. I came quicker than usual, then lay there vibrating until he'd come as well. As he cleaned me up with a warm wet wipe, I smiled sleepily at him as he touched me.

"I have something to tell you." I needed to touch him. Catching his hand carefully, I drew it to my mouth and kissed the tips of his fingers. "I think I might have a job."

"That's good. Let me clean up and put my shorts on, and you can tell me about it."

I waited, watching as he wiped himself off and climbed into a pair of boxers. When he'd finished, he lay beside me and took me into his arms. We were less clumsy now because we knew how to move together.

"Tell me about your job," he said.

I knew he didn't like David, but I told myself he'd understand. I'd work him in slowly, talking about the abstract and not the specific. "It happened by accident. But I'm going to be helping a resident here, maybe. With things that are no big deal to you and me, but everything to him. It'd be more than Sally having to find something for me to do to keep me busy. It would be real work. Taking him out into the community and everything. I think I'm going to tell them in the morning that I'll do it, after I think on it tonight."

Emmet squeezed my hand. "That's good news. Who would you be helping?"

My belly flipped over with nerves, but I told myself this one time I'd believe for once everything could be okay. "That's the craziest part, actually. It's David."

Wouldn't you know it. The one time I don't panic and think everything will fall down around me before I have a chance to try, this time it turns out everything *wasn't* okay.

Chapter Nineteen
Emmet

I sat up in bed, pressing a hand over my chest. My breath came fast, and so did my anger. Everything swirled in dark colors inside me. Jeremey asked me what was wrong, and I couldn't use words. I couldn't even sign.

I got out of the bed and stood in the center of the room. I wanted to flap and scream and yell, but I couldn't do anything.

Jeremey was working for David. David, my enemy.

It hurt so much I couldn't breathe.

Jeremey climbed out of bed and stood beside me. He wasn't wearing any clothes. "Don't be angry," he kept saying, worrying his hands in that way I always thought of as Jeremey-flapping. "I'm sorry. Please don't be angry with me for working for David."

I *was* angry. I was *furious*. I wanted to shout so much it made my ears ache. "You can't work for him. He's a jerk."

"David's not a jerk, not really. He's super nice. He's lonely, and he's scared, and he needs friends." Jeremey moved to stand in front of me. He looked ready to cry.

I didn't want to make Jeremey cry, but he couldn't work for David. "I don't want to be his friend."

Jeremey stopped fussing with his hands and wrapped his arms around his belly. "It's the perfect job for me. I'll help him get on the bus, brush his teeth, eat, get dressed—"

"You can't see David naked!"

My shout made Jeremey startle and hunch his shoulders. I thought he'd say *okay, I won't work for him*, which is what I wanted. But that's not what Jeremey did. "David's not gay. Also, he can't move most of his body. And I'm *your* boyfriend. This isn't about seeing him naked. It's about helping. I *like* helping him."

My head hurt. My *heart* hurt. I wanted to yell, to hit, but I couldn't. I felt so confused and frustrated. I didn't want to hurt or upset Jeremey, but I was so angry I also *did* want to hurt him. I needed to leave. That would upset him too, but less than me yelling or hitting. Except I couldn't be in the apartment. I didn't want to be anywhere Jeremey was right now.

I went into my room and put on clothes. My Dalek shirt and black shorts and black shoes. Jeremey didn't follow me into the room, but he talked to me through the door, begging me to listen. I couldn't listen, and I couldn't stay in the apartment, not if he was going to try to talk to me when I was this upset.

I picked up my keys and my backpack, and I left.

He called after me, but I didn't answer, and he couldn't follow me, since he was still naked. My heart raced, and I thought *I* might have a panic attack. I didn't know what to do, where to go. I stood on the front steps, trying to decide if I should go onto the playground equipment or to my parents' house, and that's when Sally found me.

"Hey." Sally stood in front of me but slightly off to the side so she wasn't blocking my way. "What's up, Emmet? Are you heading out somewhere?"

I put my hand over my left ear.

She kept smiling, and she didn't leave. When she spoke again, her voice sounded like a teacher's. "That's fine. We don't have to talk. But I can tell you're upset, even without your Dalek shirt, and it's my job to make sure you're okay. Here are your choices: I can take you somewhere safe to be until you're not upset. I can call your mom or dad. Or you can tell me where you want to be, and I can sit with you. But if you choose that option, you have to let me check in with Tammy first so she knows she has the place to herself."

I didn't care for any of her options. I wanted to break things. I wanted to yell.

The door behind me opened. "Emmet—Emmet, *please.*" Jeremey appeared in front of me, his face twisted up with loud hurt and anger. "This is a *good thing* for me. You've seen how impossible it's been for me to keep a job. Please, I need to do this."

Sally put her hand on Jeremey's shoulder and spoke quietly. I didn't listen to what she said, focusing on how she knew how to touch him, how her touch was magic. Not like me, who had to think how to do it for five minutes and talk myself into being okay doing it.

At least David couldn't touch Jeremey.

I did my best to calm myself. A whistle told me a train was approaching, and I went to the edge of the stoop to watch the cars go by. Three engines, thirty corn syrup cars, twenty boxcars. No one interrupted me while I counted, and when the train passed, I felt better.

But only a little.

I turned to Sally. I could see Jeremey beside her, his eyes red, his breathing coming fast. I was giving him a panic attack, which made me sad, but I couldn't stop being angry.

I had to get away. I had to get away right now.

"What do you want to do, Emmet?" Sally asked.

I wanted to make David leave, but that wasn't going to happen. So I'd have to leave.

I went over to my parents' house by myself. It was only a block and a half—I could see my old bedroom window from my living room at The Roosevelt. Sally tried to come along, then call my mother, but I got angry. "I'm an adult. I can visit my mother by myself."

Sally made me call when Mom was with me, though, and she asked to talk to her. That made me angrier. By the time I handed over the phone, I went upstairs to my old room. The space wasn't empty or anything, but it didn't feel like my room anymore. I didn't even have my foam hammer to beat on the bed.

Everything felt wrong. I felt wrong.

I couldn't stop thinking about Jeremey working for David. I hurt all through my insides as I thought about David smiling and laughing at Jeremey, being able to make all the right jokes, flirt without notes and special fonts. The more I thought about it, the more I hurt and the more panicked I felt. My feelings got louder and louder, angry, sharp colors jangling in my head. My brain started playing bad pictures of David walking across campus, laughing and teasing with Jeremey, putting his arm around him, touching him the way he wanted. David getting out of his chair and flirting with Jeremey with his whole body.

Taking him away from me.

The world went tight and dark and terrible, and even in my old room, I wasn't safe. I went to the corner of my closet—my mostly empty closet. All my things were over at The Roosevelt. I shut the door, curled up in a ball, and I cried. I felt as awful and scared and confused as I had when I was ten and everyone made fun of me at school. I was so sure I would go back to The Roosevelt and David would have stolen Jeremey, that they'd be boyfriends now.

I didn't want to kill myself, but a dark empty space closed around me, and if I could have stayed in there and died, I would have. I didn't die, though. I really am Super Emmet, and like the comic book Superman, I have a powerful secret weapon.

My mom.

I heard her knock on the door to my bedroom, the knock that meant she was respecting me but coming in if I didn't respond. I didn't respond. I couldn't. When she came in, she called out my name, then got quiet as she came up to my closet door. I saw her shadow underneath. For a few minutes we sat together, silent.

Then, quietly, she began to sing.

"Sleep my child and peace attend thee, all through the night. Guardian angels God will send thee, all through the night."

I shut my eyes and leaned my head against the wall. Some tears still fell, but this was our song, the one she'd sung to me since I was little. She said when I was a baby, sometimes her singing this song was the only way I could be calm. It worked okay if she played a recording, but her voice was the best. It was still as magical to me now as it had ever been, and as she sang, my anger and bad feelings went away.

When she got to the last verse, I sang with her. My voice isn't good, but Mom doesn't care.

We were quiet after we finished singing, but the quiet was easier now. I still felt sad when I thought about David and Jeremey, but I didn't feel alone anymore. I remembered that no matter what happened, I would always have my mom. Even if I couldn't be independent, I would have her. I still wanted to live at The Roosevelt and get a job, but singing with her reminded me I could still be okay.

"Jujube, can I open the door? I need to hug you."

I didn't want to hug her, but she'd probably used up a lot of her superpower to get here and sing with me. So I opened the door and let her in.

She hugged me tight, rocking me from side to side. She didn't ask me what was wrong.

When she had enough hugs, we went downstairs together. She made me banana bread with no nuts, and she bought me grape Zevia from Wheatsfield. We sat out back and had a snack.

"I got a text from Sally," she said when we were cleaning up, washing dishes together at the sink. I was washing, and Mom was drying and putting away. "Jeremey is still upset. Do you want some help talking to him? Or do you think you need a night apart?"

"I can't stay here. Jeremey will stop wanting to be my boyfriend."

"Why do you think that might happen? Can you explain to me what's going on?"

I touched a bubble of soap in the dishwater, felt it pop under my fingertip. "He has a new job, helping David."

"And why aren't you excited about that?"

I still couldn't say the words, but after the singing and the banana bread and Zevia, I was pretty sure I could sign them. *I'm afraid Jeremey would rather have David as a boyfriend.*

A lot of people would have said "oh, honey" and told me I was silly. Sally would have. Not my mom. She raised her eyebrow and signed back, *Sweetheart, he's not competition for a superhero like you. No way he can take Jeremey away.*

Yes, but Jeremey will work with him all the time. And he's a smooth-talker. Also he's very handsome. Even signing that made my chest tight again.

Mom made a *huff* sound and gave up signing. "You're pretty smooth yourself, buster. If you think David's a threat, you keep being your awesome self and there's no contest. I'll tell you one thing, though. Upsetting Jeremey and running away instead of talking to him isn't going to help at all."

She was right. It had been smart to go away and calm down, but I had to get in there and fight and be a good boyfriend, not a jealous mess.

I picked up the dishcloth and squeezed out the water. "I'm going to research more sex. That will distract him from David."

Mom kissed my hair and swatted my butt with a towel.

Chapter Twenty
Jeremey

I hung out in a strange headspace while Emmet was at his parents' house. I was upset, yes, and I absolutely had an Ativan. But I wasn't hysterical, which is what I would have predicted. I felt more numb than anything. I think if I'd been alone in our apartment, I would have flipped out for sure, but they kept me in the lounge. Tammy sat with me, and Stuart made me a smiley face out of macaroni glued on a piece of construction paper. "Happy," he told me as he presented his art project, and then he started playing Pharrell Williams on his portable stereo.

Happy wasn't an option for me at that particular second, but I did appreciate the gesture.

David hung out in the lounge too. When he asked why I was upset, I couldn't answer, so Tammy told him Emmet and I'd had a fight.

Funny, I didn't start crying until she said that.

It wasn't a loud cry, thank God, only silent tears that wouldn't stop no matter how many times I wiped them away. I didn't feel anxious at all, and even my sadness was weirdly muted. I wondered if it was the drugs. For half a second a tiny voice tried to say maybe I wasn't too anxious because I knew deep down Emmet wouldn't leave me, not for something so small. The hope drowned quickly in my usual negative thoughts, but I had enough presence of mind left to get that was a victory for me, that something this big had happened and I'd had that kind of faith at all.

David rolled closer, running his chair into the end table a few times as he navigated closer. "Hey." He touched my shoulder awkwardly with his left hand, half missing it. "What happened?"

I wanted to tell him—I *needed* to tell him. I was pretty sure I was going to have to choose between him and Emmet, and I needed to choose Emmet. But of course, though all the words banged around in my head, I couldn't get them past my mouth. It was the hospital all over again, except this time Emmet wasn't there with me. I let out a watery sigh instead.

Tammy rubbed circles on my back. "It's going to be okay. Marietta texted a minute ago and said they're coming."

That didn't make me feel better. It made me terrified. I shut my eyes and sank deeper into the couch.

Tammy slid her hand up to massage my neck gently. "Shh. Every couple has fights. You two will make it through. I know it."

"What are they fighting over?" David asked.

Tammy said nothing, but when I glanced at her, I saw she was looking at me, silently asking for permission.

I nodded. *Yes, please, tell him so I don't have to.*

Tammy ruffled my hair while she answered David. "They're fighting over you, sugar."

"What? Me? Why?"

She hesitated before answering, and I shut my eyes and leaned into her, abruptly exhausted. I wanted to go to bed, pull the covers over my head and cry. I wasn't sure I wanted to see Emmet tonight, especially if he was angry with me.

Before Tammy could answer, though, I heard a familiar loud whisper. I lifted my head in a sharp jerk and opened my eyes to see Emmet standing with Marietta at the door.

Too late I realized what would happen when Emmet saw David with me. Then I *did* panic.

Tammy gentled me as Emmet and his mom came over. I felt like a rabbit, though, my heart beating too fast, my body ready to take off at the first sign of trouble. I couldn't look at him, not even when he stood in front of me. Not until I saw his hands moving—signing.

I'm sorry.

My breath came out in a ragged rush. It wasn't quite relief, but it was close. I looked up at him, at his beautiful, quiet face, his brow knit, his lips flat.

I'm sorry too, I signed.

For a second I thought he'd say something, but he frowned with his gaze near David. He signed something more complicated than I could read, so when I looked confused, he pulled out his phone and typed instead. He passed it over.

May I speak to you in private please? When I looked nervous, he pulled his phone back and added, *I won't yell. I promise.*

Swallowing against my dry throat, I held out my hand for the phone.

Will you leave?

He read the message, then hummed as he typed.

If I'm too upset, I'll leave until I calm down. I don't want to be upset in front of you. You wouldn't like it. So yes, I'll leave if I'm upset. I'll come back when I'm calm. The way I did now.

I stared at the message for a long time after I'd read it. I had so many feelings at once, loud even through the Ativan. The hope that had winked before flared back to life, and as Emmet took my hand and led me upstairs, the feeling burned inside me.

He hadn't been rejecting me. I wasn't such a disappointment he couldn't stand me. He didn't go away because I was too pathetic and worthless to be around. He did it to protect me—from himself.

I wanted to hug him. I wanted to kiss him. I wanted to make love to him again, touch him everywhere. I wanted to dance with him, hold him, everything all at once. But he was serious as we entered our apartment, and I was too shy, so I didn't do any of those things.

He sat me on the couch, and he sat in the chair across from me. He rocked as he spoke, and flapped gently, and when he paused, he hummed.

"I'm sorry, Jeremey. *Hmmmmm.*" *Flap, flap, flap.* "I shouldn't have been angry about you working for David. I shouldn't tell you who you can work for. That's not being *hmmmmmmmm* a good boyfriend."

"No," I said, aching for him. I could feel how difficult this was for him, and I wanted it to stop. "No, I should have thought it through. I was being selfish. I'll tell David I can be his friend, but I can't work for him."

"You need to be selfish. *Hmmmmm.*" He flapped so hard I thought he might fly. "You should work for him. You're right. It's a good job for you."

His voice was gruff, and I panicked. I pulled at my fingers as my insides tangled into knots. "But I don't want you to be upset. I don't want you to be angry with me."

"I'm not angry with you. *Hmmm.*"

"You sound angry. You're upset. You can't stop humming." I put my hands on my thighs and dug my fingernails in until it hurt. "It's okay. There are other jobs. I can get a different one. No job is worth losing you."

His gaze flickered to my face, almost my eyes before darting away. He rocked once, then stopped, as if he'd tripped over something. "It's not right for me to ask you to quit a job because I don't like it. That's...*hmmm*...abusive behavior."

The way he said it, I knew his mom had told him that. Now the panic was a squirrel climbing to the top of my head, ready to eat off my face. "I don't care." I paused, realizing how that sounded. "I mean—it isn't. It's fine. I don't want to work for him anymore."

"Yes, you do. Don't lie, Jeremey. You suck at it."

The tears, never far, spilled over. "Please, Emmet—*please*. I don't want him. I want you. I love you."

He stopped rocking. Stopped humming. Holding still as a statue, he stared at my chin. He looked...shocked. It was subtle, but I was getting good at reading subtle.

I signed it. *I love you, Emmet.* "Always," I added in a whisper.

He let out a heavy breath, then rocked gently. "David's handsome. Flirty."

I blinked. What—*really?* "Are—are you *jealous?*"

Still staring at my chin, Emmet nodded.

I couldn't believe this. "But, Emmet—he's not gay."

"You are. You could like him better. And he's a bully. He could take you away for fun."

I couldn't imagine a universe where David would try or I would go. "I don't care for him that way."

"You might get to know him and change your mind."

"Well, unless he turns into you, I'm not interested. He's too scruffy and loud for me. For a boyfriend."

Emmet rocked more, but it was almost a sway now, no longer jerky. "He's sassy."

He was. "The wrong kind of sass for me."

Emmet's gaze moved to my knees as he went still. "He doesn't have autism. His spine is broken, but his brain is fine."

"So is yours," I whispered.

He shut his eyes and put his hand over his heart as he resumed rocking gently. "Say it again."

I smiled, loving that I knew him well enough to know what he was after. "I love you, Emmet. I'll love you always. I'll love you always *best*."

Eyes still shut, he smiled, so wide and bright it was like sun burst into the room.

I love you too, he signed.

I crept quietly over to him. Kneeling between his legs, I kissed the hand over his heart.

Emmet and I were better after our conversation, but he didn't like David any more than he had before. This didn't surprise me, but David's reaction did.

"He seriously hates me. Why? What the hell did I do?"

David asked this when he and I were taking a trip to Wheatsfield on our fifth day of working together. I didn't have a set schedule, as David wasn't sure what he needed, and I was too worried about letting everyone down. For now, I was officially available when I wasn't otherwise occupied during the day, when Emmet was in school and during the time he studied. David texted me when he wanted help, and I came when I could. So far that was every time, but he kept saying I could say no if I needed to.

I hadn't answered David's question, and I didn't know how to. I'd tried several times, and David didn't understand. "He calls you a frat boy."

David snorted. "Not quite. I was going to pledge, but I drove into a tree first. What would that have to do with anything, anyway? Is this about me being a bully? All I've done is tease him."

I thought about pointing out to David that this is what bullies did, but he didn't see things that way, and in any event, this conversation made me nervous. "You'll have to ask him about it." I started saying that every time he asked, but he didn't stop asking.

A few times I saw David try to approach Emmet, but if anyone was oil and water, it was these two. Sometimes I sat with Tammy on the other side of the room and watched them interact badly with one another. We could see the train wreck a mile before it happened, just as clearly as we could tell there wasn't any way around it. Emmet was sure he knew exactly who David was, and as much as David tried, he seriously had no concept of Emmet.

"I think you should study autism," I told him one day when Emmet was at school and we sat together in David's room, David venting frustration at how antagonistic Emmet was to him. "His disorder isn't everything about who he is, but it's a huge part of him. Learning might help you see him more clearly."

"Like read a book?" David hated reading.

I remembered "Carly's Cafe" and pulled it up on YouTube.

David had the same kind of visceral reaction to it that I had—more so, even. The first time he watched it, he didn't say anything, only fumbled on the iPad's screen to make the video play again. On the second viewing it was as if something cracked on his face, pain breaking through the clay he'd packed around his emotions. I didn't let him try to replay it a third time. I simply restarted it for him. I wasn't surprised when tears ran down his face.

He closed his eyes and sat still for almost half a minute before he spoke. "Okay—shit." He pulled his forearm up to wipe his face. I got the sense that if he'd had full use of his hands, he'd have pinched his nose. Instead he covered his eyes for a second as his lip quavered. Then he lowered his arm with a heavy sigh. "*That's* autism? She doesn't seem anything like Emmet. She's a hell of a lot more like me. People treating you as if you're their fucking pet. Weird shit getting to you. Everything being too loud. It never used to be that way for me, but with my spine shut down, everything else is turned way up. The not being able to do what you want or explain it right—I swear I'm speaking English, but nobody hears me when they see the chair."

I remembered watching the first time and feeling the same way, that Carly was more like me than Emmet. And yet now that I knew Emmet better, had read Carly's father's book, watched her other videos, I understood how he and she were similar. I thought it was interesting, though, how we all three saw her experience as ours.

I showed him more videos, and we downloaded the audiobook of *Carly's Voice*. Over the next few days, whenever he'd advanced a few chapters, he asked me questions. I showed him other books about autism, some websites, and he asked more questions, especially about emotions.

"This stuff keeps saying he has a difficult time expressing emotions, but he doesn't have any trouble showing me he hates me."

I wasn't sure why David cared so much that Emmet didn't like him. *I* liked David fine—he was bossy a lot, and intense, but I was impressed with how much he refused to let his disability define him or limit his life. We were venturing out deeper and deeper into Ames, taking the bus anywhere it would go. We'd gone all the way out to west Ames and gone bowling, which I had been sure would be a disaster, but David talked me into helping him roll a ball down the lane—always into the gutter, but he did it over and over again, taking pride in the fact that he'd figured out a way to roll the ball with a broom strapped to his wrist. We went to campus sometimes, but not often. It depressed David, the way people looked at him.

It occurred to me he and Emmet had that in common, but I didn't bring it up.

All through September and into October, I watched the two of them dance around each other. Everyone did. David tried to get Emmet to like him, but he tried too hard, and the wrong way, and Emmet only disliked him more.

"One of these days, the firework they keep throwing at each other is going to go off," Tammy said.

The first week of October, it did.

Chapter Twenty-One
Emmet

I love the season of autumn the best. I like the cooler temperatures, warm but not as humid, and I love the sound of leaves as I walk down the sidewalk from the bus stop to my house. The street where my parents live has a lot of trees, so a lot of leaves, but the sidewalks around The Roosevelt have the best leaves because the trees are so big and old. Most of the trees were oaks, and they dropped their leaves early. There was one tree by the playground, though, that hadn't turned color yet, and so all the leaves were still on. I watched it every day, wondering if I could catch it turning.

I checked the tree once I'd dropped my backpack off in my apartment. I always went into the apartment first, even if I saw Jeremey outside. I'd wave to him and sign *be right there* if he saw me, but otherwise I went straight in. I did this on October 5, same as always. Except on that day, before I could go to my room, I ran into David.

He was rolling down the first-floor hallway, heading from the laundry room toward the door. He waved when he saw me, though his waves are unusual, since he can't really use his hands. "Hey, Em. Come on outside. We're carving pumpkins. Jeremey's already out there."

I tried not to be angry when I talked with David, but he made my teeth itch every time. Also he never called me by the right name. "I have to go to my apartment now."

I headed for the stairs, but he cut me off. "Seriously, you should come. They said they'd let me strap a knife to my wrist and do some of the carving. I might end up taking off part of my arm. Could be exciting."

I don't know why David thought I'd want to see him cut himself. I didn't want to talk to him, and I was anxious. He always pushed me, especially when I said no. It made me angry. Usually someone was around to help me get away, but today there was no one. Everyone must be outside already.

I covered my ears with my hands. That's not the proper sign for *don't talk to me right now*, but David is dumb about my signs, so I thought I had to make it louder. I tried to go around him and go to the stairs.

He rolled into my way. His face was angry, and his voice was so loud it cut through my hand barriers. "Hey. Listen, I'm trying to be nice. I'm inviting you to come out and hang with us. I'm trying to be friendly."

He wasn't friendly. He was an asshole. I shut my eyes and pressed my hands tighter on my ears. "Go away. You're a jerk. I don't like you. I don't want to hang with you." I wouldn't go help carve pumpkins now, though I wanted to. I couldn't stand to be around David. Not even for Jeremey.

"I'm not being a jerk. *Jesus.* What the fuck is your problem, anyway?"

I shut my eyes tighter and started to hum and rock. He'd think I was the R word, but I didn't care. I had to shut him out.

Except his voice is so loud I couldn't block it, which is why I heard him say, "Fine. I'll go flirt with your boyfriend then. See how you like that, asshole—"

He stopped talking then because I'd unblocked my ears, opened my eyes and punched him in the face.

It hurt my hand, but I didn't care. I bunched my fist up and pulled it back by my head, ready to hit him a second time. I made my yelling noise. I hadn't made it in a long time, not since I was fourteen, but I hadn't forgotten how good it felt, all my anger rushing up my throat and out of my mouth. He swore and flailed his arms, but he couldn't hit me back. I moved too fast. Also because his arms don't work.

"*Fucker—*" He fumbled with his chair controls, trying to get out of my way. "Knock it the hell off."

I chased him, more angry all the time. "You won't leave me alone. I told you I wanted to go to my room, that I didn't like you, but you won't stop. You never stop." Soon he'd hit his help button on his tray and I'd be in trouble, but all my anger was out now.

"I'm being good for Jeremey. He said he loved me, not you, but you're an asshole and you're going to try to take him. I don't care if you're in a chair and can't move. I don't feel sorry for you. I hate you. You're just like the jerks at school who make fun of me and call me the R word. You probably call me the R word all the time and laugh at me. You think you can take Jeremey from me. *Hmmmm.*" I got so angry I had to rock a second and pull the anger back. "You can't have him. I'm being a good boyfriend. You can't have Jeremey. I won't let you take him from me, *ever.*"

He was going to say something. He had his mouth open, his clumsy hand held up like it wanted to say *wait*, but I didn't wait. He'd moved away from the stairs, and I went up them as fast as I could. I locked the door to the apartment, went into my room and locked that door too. I grabbed my foam hammer and pounded, pounded, pounded—but it wasn't enough.

All I could see in my head was Jeremey holding David's hand. Jeremey said he loved me best, but now I knew David wanted Jeremey too.

David had lied. He was gay. He wanted Jeremey for himself. Jeremey liked how David talked. How he flirted. It didn't matter that I was almost ready for anal sex or that David was in a chair. David would find a way to make it not matter.

David wasn't autistic, and neither was Jeremey. David would find a way to change Jeremey's mind, and I wouldn't be able to fight it.

Because I was autistic. Because there was so a normal. And I couldn't be it, ever.

I threw the hammer at my bookshelf and yelled more. I ripped up my bed, throwing the sheets all over. I banged a pillow on the door until it broke into pieces, all the fluff falling out around the room. My anger and sadness was my ocean, and I couldn't carry it. Not anymore.

No one could really love me. Not when they could love somebody else instead.

Here's another example of why it's wrong to say autistic people don't feel emotions. I felt very emotional about David, but usually I could make modifications so I didn't have to let my emotions take over. Though I yelled and hit him, I still kept most of my feelings to myself, until I went to my room and could let them out. It's not nice for people to say I'm unemotional because I'm better than they are at management.

I didn't feel like I was good at management that day, though. Even after letting myself get extra angry and break some things, all the feelings were still loud inside me. Too loud. I wanted to shut down, to go into my closet and be in the dark and quiet until everything calmed down. But I could hear people in the apartment outside my door. I felt Jeremey's text pulse against my leg in my pants pocket. They'd know I hit David, that I'd lost my temper. I hadn't lost my temper like this in front of any of them, and I didn't know how they would punish me. Sometimes nice people are not nice at all when autistic people get angry.

I didn't know either how Jeremey would feel when he found out I hit David. I thought about him maybe not loving me anymore, and I wanted to go into my closet. I didn't, even though I was scared. I sat on the end of my bed and rocked with my eyes shut, waiting to see what bad thing would happen. Would Tammy try to talk to me? Sally? Mom? Would

Jeremey talk to me, or was he already so angry with me he was talking to Bob about moving out? Would they kick me out and send me home, since I was the bad one?

How was it fair that I'd tried to get away from David, but I would be the bad one?

It got quiet on the other side of the door. I was wondering if they'd all left when the knock came.

Knock, knock-knock.

It was a strange knock. Not any of my signals, but it was rough and uneven.

"Emmet. It's David. You don't need to let me in, but I wanted to talk to you."

I froze but didn't say anything. I didn't want to talk to him, or listen. But I didn't know who else was listening, and I didn't want any more trouble. I kept quiet and waited to see what would happen next.

What happened was David kept talking. His voice was softer, more sad than usual. He almost sounded like a different person.

"I...I'm gonna assume you're listening. Probably I'm talking to myself more than anyone else anyway, so...whatever." He sighed. "I'm sorry, and you're right. I'm a jerk, and I didn't listen to you when you said you wanted to go. I was being selfish. I wanted to bring you out for Jeremey. He'd been waiting for you, to show you the pumpkin he'd made. It's pretty special. You should go see it."

I kept my eyes shut and rocked gently. I wanted to hum, but I didn't want him to know I was listening, so I kept quiet.

"Anyway. I didn't mean to be a jerk. I'm trying with you, to get along, but I keep doing it wrong. I'm sorry. I think I do it because you *don't* like me. Though it's more you don't give a shit that I'm in a chair. Jeremey's not bad, but do you know you're the only one in my life right now who sees me before they see my injury? You don't like what you see, but...well, this sounds pathetic, but that's my favorite thing. You don't feel sorry for me. You think I'm a jerk and don't want anything to do with me. I think part of me has it worked out if I could win you over, if I could sweet-talk you...well, see, then the one person who saw me for me would be on my side. Which is probably dumb. And selfish. But I guess that's what I am. A dumb, selfish jerk."

I did hum a little now. I wasn't sure what to think. Was he lying, saying he wanted me to like him? It felt like a trick. But he didn't sound like he was joking.

He kept talking. "As for Jeremey—that was a joke, me saying I was going to flirt with him and steal him away. I didn't mean it, but I should have known better than to tease you that way. You gotta understand in my own head that's the most obvious joke there is. I could never steal anybody away from anyone. Even if I were gay or he were a girl, I don't think I could. How would I do it, huh? Forget sex—which is something I don't know how I'll ever have again—how exactly am I supposed to put the moves on somebody? Headbutt them? Whack them with my arm? Strap a spoon to my wrist and pet them with it?"

He laughed, but it wasn't a funny laugh. More sad. "Dude. Even if I could, he wouldn't leave you. He loves you. He said you're jealous of me—fuck, man. I'm jealous of *you*. And not only because you have somebody like Jeremey who cares about you. I'm jealous because you've always had your disability. It's always been part of you, so you don't have this memory of what you used to be, of what you could have been if you'd driven the speed limit or that deer hadn't jumped out in front of you. It's easy for you to make autism part of who you are. You don't know anything different. But me, every single day I think about what could have been. Should have been. Every day I think about how much life I have in front of me, and yet the nineteen years I was able-bodied hang around my neck like a big yoke, holding me back."

I didn't feel as angry at him, but I worried he was tricking me. "You're still a jerk," I said, but not as angry. I hummed and rocked.

He laughed, the sad laugh, but it was a little brighter this time. "See, Em? This is why I want to be friends with you. I tell you all that, and you don't feel sorry for me. You think I've been flirting with Jeremey? Fuck that shit. I'm flirting with you. You're the one I want to win over."

That sounded good, much better than him wanting Jeremey, but I couldn't trust him. And I didn't care for the nickname *Em*. "I don't want to be your boyfriend. Jeremey is much better than you."

"How about regular friends? How about we hang out sometimes, and you call me a jerk and hit me when I'm out of line, but we say we're on the same side?"

I opened my eyes and stared at the back of the door, rocking. "It's a trick. Guys like you don't have autistic friends."

"It's not a trick. I'm outside your door begging like a dog." He paused. "And fine. Before my accident, I wouldn't have asked to be friends. I maybe would have been mean to you, just as you say. Except I've had my accident. I'm not that guy anymore. Or I'm that guy with his eyes open. Let's have a do-over. If not for me, then for Jeremey. I think he'd be less nervous if he didn't think this was going to happen every day."

I did worry about Jeremey. "Is he there? Is he upset?"

"He left with the others to wait outside, but I bet he's in the hall. They didn't want to let me talk to you. Everyone worried I'd mess it up more than I already had."

They worried *he* would mess it up? "They aren't angry I hit you?"

"I didn't tell them."

I stopped rocking and stared at the door.

"I didn't tell them," he said again. "I have a big red mark on my forehead, but I said I slammed it into the doorway trying to follow you. I don't think Jeremey believes me. But if he figures it out, I'll tell him I had it coming, that it's not your fault. It isn't. To be honest, I needed it."

"No one needs hitting. It's bad."

"Sometimes we jerks need a bonk in the head to keep us in line. Thanks for having my back."

I didn't say anything to that, only kept staring at the door, rocking and humming. He went quiet too, but I didn't hear him roll away. I wasn't sure what to do now. I was pretty sure he wasn't tricking me, but I still felt strange saying I was David's friend. I decided if we were going to be friends, we should talk a little more. Get to know one another.

"David's my middle name," I said at last.

"Oh? Nice. Emmet David Washington. Good ring to it. Mine is Samuel. After my grandpa."

"Mine is after my mom's brother. He died when she was in high school. Emmet was her grandpa."

He didn't answer right away, but it was a good pause. "Jeremey showed me websites and books about autism. I started following that Carly girl on Twitter. I keep trying to think of a tweet to say to her, but I can't think of anything."

"She doesn't reply to anyone. Not on Twitter or Facebook."

"Oh. Huh. Bummer."

I hummed and rocked while I thought about what I wanted to say next. I replayed the conversation in my head, pausing at the part where he talked about sex. "You should look on the Internet about how to have sex as a quadriplegic. The Internet has everything."

He made a grunt noise. "Yeah, mostly it has people being sad and pathetic, and it bums me out. I haven't had the courage to dig in."

"I could research it for you. I'm good at research. Especially about sex."

There was a pause before he answered. "I'm serious about not wanting to have gay sex. I don't knock it for you and Jer, but I'm talking sex with girls."

"There's information on the Internet about everything. Even sex with animals, but I don't read those articles."

He laughed, not a sad laugh this time. "Okay. If you find me stuff about quad sex that isn't depressing, I'd love to hear it. Thanks."

I rocked some more. "So we can be friends now. Unless you're a jerk."

"Please be my friend even if I'm a jerk. Hit me. That will always get my attention."

"I can't hit you. Hitting is wrong." I hummed and flapped. "I could make a sign and teach you. A sign that means, *David, you're a jerk and need to stop right now.*"

"They have one of those already. It's called your middle finger."

The middle finger is a rude gesture, and I'm not supposed to do it. But I decided that for David, a rude gesture was probably exactly what I needed. "Okay."

"Great. Now will you open this door and come out?"

I opened the door. He backed up so I could get through. I tried to read his face, and I think he was relieved.

He was right. Everyone was in the hall outside our apartment, and Jeremey was at the front of the group. He looked nervous, so I signed *it's okay* to him. When he still looked nervous, I took his hand and held it. "Please show me your pumpkin surprise, Jeremey."

He took me outside, and everyone else followed. The surprise was that Jeremey had carved his pumpkin with a train on it. It was delicate and must have taken him a long time. It was beautiful.

I told him thank you and kissed him on the cheek. He smiled.

David rolled up, looking more like himself. "What did I tell you? It's perfect for you. A train pumpkin for Train Man."

Tammy and Sally made angry faces at him when he said this, and Jeremey looked nervous too. But David grinned at me, not a mean grin.

I liked the nickname Train Man. I smiled at my friend.

Then I smiled wider, because when the wind blew, it drew my attention to the trees. The big maple had yellow tips on the ends of some of its leaves. They hadn't been there when I'd checked that morning. The tree was changing at last.

I'd known it would, eventually. Everything will change, if you wait long enough.

Chapter Twenty-Two
Jeremey

I'm not sure exactly what David said to Emmet through his door, but whatever it was changed everything.

They went from near-nuclear war to careful allies in the span of one afternoon. Sure, they still fought, but how they fought was different. It reminded me more of the way Emmet was with Althea, fighting with an understanding beneath it. David, I'd already learned, loved a good argument, so he enjoyed the conflict. I wasn't sure if it was Emmet's favorite part, but it hurt nothing that David treated him firmly like an equal.

In turn, Emmet let David in on his secret codes, and as we started hanging out together, Emmet began problem-solving for David the way he did for me. He was good at imagining modifications to David's chair or tray. There was some wheelchair called a Tank Chair that David apparently wanted, but it wasn't appropriate for most quads. Emmet had ideas on how that could be changed. I wasn't sure they'd work, but David appreciated the effort to help him feel less dependent on others.

Emmet was fascinated with David's quadriplegia. He researched it as industriously as he did anything else, and he showed David what quickly became his new favorite place on the Internet: the Mad Spaz Club. It was a website with information and a forum for para and quadriplegics. It had a lot of information about how people with SCIs could have sex. David read those web pages almost every day.

We started hanging out together in the evenings, and one of those evenings we watched *The Blues Brothers* together.

David loved the movie already, but Emmet's quotes cracked him up. He loved the dancing too, and he was always trying to get Emmet to dance like Elwood Blues to any pop song David played.

"You gotta dance for me, man. I can't dance. I'm gonna live vicariously through you now."

"You can dance," Emmet told him. "You can dance with your head and shoulders."

They started doing a kind of karaoke routine in the lounge before dinner, Emmet dancing and David head-bobbing and singing. Sometimes they got me to dance too. The other residents loved it, especially Stuart, since he could usually get us to dance to "Happy".

One day, though, David and Emmet and I discovered we all shared an obstacle: overstimulation in public places.

"It's not the end of the world," David clarified when I'd expressed surprise over his confession. "But the thing is, when you lose a sense, your others pick up. They also think part of my brain got damaged in the accident too, making it easy to stimulate me. I hear and see too well sometimes. I used to love stock car races, but I can't handle them now. Way too much input. The smells almost get me more than the sounds, but those are pretty bad." He shifted his shoulders. "I do pretty well in public most of the time, but I've learned I have to mentally prepare and shop when it's not super busy. Partly so I have room to drive, and partly so I have room for my head."

"I can't handle any store bigger than Wheatsfield." I leaned into Emmet as I confessed this, feeling ashamed as usual. "I keep trying to make Target work, but I have panic attacks every time."

Emmet didn't push me away, but he tapped two fingers on my leg, which was his code for *I love you, but I need my space back.* I moved away, and after signing *thank you*, he rocked as he took his turn to speak. "Stores bother me, but counting helps me be okay. Everywhere can be overstimulating, so when it is, I find something to count. When we have to go somewhere busy, like an airport, I put in earplugs or headphones, and sometimes I wear sunglasses. It makes the light less, plus it makes me look like Elwood Blues."

"Headphones?" I thought about it, wondering if it would work for me. I couldn't quite imagine it. "Isn't that just a different overstimulation?"

But David looked thoughtful. "No, it's controlled stimulation. That's brilliant, Em. I'm gonna try it. It's an added bonus of not having to hear people's pity whispers, either. Now if I could get them to stop making sad eyes at me, I'd be set."

Emmet grinned and hummed as he rocked. "You should make your chair more of a jerk chair. Mean bumper stickers and signs."

David's laugh made me startle, but I smiled as he maneuvered his arm into place for an awkward high-five with Emmet. "You're my man, Train Man."

Emmet met David's hand in more of a carefully applied pressure than a clap, but it counted.

They spent the rest of the week hunting down rude stickers online, ordering more than David could put on five wheelchairs. His favorite was one with the familiar silhouette of a busty reclining woman straddling the stick figure in a wheelchair, but he also liked *If you stare long enough, I might do a trick.* He wasn't sure if the wheelchair figure holding a machine gun or the one tumbling out of its chair drunk were making the final cut, but he got a patch for his backpack that had a wheelchair rider moving so fast he trailed flames. There were at least eight other ones in his various online carts, all of them with the same underlying message of *fuck you, don't pity me.*

One actually said it word for word.

I enjoyed watching them hatch plans both for surviving public experiences and pissing off David's hated pitiers, but when I learned they planned to take *me* along on their adventures and find a way for me to ride out Target, I balked.

"No. I don't want to go. I'll look like an idiot."

David wouldn't give up. "Come on. We'll be there with you. We've got your back. It won't be as fun if you don't go."

I tried over and over to convince them it was a bad idea, but it was tough when they both were having so much fun and were so sure I could do it. When they saw I was weakening, they got serious about setting me up.

"We'll go to Target early on a Sunday morning, when it's quiet." Emmet smiled and rocked. "We'll give you my noise-canceling headphones and sunglasses. You can test out songs. You could do a playlist, or put one on loop."

"I vote for loop," David said. "And honestly, I would say don't listen to something chill. I'm gonna blast some old-school metal, but I don't think that will work for you. Go for something upbeat."

We were having this conversation in David's room but with the door open, and Stuart's Pharrell Williams played in the background as usual. "I could try 'Happy', I guess."

Emmet laughed and clapped his hands. "Yes. That's a good idea. I think you should play Pharrell Williams's 'Happy' song on repeat."

"I'll probably end up hating the song. Of course, as often as Stuart plays it, I'm half there already."

"You know, it could work in your favor." David tilted his head to the side and grinned at me. "You feel safe at The Roosevelt, right? And the song makes you think of The Roosevelt. That might be handy when the panic tries to get its hooks in."

It all sounded fine in theory, but whenever I thought about actually walking into Target, ready to fail, I discovered my fear of big box store shopping didn't require being present to win. Of course, that was also when I learned how much of a friend David had become. Emmet had a difficult time comforting me, and my stress sometimes consternated him enough he had to spend time alone in his room. David, though, was right there with me every step of the freak-out.

"You might not make it the first time you try. No big deal. But you need to try. You've made this too big of a bogeyman in your head. Take it in small bits. Get in the front door and order a coffee at Starbucks and get out. Then go in for toilet paper and leave. Keep adding one item to the list, one day at a time, until you have to go through the whole store."

We were sitting outside behind The Roosevelt, where it was technically a little too chilly, but we both liked sitting in the quiet near the playground. I sat on a long bench with multicolored elementary-sized handprints along the length, my knees drawn to my chest, shoulders hunched. "I'm afraid I'll never be able to make it. That my public anxiety will keep getting worse and I won't be able to go out in public with you as your aide."

"How the hell will not trying to conquer Target keep that from happening?" When I said nothing, only shrugged and buried my face deeper into my legs, he sighed. "Look. I get the whole terror-of-failure thing. I get it's not as simple as willing myself a positive outcome. Believe me. The thing with incomplete injuries is sometimes some people get better. For a year we tried surgeries and procedures, hoping for a miracle. I got a few minor ones, but in the end, what you see is what I got. Sometimes, yeah, you try only to find out you can't ever succeed. But you've got to quit thinking if you simply don't try you've saved some possibility of a win. Not trying is the only guaranteed failure."

"I'm going to feel so stupid if I fail this one, David. *So stupid.*"

"You know I won't ever think that. Or Emmet. Or anyone here." He was quiet a moment, then added, "Is this about your mom?"

I shrugged and averted my gaze. Of course he'd hit it on the head.

"You're the one who decides what a good life is. What enough trying is. What happy is."

I rested my chin on my knees and stared off toward my family's house. I couldn't see it from there, but I saw it crystal clear in my mind's eye. "I can't shake my fear she might be right. If I tried more, I'd be fine. I wouldn't be so limited in life."

"Everyone is limited in life. Some people are simply more aware of it than others." David moved his chair closer and nudged my toes with his elbow. "There's no rush on trying Target. We'll go whenever you're ready. Just don't stay away because you're afraid you'll fail. And remember, Emmet and I will both be there every time you want to try."

I wasn't ready that week, or even the next. But I thought about it all the time.

When I brought up Emmet and David's plan to take me to Target with Dr. North, I half-hoped he'd tell me it was a bad idea, but he said exactly the opposite. "If you feel you're ready for it, I think it's a fantastic plan. Before you go, however, I'd like to talk about the AWARE strategy with you. I've been meaning to bring it up for some time, but I wanted to introduce it at a moment when I thought you'd be more open to it. I think we might have come to that fork in the road."

"What's an AWARE strategy?"

"It's an acronym for a technique to walk yourself through panic attacks."

I brightened. "To get rid of them? Why didn't you tell me before?"

"You can't erase your panic attacks. You can control them, but not delete them. They're part of you. They're your brain's reaction to too much stimuli. You must respect panic attacks, not try to make them go away."

I didn't care for that idea at all, and I learned quickly why he hadn't told me about AWARE before.

The first A stood for accepting—something I didn't much care for. When I had a panic attack, I was supposed to accept that it was happening. Not try to stop it, if you can believe *that*. Only accept that it was happening and that they were normal.

Whatever.

Then I was to move on to the W, which was *watch and rate.* But the worst was the next A: Act. *Keep doing what you're doing.*

"You mean I'm supposed to sit in the middle of the aisle at Target and be the resident freak show?"

Dr. North raised his eyebrow over his glasses. "The technique asks you to remain where you are as much as possible in an effort to take control. You cannot stop the panic attack, but you *can* keep it from consuming you. Much like the time when you went with Emmet to Target, you insisted on staying in the store. You were *acting* then."

"I wasn't able to shop. I can't ever shop."

"Well, it will probably take practice to get that far."

I hated this already. "What's the R and E for?"

"R stands for repeat A-W-A. Ideally you continue doing whatever you were doing which inspired the attack, though sometimes you have to modify what you're doing. Often, in fact. Maybe you don't have to sit in the food court, but you close your eyes in the aisle and practice breathing deeply. Maybe a busy section of the store is what sets you off, so you use A-W-A and repeat them in a quieter part until you feel you have more control. The final letter, E, is to remind you to expect the best, to not make the attack worse by expecting bad outcomes. Try to surf the attack. Ride it, instead of it riding you. Above all, remember success isn't elimination of occurrences but managing them."

"I will never be able to do that."

"Yes you can. *Expect the best.* The brain can change your whole life, for better or for worse, and *you* can change your brain. You can rewire it. Retrain it."

It sounded great, but I have to admit, I wasn't ready to be AWARE.

On Halloween, for the first time in ten years, I went trick-or-treating. Emmet, David and I all went with other residents of The Roosevelt, with Tammy and Sally escorting us. We went to the Washingtons' house, several of their neighbors, and a few houses across the street from the playground. Several residents were overstimulated after that and wanted to go home, but Emmet, David and I got permission to keep going.

The three of us had dressed up as the Blues brothers, which didn't quite work since they were two, not three, but David said not to obsess over details and have fun. Without discussing it out loud, when we went off on our own, we headed down my family's street. We trick-or-treated at a lot of my old neighbors', and they all smiled and said it was good to see me looking happy. The woman who used to babysit me gave me a big hug and a kiss on the cheek.

My parents didn't have their porch light on, so we didn't ring their bell, but we stood on the sidewalk in front of it, staring at the darkened doorway.

"You're happier than they are, you know that," David said at last.

"You have other family," Emmet added, rocking back and forth as we stood. "Better family."

We went to The Roosevelt. David went to his room, and Emmet and I had sex in my bed. He stayed with me after, holding me. I was happy and sleepy, but despite the rosy glow of too much candy and great sex, I kept thinking about my mom and dad's dark, quiet house. I thought about how many people on our block had given away candy and hugs and smiles though they had no children or theirs were grown. I thought about how happy most people were, even when they didn't have reason to be.

I wondered how much of what I feared about shopping at Target and life in general was my anxiety, and how much was the bad habits I'd learned in my parents' house.

"I want to try Target tomorrow," I whispered to Emmet. "I'm scared, but I want to try."

Emmet hummed, then bussed my ear awkwardly. "I'll be with you."

I turned in his arms and held him tight, loving him, hoping he would always be a part of my family.

I had this idea that when I said I was ready to try going to Target, David and Emmet would rush me off immediately in case I changed my mind. It surprised me when Emmet told me to tell Dr. North first and make a plan.

Dr. North crossed his legs. "Do you want my help to explore AWARE more, or are you here because Emmet told you to ask me?"

I considered that, wondering which one was the right answer.

Dr. North raised an eyebrow, which was his way of reminding me there wasn't a right answer except whichever one was the truth.

Trouble was, I didn't know why I was telling him. I stared at my hands in my lap and scraped at the cuticle of my thumb. "Because he told me, I think, but if you really would have good ideas, I'd like to hear them. I guess I didn't know I'd need a plan. I thought I'd sort of think about the AWARE thing a little, and see what happened."

"Well, I don't know that you *need* a plan. But it's not a bad idea to consider strategy. Why don't we start with what techniques you've used in the past, and what ones you're thinking of now? And I'd like to talk more about AWARE. I can tell you're not convinced."

Techniques? "Mostly my mom made me go, I freaked out, and she got mad. I guess there was the one time with Emmet and his family, but we didn't have a plan. I just tried not to get upset, but I did anyway. They were nicer about it than my mom, but I was embarrassed." I twiddled my thumbs so I'd stop picking at my nails. "Emmet and David think I should use headphones. Play happy music. David says don't do it all at once. Make it a short trip and then try to make it longer every time." I frowned. "I guess I already have a plan."

"How do you feel about your plan?"

"Nervous." I gave up and dug at my cuticles again. "I'm worried I'll screw it up."

"What does screwing it up look like?"

"Having a panic attack. Embarrassing myself in front of everyone."

"Remember, having a panic attack isn't a failure, and not having one isn't a success. Success is not letting the attacks run your life." He let that sink in before he asked his next question. "Do you believe Emmet and David will react the way your mom did?"

I tucked my thumb into my fist, as it had started to bleed from being picked at. "Maybe not right away. But eventually they might, if I can't get it right." The thought of David rolling his eyes in disgust at me made me hollow inside. The thought of Emmet turning away left me cold.

"What about their behavior has led you to think this is how they'd judge you?"

I shrugged, not looking up.

"Let me ask you another question, then." His voice was so gentle, so comforting. Sometimes I wished I could have an appointment with him every day. "Why do you think when you told Emmet you were ready, he suggested you talk to me?"

It was funny. I'd wondered that ever since Emmet said it, but now I wondered about it in a totally different way. I glanced up at Dr. North, wanting to say that but finding myself unable to articulate what I meant. I could barely get it straight in my head. It was an odd little nugget, like a spark of light in fog.

Emmet hadn't been correcting me. He hadn't been judging me. He wasn't suggesting I do this because he wanted to help me. He and David—and Sally and Tammy and Dr. North, and the Washingtons—only wanted me to succeed. Not fix me because I was broken.

For a bright, shining moment I could see it so clearly, feel it all the way to my feet. But then doubt crept in, and the light winked out.

Dr. North smiled gently—not sadly, but in his way, which left space for me to feel. "It's difficult, sometimes, to get out of the habit of believing everything is a test, a challenge. That everyone is a judge. Difficult to trust that people might be there for us out of love."

Well, now I felt bad. My cheeks got hot. "I don't mean to not trust Emmet. Or David. Or you."

"I would suggest, in fact, the greater issue is sometimes you can't trust others because your greatest difficulty is in trusting yourself, that a good-faith effort is enough. That saying you want to attempt to climb this mountain of your fear is something to be proud of. That the work you do with David is precious to many people. That in the months since we met, you've covered a great deal of ground. That you don't have to compete with other people and their expectations of you. That first and foremost you should seek to live a life which gratifies and completes you—and striving is more than most people ever do."

His words swam in my head, beams of light through my omnipresent fog. I let out a long, slow breath as the ideas took root where they could. When I was ready, I glanced at him, and this time it was me who raised my eyebrow. "So if I say learning how to survive Target gratifies me, and I try to do it, even if I don't make it, I'm doing a good job? And that's not stupid, or pathetic, though a lot of people survive Target every day?"

"You aren't a lot of people, and they aren't you. Trust me when I tell you many, many people would cower at the mountains you face, if the struggles your depression and anxiety give you were as visible as David's quadriplegia." He uncrossed his legs and leaned forward. "*I* see you, Jeremey Samson. I don't see all of it, but I see more than most, and I'm impressed."

Our session ended not long after that. It was funny how we hadn't mapped out a plan, and yet I'd never felt more ready to go.

We made our first Target run on a rainy November Sunday morning.

Emmet and David went with me, and Sally drove us in the van that let David's chair drive up the ramp. Sally came along too, since my job was to go to Starbucks and get her a coffee.

"But I've gone to the Target Starbucks a lot," I tried to point out. "It's where I sit and wait when I get overwhelmed."

"Right. This first time, we want to all but guarantee a positive outcome." Sally patted my shoulder. "Get going, hon. I'm ready for a latte."

I felt kind of dumb, putting in my headphones to walk twenty feet through the doors to the Starbucks counter. The chairs were too close for David to go up comfortably, so he waited by the tables as Emmet went up with me. I took my headphones out as the barista smiled and asked me for my order.

"A grande vanilla latte with skim milk, please." I gave her Sally's Starbucks card and put it in my pocket once she'd swiped it. Then I put my earbuds in while Emmet and I waited at the other end of the counter.

I didn't listen to "Happy" this time. I listened to "Welcome Home, Son" by Radical Face on repeat. It felt right. I'd say it worked, except like I said, I'd never melted down ordering coffee.

They all applauded me anyway when I went to the van.

"We'll come tomorrow morning before Emmet goes to class," David said.

I frowned. "I could go again now. Maybe go to the card section."

"Go slow. Don't push it." Emmet's gaze was over my head, but he smiled. "You did a good job. Be happy."

I thought it was pretty pathetic, but they kept telling me I was awesome, and I admit, it was nice.

We did go the next day. I wanted to go to the cards, but Emmet pointed out that was where I'd started to get nervous last time. "Let's walk down the first aisle to the end. We'll go to the men's underwear and turn around."

I got nervous by the time we passed women's pajamas, which was only halfway to the underwear. I started to breathe heavily, and David nudged Emmet to take my hand. Emmet did, but first he signed for me to look straight ahead and listen to my music. Nodding, I fixed my gaze at my goal and listened to the lead singer. It was "Welcome Home, Son" again.

I made it to the underwear, but my breath was shallow and fast. I tried to practice AWARE, and it helped a little to think of the things the acronym stood for, but mostly I focused on not passing out. Sally had me stand there a second and recover with my eyes shut. I tried to *act* as long as I could, but eventually I gave the sign that I needed to leave. Then we got the hell out of there. When we got to the van, they all cheered, but mostly I felt as if I'd been through the wringer.

"You did great," Sally said over and over. "You didn't melt down. You were nervous, but you did what you said you would. That's excellent progress! I think you deserve ice cream."

We went through the Dairy Queen drive-through. David got a malt, which we had them thin a bit more and put in his special cup that he could strap to his wrist. He grinned at me as I clutched my Blizzard, still too shaken to eat.

"You were awesome, buddy. Give it a day or two, let yourself recover, and we'll do it again."

And that's exactly what we did. Over and over and over. Every time we went, Emmet and David and either Sally or Tammy went with me. We went to men's underwear four times, until I could get there and back as easily as I could order a latte, and every time, whether I panicked or not, we went to get ice cream. Every time, I listened to "Welcome Home, Son".

"I still think you should listen to Pharrell," David told me one afternoon when we were riding the bus to campus.

"I'm waiting to use it for a victory lap," I confessed.

He grinned. "I like that you're thinking about victory laps."

It wasn't always easy to think about success, though. Emmet was right—there was something about the card section that tripped me out. When we started heading that way, I panicked every time. I was mortified, but Emmet never was.

"I think you should switch your song. And try sunglasses."

"I'm sorry I keep messing up," I said.

Emmet rocked on the couch beside me. "You're not messing up. You're learning. Are you using AWARE?"

I was a little sorry I'd taught him the acronym, because he hounded me mercilessly to use it. "Yes. I'm trying."

"You need to expect the best, but don't be so upset when things aren't perfect. But I still think you need a new song."

Emmet sat up with me that night trying to find another song to play in the aisles. After considering a lot of popular songs that didn't feel right, Emmet pulled up someone I'd never heard of on Spotify.

"His name is Derek Paravicini," Emmet said. "He's autistic, like me. He's a savant, which means he has a mental disability, but he's good at a skill, better than people on the mean could ever be. He's blind too, but that has nothing to do with how he plays." He held out his headphones. "Here. Try this song."

It was simple piano, and I didn't know the tune, but the readout said "It's Only a Paper Moon". It was light, bouncy and simple. Paravicini was amazing. I watched the TED talk about him and understood the kinds of obstacles he'd had to overcome—and did. Beautifully. I read the lyrics to the song, about how everything is fake, except for belief. I listened to that song and others of Derek's over and over. I lay in bed, on the couch, curled up beside Emmet or by myself, listening to the music and imagining myself making it past the greeting cards.

Just past them, I told myself. *Just to the wrapping paper.* I shut my eyes and imagined myself doing it. With my friends. Alone. With headphones. Without. I imagined it over and over.

And eventually, I did it.

Playing Paravicini's "It's Only a Paper Moon", I made it past the greeting cards. The first few times I huddled in a ball in the van after, David and Emmet and Sally reassuring me, but I managed it only shaking a little. I was AWARE. And then I went farther. And farther, and farther.

I never told anyone about it, but I figured out the places which were the worst were the ones where I'd been with my mom or dad and they got angry over my panic attacks. Sometimes I could see them in my head, like they were hovering at the end of the aisle, frowning at me. I did what I could to erase them from my mind. I wore sunglasses so they weren't as bright. I accepted that they were there with me whether I wanted them there or not. I watched them and rated how upset they made me...or didn't. I listened to Derek Paravicini, imagining him learning music without being able to see, unable to understand the world in the way even I could. Sometimes I imagined Derek walked with me, holding the hand Emmet wasn't.

David and Sally and Tammy always cheered me when I did well, but Emmet only smiled and said, "Good job." His praise made me feel the best.

I had to take a break on my "Target practice", as David liked to call it, during the Christmas shopping season. It was too busy and crowded and sent me backward on some of my progress. I also had some tension with my parents during that time. They wanted me to come home for the holiday. I wanted to stay at The Roosevelt, or go to the Washingtons. Or David's house. Anywhere but what had been my home.

For most of December, I was busy practicing telling my parents no, then processing through feeling guilty because I finally did.

After Christmas, though, everything changed. It helped I'd had a good holiday with my boyfriend and my best friend, and the residents of The Roosevelt. I'd made cookies, sung carols, helped David shop online for his family and do the wrapping. I got Emmet a gift with money I'd earned from working with David: it was a complicated, angular art piece I'd seen in the window of a gallery downtown. It was unusual but beautiful in a way that reminded me of Emmet.

David convinced the artist to give me a break on the price, and I'd bought it. Emmet loved it. His present to me was a computer program that had an image of me—with my real head on a cartoon guy—dancing down the aisles of a busy store while "Happy" played in the background.

During the second week of January, that's exactly what I did.

We'd been to Target a few times where everything had been fine, and I'd played "Happy" for those trips. David was right, playing it reminded me of The Roosevelt, and I danced a little while I went through the aisles, like I did in the lounge with David. David saw me one time, and I could tell he had a plan from the wicked look on his face. On the way home, he told me.

"I think we should go to Target again tomorrow. You, me and Emmet. And Sally or Tammy. They're going to take a video. We're gonna be a baby flash mob, you, Emmet and me. We're gonna play 'Happy' on my iPad with a Bluetooth speaker to boost it, and we're gonna dance in the fucking aisles and put that shit on YouTube after."

I balked, but before I could say what a crazy idea that was, Emmet grinned and said, "We should wear our Blues Brothers costumes while we do it."

David barked out a laugh and held up his hand for one of his and Emmet's awkward high-fives. "*Fuck yeah.* Oh, shit. We might go viral for that. Come on, J. What do you say?"

I wanted to say no, but they looked so excited. "What if I can't do it without headphones?"

"You keep your headphones," David said. "The speaker is for everybody else."

"But what if they're not in sync?"

"I can make them play the same," Emmet said. "No problem." He grinned and rocked in his seat. "I want to be a viral video as Elwood Blues. Too bad we can't sing 'Everybody Needs Somebody'."

"'Happy' is more flavor of the month. Well, it's a little passé now, but it's closer than the other one. Plus it's more fun to dance down the aisle to, and it happens to be the song getting your man through big box stores." David raised an eyebrow at me. "So?"

Of course they convinced me.

We didn't go the next day, since Tammy wanted us to practice. She taught us some choreography, helped David figure out how he could safely weave through Emmet and me. Emmet did his usual Blues Brothers dance, but I needed help so I didn't feel so self-conscious. I worried I would freak out with that much attention, but I did want to try. For Emmet, for David and for me. I could see it in my head. If I could do it, it would be amazing. I expected the best as much as possible.

The day we went to do the flash mob video, Emmet and David and I went alone to the store. We took the bus, which meant we had to walk from the stop to the door, but that was okay. We laughed and teased each other, and I gave myself a pep talk, saying I could do it, and if it turned out I couldn't do it yet, that was okay.

Tammy was there waiting, and so was Bob, and Marietta and Doug and Althea. They were so excited, waving and grinning as we walked past the jewelry counter. The Target employees were looking at us curiously, but when David started flirting with the female clerks, they smiled and followed us.

At the greeting cards, Emmet started our music, and we danced.

David wiggled his shoulders to the beat and made his chair swerve as part of his dance step, the way we'd practiced. I couldn't hear them, only the music in my headphones, but I saw David singing along, or at least moving his lips. Emmet moved in front of us, doing his Elwood dance.

I laughed and wiggled my butt a little, then weaved with Emmet and David as Tammy had taught me. Ahead of us Sally and Doug were both filming. A guy I didn't know was smiling and filming us too.

A woman shopping nearby smiled at us. David said something to her, and the next thing I knew, she was blushing, but she was dancing too. She danced with us all the way to the grocery section. First it was that woman, then another, then a grandpa and his grandson, then four employees, and the next thing I knew, Emmet and David and I were leading a dance line through the store, like something out of a movie. We were a real flash mob. We were cool. We were making everyone happy, including ourselves.

I was nervous the whole time, I'll admit. I never once had gone to Target without knowing a panic attack was a possibility, a pit waiting for me if I wasn't careful. I had to be so, so careful while we danced, while we were such a public spectacle. On the one hand, it was easier, since the stimulus was controlled—*we* were the stimulus. But sometimes I simply got nervous from exposure, and when that happened, as we'd agreed, I fell back behind David's chair. Every time I did, he hammed it up more, egging Emmet on to dance more aggressively, swerving his chair more wildly. Basically, they took attention off me, gave me space to get my head back in the game.

Maybe I wasn't ever as flashy as either of them, but the fact that I was willing and *able* to dress up and dance in a store that had made me tremble at the thought of it only a few months ago was an out-and-out miracle.

When I had courage enough, I got in front of David and boogied down like I was dancing by myself at home in my bedroom.

I was happy. I was amazing. I'd conquered my fear—or at least learned how to drive it a lot better.

When the song ended, everyone clapped. Everyone took pictures of us, with us. We were the Blues Brothers. We were the cool kids.

As the barista brought me over a free coffee, smiling as if I'd made her day, I realized I was always this cool. I'd just been waiting to figure it out.

Chapter Twenty-Three
Emmet

When the second semester of classes started, Jeremey was really good at being in public. David started going to ISU, and he took Jeremey with him.

Jeremey wanted to take an online course through Des Moines Area Community College over the summer, but otherwise he wanted to help David. One night when we were talking on the couch, he told me what he wanted most for a job was to be David's aide, one who would work all the time and would stay. That would mean getting his Patient Care Technician certification, which wasn't a lot of school, but still made him nervous. I thought about how he'd conquered Target and learned to manage his panic attacks, and I told him to start with the one class and see how it went.

I liked having Jeremey and David on campus at Iowa State. We had no classes together, and David was only part-time, but on Wednesdays we met for lunch in the Memorial Union or at the Hub, if the menu was good. I enjoyed having lunch with them, though if they weren't along, I kept to myself on campus. I knew people in class, but I didn't have any friends in my classes. When David and Jeremey were with me, we were the Blues Brothers, even if we didn't have sunglasses on.

One day in early February, we were going to the bus stop to go home, singing, when some frat boys went by. They muttered something mean under their breath and laughed at us. That was when I found out I'd been right about David all along, that he was one of those guys. What I hadn't understood until then was that he was one of those guys on my side.

David stopped his chair, spun it around. "Excuse me, asswipes. Were you saying something?"

The frat boys glanced at each other, their faces too complicated to read. They started to go faster, but David's chair can go up to fifteen miles an hour, and he caught them. He almost ran them over.

"Hey. Pencil dicks. Talking to you. Did you have something you wanted to share with the class, or do you get your jollies picking on crips?"

He was talking really loud, and everyone on the sidewalk watched us. They were pointing and whispering. Jeremey was nervous, but I wasn't. David was being mean, but he was good at it. He was winning. I smiled, hoping he would keep going.

He did.

He backed the guys up to the edge of Lake LaVerne. "Come on. Let's hear it. Give me your best shot. It must have been good, the way you were giggling. Look, you've got everybody's attention. Those four girls over there look really interested to hear what a pack of assholes have to say to a quad and his autistic wingman and his friend with social anxiety. Go ahead. Wow them with your Rainman joke."

"I'm Train Man," I told David. I liked his nickname for me.

"There you go," David said. "My man Emmet's setting you up. He's autistic. He loves trains. Train Man. Get it? Oh wait. He thinks that name's funny. So if you want to mock him, you'll have to try something else."

"Let's get out of here," one of the guys said.

They hurried off, but David chased them. "Fuck off, assholes. I don't need a functioning spine to kick your ass." He stopped, watching to make sure they were gone. His face was angry, and his cheeks were red as he turned to us. "You guys okay?"

I laughed and clapped. "Yes. You're my favorite bully, David."

"Damn straight." He turned his head, then spoke quietly. "Hey. Don't look now, but those girls are checking us out."

"Jeremey and I are gay," I reminded him.

"Oh, damn." David grinned. "I guess that means they're all for me."

He went over and talked to them, calling over his shoulder for Jeremey and me to come along. The conversation was boring, so I counted the cars passing by and memorized the license plates. Eventually, though, Jeremey tapped my shoulder.

"Emmet, David wants to know if we want to go to a bar with him and the girls."

I frowned. "We aren't old enough to drink alcohol."

"David is. He says there's a bar we could go to that isn't too loud at this time of day, and they'll let minors in. What do you think? Should we go?"

I didn't really want to go to a bar, but Jeremey signed something extra. *Please, Emmet? David wants to go, I can tell.*

So I nodded, and that's how we went to a bar.

It was a place called Bohemia on West Street, which was a long walk, but it was a nice day, not too cold, and there were five hundred and six cracks in the sidewalk on the way there. The girls walked with David, making a circle around his chair. They giggled a lot. Jeremey and I walked behind, and Jeremey kept having us slow down to put more space between us and them.

"He's having fun," Jeremey whispered. "This is his dream, having all those girls hanging on him."

But when we got to the bar, David sent the girls in to find a table, and he hung out with us for a minute, just the three of us.

"You guys okay with this? If it's too much, tell me, and we'll bail."

The bar was dark, but it didn't make me nervous. I wasn't sure about Jeremey, but he said he'd be okay. "Maybe not too long. I can do a little while, if there's no loud music."

"Just some piped-over stuff, as far as I could hear, and not loud." David's face was red, but his eyes were very alive. "I appreciate this. I don't think I'm going to get lucky or anything—not sure what I'd do yet if I could take somebody home, despite your websites. But it means a lot to me to flirt. Feel normal."

"Let's go be normal," Jeremey said, smiling.

"Okay." David turned his chair around for the door and let out a big sigh. "A quad, an autistic and a depressive walk into a bar. We're the opening line of a joke."

Jeremey laughed, but I didn't get it. He tried to explain it to me after, but I didn't care. David was right. It was nice to feel normal. To be three friends hanging out in a bar. To be with my boyfriend, to hold his hand and let him lean on me, even if he was a little too much in my space.

There is no normal, not really. Not a right and a wrong way to be. But there is belonging. That day in Bohemia with Jeremey and David and the girls, I belonged. I belonged as much as anybody on the mean.

Maybe even a little bit more.

When we got home from the bar, on the day I felt as if I belonged, I asked Jeremey if he wanted to try anal sex, and he said yes.

I wasn't surprised. Jeremey always said yes to anything about sex. He wasn't nervous about anal penetration now. We'd ordered a dildo from a reputable online sex store, and he said it felt great. I tried it too, but I don't care for things in my butt. Jeremey does, which is good. I wanted to be in him that way.

We took a shower together, which we hadn't done before. It was weird at first, but then it was fun and sexy, because we kissed with water coming down on us. It was a lot of sensation at once, and it made me so excited. I wanted to make love with him more. I wanted to be the dildo in him. My cock inside him, in the hot place.

We didn't use a condom, since we were monogamous and disease free, plus I didn't like the way they felt. No *used prophylactic* for me like Jake Blues. I wanted to feel my cock naked inside Jeremey, but first I had to get him ready. I used gloves and lots of lubricant, and I pushed my index finger carefully inside his body.

It's still a little weird to me to put something in someone's anus, except when I watch Jeremey's face as I do it, I don't think it's so gross. It's not much different than all the germs in someone's mouth, but we kiss them anyway. An anus has fecal matter, but if you use proper precautions, it can be okay. Plus many people don't wash their hands, so we all probably have more fecal matter going around than we want to know about, Mom says.

I'd watched videos about anal sex, some porn and some that were more instructional. I'd gotten good at loosening Jeremey's anal ring for the dildo, but this was the first time I was doing it for me. For my cock to go inside him.

It made me excited to think about going inside Jeremey.

When I did it, I jolted like electricity, it felt so good. It was tight and extra hot, like spicy peppers. Jeremey was facedown, and his gasps and cries made me more aroused. I pushed my cock in deeper, and he gripped the bedspread and arched his back.

"Oh God, Emmet—*fuck me.*"

I did. I pumped my hips into Jeremey over and over the same as a porn video, but it wasn't a porn video. It was a love video. I loved him. We were making love. We were boyfriends, a couple. I was the top. He was the bottom. Some people don't care for labels, but I like this one. I enjoy being a top. And I know Jeremey enjoys being a bottom.

I came a little faster than usual that first time we had anal sex, and it had me so overstimulated I had to make the sign to lay by myself a second until I could calm down. Jeremey didn't mind. He jerked himself off, then lay quiet on the bed, looking like he might fall asleep. When I made the sign that I was ready to cuddle, he snuggled against me and kissed my chest.

"Did you like the anal sex?" I asked him.

"I loved it, Emmet." He leaned up to kiss my chin. "I love you."

"I love you, Jeremey." I got the wet wipes to clean us up, and then I held him until he fell asleep.

I am normal. I belong. I have a friend who can kick ass from a wheelchair. I live independently and get good grades. I'm an excellent lover.

Like I said. I'm awesome. I'm Emmet David Washington. Train Man. The best autistic Blues Brother on the block.

Chapter Twenty-Four
Jeremey

On the one-year anniversary of my meltdown at school, I had a family meeting with my parents.

It was at my therapy session, and Dr. North was there, but I almost thought I could have done it without him. He'd given me that option, but I decided it was the same as my Target practice. Best to start the first try with something I was sure would work out.

My parents were nervous, and I couldn't blame them. The last time we'd had a family meeting, Emmet had panicked, and I'd shouted. This time he wasn't with us, though. He waited in the lobby, probably counting ceiling tiles or figuring pi.

This was a meeting I wanted to do by myself.

"Thank you for coming," I told Mom and Dad as we sat down. "It's good to see you."

My mom frowned and brushed invisible lint from her trousers. "You never visit us. You don't call often."

It wasn't a friendly start to our meeting, but I'd talked a lot about my parents, especially my mom, with Dr. North. I'd expected this kind of greeting. Worse, to be honest. I hadn't been sure they'd come at all.

"Well, I want to talk to you about visiting you more." I had my hands in my lap, carefully not making a fist or fidgeting. I wanted to present calm, controlled body language. It was difficult to do, but I wanted to try. "But I also wanted to tell you what I've learned in the last year. Since the day I had to leave school. Would you care to hear what I've learned? What I've done at The Roosevelt?"

My mom crossed her arms over her body and glanced at my dad, still frowning. "I suppose."

I admit, I wanted her to be eager and happy. I will always watch Emmet's parents and David's and wish mine could be like theirs. But that wasn't who my parents were. And though they made me nervous and were, I'm pretty sure, the reason I got as out of control as I did, I did love them, and if I could have a relationship with them, I wanted one.

This was the first step toward that. I wasn't sure success here was any more likely than me being able to go to a rock concert and dance in the pit, but I wanted to try.

I told my mom what I'd learned.

"Well, there are a lot of things. Most of them are little to most people, but they're big to me. I've learned how to live by myself, for one. I know how to balance my checkbook and make sure there's food in the fridge. With Emmet's help, I keep my room clean, and the apartment too. I help residents at The Roosevelt, especially David, my friend who is a quadriplegic. I want to go to school to be his aide. I signed up for an online class this summer. I want to go to the classroom in Ankeny, but I'm going to work up to it slowly.

"That's the big thing I learned this year: it's okay to go slow. That everybody else's pace and definition of success isn't mine. What is easy for other people isn't necessarily so for me. Though some things are easy for me and hard for other people. This year I learned I'm good at feelings. Emmet calls these our superpowers—his are listening and seeing and math and remembering. Mine is feelings. I can tell what everyone is feeling all the time, and I almost feel it with them. So I have to be careful, because if there are too many feelings around me at once, I get overwhelmed. This is why shopping is challenging for me. It's as if every aisle has strangers with too many feelings, and I can't always stop them. But I've learned how, sometimes.

I take headphones and wear sunglasses. I take my friends. I take my boyfriend."

I smiled, thinking of Emmet. "That's another something I learned this year: how to be a boyfriend. How to listen to someone else, what they need, how to give it to them. What I need. How to love them. How to handle it when they get jealous—or when I do. How to make a life with someone. How to help someone else through their struggles, and let them help me with mine."

I stopped then, waiting. I wasn't sure if they still didn't like Emmet. I watched their faces, trying to read them. They weren't happy, but I couldn't tell if it was Emmet, or because this meeting made them uncomfortable.

That seemed a good time to move on to the next part.

"The other thing I learned, Mom and Dad, is that I need to protect myself. There's nothing wrong with me and who I am, but I do have depression and anxiety, and they're both pretty severe. I have major depressive disorder. I have clinical anxiety. They're real things. They're invisible to everyone but me, but I have to tell you, most days Emmet's autism and David's quadriplegia don't hold them back as much as my depression and anxiety do me. I have to fight every day, and some days I can't win. There are days I have to tell David I can't help him go to school when my depression or anxiety is too bad. And you know what? Those days he usually stays with me, unless he has a test. He sits with me or helps Emmet make my lunch. Until I can climb on top again. He's my employer, but he's also my friend. One of my two best friends."

My mom was frowning, and my dad seemed disgusted. I was sad, since it was clear this meeting wasn't going to be a success at all. I felt the dark clouds coming over me, as if the lights in the room were going dim. I didn't panic, but I felt tired, and I wanted to withdraw.

Dr. North, sitting beside me, rubbed my shoulders.

I glanced down at my hands, which I held still, but they were clenched in fists now. I stared at a bracelet Emmet had made me, an intricate weave of patterns that he said reminded him of me. I touched it, thinking of him in the lobby, wondering what he was counting now.

I considered going to sit with him, leaving my parents. Not trying anymore. I told myself I still had a family. I had Emmet. But it still made me sad.

"I only wanted you to be happy."

The voice was so quiet I almost didn't hear it. I looked up, wondering if maybe I'd imagined it, but my mom was watching me. Crying silently. Whispering. To me, while my dad held her hand.

"I only wanted you to be happy," she said again. Her face was twisted up in misery. Her mascara ran down her cheeks, until she wiped at it with a tissue and made streaks. "You're always so withdrawn, and I knew how you felt, because I felt that way too at your age. I didn't want you to be sad. I wanted better for you." She blew her nose, and my dad put an arm around her shoulders, drawing her close. She put her forehead on his cheek, crying harder. "I didn't want that for you. I didn't want that for my baby."

I stared at my mom, my head spinning, too light, like it wasn't on my body. Was this actually happening? Was this my mom? My dad? It felt unreal. I'd imagined her hugging me a million times the way Marietta hugged Emmet, of magically becoming somebody else, but I'd never envisioned this. Her telling me she wanted me to be happy. That she understood. And crying as if someone had taken everything away.

In the same way that one day I'd had a glimpse of Emmet only wanting good things for me, helping, not waiting for me to be fixed, I had a new look at my parents, especially my mom. I watched her crying, as upset as I felt sometimes, more upset than I'd ever seen her. *I felt that way too at your age.* Did she still feel that way, I wondered? Had her mom talked to her the way she'd talked to me? Had she been lumbering through life in the dark, heavy fog, the same as me?

Without an Emmet to light the way?

I don't know if I was right, or even close. But at that family meeting, I didn't wish my mom were somebody else. I didn't get nervous about what she might say that would upset me. That day I got up from my chair, crossed the room and hugged her tight. I let her cry on my shoulder. Felt the bad feelings with her, and did my best to make them go away.

"I'm so sorry," she said, and buried her face in my shoulder.

I patted her back and rocked her side to side like Emmet rocked me. "It's okay, Mom. It's okay."

And you know what? It really was.

Chapter Twenty-Five
Emmet

A lot happened to me, and to Jeremey, after his family meeting with his parents. All kinds of things happened to David. But those are other stories, and David will get mad if I tell his for him. So I'll tell you about my job, and the train.

When I started my junior year of college, one of my professors told me about this company in Ames called Workiva. It used to be WebFilings, but they changed their name. A supervisor from Workiva asked me if I wanted to get an internship there. I didn't get paid for it, but I learned all kinds of things about working and got real-world experience, which is important for getting a job that pays. Except when I did my internship, they liked me so much they asked me if I wanted to stay and get paid once my internship was finished. I told them no thank you, I still had school. So they said they'd pay for me to complete my schooling if I promised to work for them part-time until I was done and stick around after.

I had to talk to my parents, because it sounded more complicated than I could agree to in a meeting, and it was. My dad talked to my supervisor for hours and hours, and he brought a lawyer once too. While they talked, though, I researched the company. I'd learned a great deal from my internship, but I found out they were growing quickly and had offices all over. I enjoyed working there. They generated reports for other companies, and they liked how good I was at writing programs and noticing patterns. They were excellent at modifications too. Even when I was an intern, they made sure my space was comfortable, and they changed a few of the company rules for me so I didn't feel unsafe. They told my dad's lawyer, who was my lawyer now too, they would make more accommodations for me if that was what it took to get me to sign on.

I said I wanted to learn to drive a car, but dad says they can't promise that.

They gave me all kinds of other things, though, and so after my internship, I did work there, for money. They gave me rides to school, and sometimes they did it in a fancy car, which made me feel like a Blues Brother for sure. Even if I didn't drive.

They also gave me so much money I was able to take Jeremey, David and our families on a train.

I'd been on Amtrak before, but never on the train with my boyfriend. Jeremey and David hadn't been at all. David worried he couldn't do it with his chair, but the train staff was helpful, actually. They brought bridges for platforms that had gaps and ramps to get on and off the train. They would bring him his meals in his car, or he could transfer to the lounge car at a scheduled stop, since the dining car was on the second floor.

We were taking a trip to Chicago, to see the sights and eat deep-dish pizza. We'd visit Jeremey's sister Jan, and Dad said we could see some places from *The Blues Brothers*. I took Jeremey to the lounge car as soon as we were settled. David said he'd join us there when it was time for dinner. I was glad he wasn't coming right away. I wanted to be with Jeremey by myself for a while.

We sat on a seat together, holding hands while we watched the world rush by. I was excited and rocked, and I didn't care if people looked at me when I hummed. Jeremey was with me, and smiling. My boyfriend. And I had a job that let me take him on nice trips.

"I love you, Jeremey," I said. I tried to look him in the eye, but it was too intense a moment.

He didn't care. "I love you too." He kissed me on the cheek.

Heidi Cullinan

I wanted a bigger moment, though. I picked up his hand and kissed it. "I want you to be my boyfriend forever."

Jeremey got quiet. He touched my face, reading it with his superpowers. "Just your boyfriend?"

I smiled big. I felt like my whole face was a smile. "You have a better idea? Maybe something else you could be?"

He blushed, but he smiled too. "Yeah. I have some ideas. But when we're ready. No need to rush. I'm not going anywhere, and neither are you."

I kissed him on the mouth. "'It's a hundred and six miles to Chicago, we've got a full tank of gas, half a pack of cigarettes, it's dark, and we're wearing sunglasses.'"

Jeremey tweaked my nose. "Hit it."

About the Author

Heidi Cullinan has always loved a good love story, provided it has a happy ending. She enjoys writing across many genres but loves above all to write happy, romantic endings for LGBT characters because there just aren't enough of those stories out there. When Heidi isn't writing, she enjoys cooking, reading, knitting, listening to music, and watching television with her husband and ten-year-old daughter. Heidi is a vocal advocate for LGBT rights and is proud to be from the first Midwestern state with full marriage equality. Find out more about Heidi, including her social networks, at www.heidicullinan.com.

Sometimes you have to play love by ear.

Fever Pitch
© *2014 Heidi Cullinan*
Love Lessons, Book 2

Aaron Seavers is a pathetic mess, and he knows it. He lives in terror of incurring his father's wrath and disappointing his mother, and he can't stop dithering about where to go to college—with fall term only weeks away.

Ditched by a friend at a miserable summer farewell party, all he can do is get drunk in the laundry room and regret he was ever born. Until a geeky-cute classmate lifts his spirits, leaving him confident of two things: his sexual orientation, and where he's headed to school.

Giles Mulder can't wait to get the hell out of Oak Grove, Minnesota, and off to college, where he plans to play his violin and figure out what he wants to be when he grows up. But when Aaron appears on campus, memories of hometown hazing threaten what he'd hoped would be his haven.

As the semester wears on, their attraction crescendos from double-cautious to a rich, swelling chord. But if more than one set of controlling parents have their way, the music of their love could come to a shattering end.

Warning: Contains showmances, bad parenting, Walter Lucas, and a cappella.

Available now in ebook from Samhain Publishing.

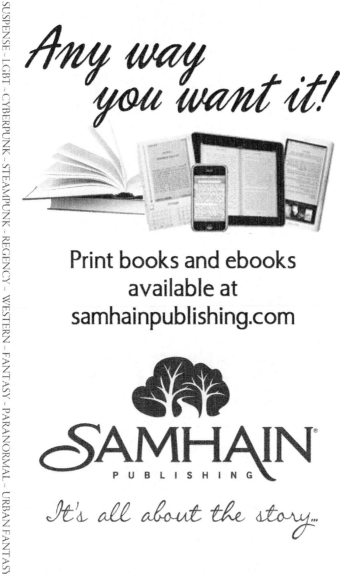

PUBLISHING

It's all about the story...

Romance

HORROR

www.samhainpublishing.com